eard the front door open. …vers, brushed her hands together, and picked up the hand-knit hat.

"But he hasn't gone to any of the hospitals in the area," a woman said.

"It's a pretty big leap to assume he would be with us," Dr. Grace told her in a soft voice.

They came into view on the top step. The woman's face was tear-streaked, and she dabbed at her eyes with a crumpled tissue. Dr. Grace had a comforting hand on her shoulder.

"You said he's only been gone since dinnertime last night, right? You said a friend called him asking for help? Maybe the friend needed more help than expected. Maybe they had to leave town for some reason," Dr. Grace suggested.

"He wouldn't do that without telling me. He knows I worry. Besides, he left his cell phone charging on our dresser. He would have come back to get it. Something horrible has happened. I can feel it."

Permelia stood to the side of the landing, still clutching the hat, as Dr. Grace guided the woman down the stairs. The woman stopped halfway down.

"What are you doing with my husband's hat?" she demanded.

"I found it at our dumpster out back," Permelia said and held it out.

The color drained from the woman's face, and she fainted, tumbling down the two remaining steps and landing on Permelia, knocking her to the pavement.

ALSO BY ARLENE SACHITANO

The Harriet Truman/Loose Threads Mysteries

The Harley Spring Mysteries

DOUBLE KNIT

A Permelia O'Brien Mystery

ARLENE SACHITANO

ZUMAYA ENIGMA   AUSTIN TX

2020

DOUBLE KNIT

© 2020 by Arlene Sachitano

ISBN 978-1-61271-423-3

Cover art & design © April Martinez

"Zumaya Enigma" and the raven logo are trademarks of Zumaya Publications LLC, Austin TX

https://www.zumayapublications.com

For Cordelia's Knitters

Chapter 1

Permelia O'Brien stood on the tree-lined sidewalk and looked at the building in front of her. It sat in a neighborhood of stately old homes, and if not for a discreet sign that sat to one side of the porte-cochere, she would have never guessed it was the city morgue.

Her oldest daughter Jennifer spun around and glared at her, the silver bangle bracelets stacked on one wrist clanking as she turned.

"You have to be joking. Please tell me you haven't signed anything."

Second daughter Katy smiled, and her eyes lit up.

"Your apartment is on the third floor, right?" She paused, and Permelia nodded. "I think it's fabulous," Katy continued. "This is a great neighborhood. You can walk to lots of stuff from here."

Jennifer tapped her Manolo Blahnik-shod toe on the sidewalk.

"Look at these old sidewalks. Mother, you could fall and break your neck. And the trees will block the streetlights at night, making this a very unsafe place."

Katy looked up and down the street.

"This isn't an unsafe neighborhood. Look at the houses. There are bikes in driveways and kids playing. Mom will be fine. She can make friends here."

"Mother can make plenty of friends at the independent living center. And they have organized activities to ensure the residents do meet people," Jennifer argued.

Katy rolled her eyes at her sister.

"Mom is waaayyy too young for shuffleboard and Wii Bowling."

Permelia cleared her throat and straightened her spine.

"Unless I'm mistaken, I've not been declared incompetent yet, which means this decision is still mine to make. And while I haven't signed any paperwork, I've agreed to take the apartment and the job, pending an inspection of the space."

"What job?" both girls said at the same time.

"Well, it's not exactly a job. To rent the apartment, you have to agree to take phone calls for the morgue at night. In return, you get a reduction in your monthly rent."

Her daughters were speechless.

"I'm going in to have a look," Permelia said. "Are you girls coming?"

◦—————◦

A cement walk led to a wide flight of steps with Japanese vine maple trees in beds on either side. A small white-haired man came out through the clear glass entry door and waited until the three women reached him. Then he held a hand out to Permelia.

"I'm Dr. Harold Grace, the assistant medical examiner. You must be Mrs. O'Brien.

Permelia took his hand.

"Please, call me Permelia."

He smiled.

"I met you out here so I could show you your private entrance."

"It's not hers yet," Jennifer muttered.

Katy elbowed her; Jennifer rubbed the arm and glared at her sister, but didn't say anything else.

Dr. Grace led them through a small parking lot along the side of the building and then around to the back.

"Here we are." He pulled a set of keys from his pocket and unlocked a plain white door. "This parking spot next to the garage is for your use, and you can park in the end spot in the garage."

He held the door open and stood aside to let Permelia and her daughters ascend the stairs then followed them up to a small landing with three doors. He used a second key to open the one directly in front of them.

"The other two doors are storerooms."

"How often will people be up here digging around in those rooms and disturbing my mother?" Jennifer demanded.

Dr. Grace's mouth lifted slightly on the left side.

"I think the last time someone looked in either one of them was about three years ago. It's mostly old records from before we were computerized." He pushed the center door open, and Permelia stepped inside.

Katy stepped past her into an office space.

"I love it," she said and twirled in a circle with her arms out. "Mom, don't you love it?"

"This is where the office phones are, of course," Dr. Grace said and gestured to a built-in desk on the left. "The door here to the right is the bathroom and then one of the two bedrooms. The door to the left beyond the desk is the second bedroom. It's slightly smaller but has its own bath." He continued into the center of the apartment. "As you can see, this is the kitchen and then the living and dining area."

Permelia crossed through the kitchen and into the living/dining area.

"It has a very lovely view and is quite spacious."

"Our building is on the National Register of Historic Homes," Grace said proudly. "And she's been very well cared for."

Jennifer tapped a manicured forefinger on her pursed lips.

"How is the...odor when you're working downstairs?"

"Jen," Katy scolded her sister.

Dr. Grace smiled at Katy.

"It's a reasonable question, but not to worry. Our workspaces are very well ventilated, and the air in our examination rooms is routed through scrubbers."

Jennifer spun on her heel and strode back to the entrance door.

"I think it's cool," Katy told her mother. "I can see you sitting in the front window with your spinning wheel or your knitting needles."

"It *is* a very lovely space," Permelia said thoughtfully. "Could you tell me a little more about the phone calls?"

<hr style="width:10%" />

Permelia put her checkbook and pen back in her purse and stood up. Dr. Grace slipped her check and the lease agreement she'd signed into the top drawer of his desk. He came around the desk and handed her two sets of keys.

"The big key opens the downstairs door, and the smaller brass key unlocks the garage; the one with the green rubber around the top is the apartment key. I've given you a spare set just in case."

"How soon may I move in?" Permelia asked as she dropped the keys into her purse.

Grace smiled.

"This afternoon, if you'd like."

"I'm afraid my things haven't arrived yet. Will Saturday work?"

"That's perfect. Unless something unusual happens, the parking lot will be empty, so you'll have room to maneuver a truck. I assume you will have a truck?"

"Yes, my son is driving it over Friday night."

"Well, welcome to Pearson House. If any questions arise, you have my number."

"Thank you."

Permelia left the office of the assistant medical examiner and exited through the front door. Katy and Jennifer were waiting on the porch.

"Congratulations on your new home," Katy said and hugged her.

"I think you can break the contract in the first three days without penalty, Mother," Jennifer said. "Please promise me you'll at least think about it."

Chapter 2

In a city known for its rain, Saturday morning dawned clear and sunny. Permelia stood by her apartment door and watched as her eldest child, Jennifer's twin, Michael O'Brien Junior, guided the box truck full of her furniture and possessions into the driveway at nine o'clock sharp, as they'd agreed.

The truck's passenger door opened, and Michael's teen-aged son Trey jumped down, ran over to his grandmother, and wrapped her in a bear hug.

"Grandma, I'm so happy to see you. It seems like it's been forever."

"Was it that bad at Aunt Jennifer's?"

Trey released her and took a step back.

"She's really unhappy that you're moving here. Poor Dad. She kept him up past midnight."

They both watched as Michael maneuvered the truck until its back door was lined up to the lower apartment door.

"What did your dad say?"

"You know Dad," Trey said. "He didn't say anything. I mean, what could he do? She's his twin; he had to listen."

"Well, I'm sorry you and your dad had to deal with that."

"It's not your fault. She's not the boss of you. Besides, I put on my earphones and listened to tunes. Dad's the one who had to suffer through it."

"Your Aunt Jennifer needs to let it go."

Trey laughed.

"Like that's going to happen."

Michael rolled up the back door of the truck.

"Are you going to stand around talking to your grandma all day, or are you going to help me unload?"

Permelia patted Trey on the back then led the way inside.

+•———•+

Michael came into the kitchen as Permelia was unwrapping dinner plates and putting them in a cupboard.

"Katy sent sandwiches if you're hungry," she told him.

Michael raised an eyebrow.

"They aren't that burned tofu stuff, are they?"

Permelia smiled.

"I wouldn't do that to my work crew. I had her stop by the deli last night and pick up some meat and cheese."

"Bring 'em on, then."

Michael wiped his mouth with the paper towel his mother handed him when he'd finished his first sandwich. He reached across the small kitchen table and flipped up the brim of his son's baseball cap.

"Did you get enough to eat?"

Trey grinned.

"I'm never full."

Permelia brought the plate of sandwiches from the kitchen counter back to the table. Michael watched his son devour a half-sandwich in three bites.

"I don't remember ever being that hungry," he said with a shake of his head.

"You ate your fair share," Permelia assured him. "You lot were like a bunch of wild animals at mealtimes."

"The girls always got the best stuff, though. Anyway, not to change the subject, but have you decided where you want the dining table?"

"I think the apartment is designed to have the right half of the front room be the living room and the left half where you come from the kitchen as the dining room."

She paused.

"But..." Michael prompted.

"Tell me what you think of this. You know my fiber co-op ladies are keeping our business going at the ranch. I'm going to be spinning here; and if I can manage it, in the kitchen, I'll do a little custom dying. I also need to do the bookwork and some distribution if I build the business here in the city. You may have noticed I brought two large armoires."

"I wondered," Michael interrupted. "They sure aren't going to fit in either of the bedrooms."

"They will go on the east wall. I brought that library table to put on the north wall. The two slipper chairs and the small round table should face the window, and if you just bring my two larger spinning wheels to the general vicinity, I'll find their spot when everything else is in place."

"And the dining table?" Michael asked.

"I'm going to try it on the north wall in the living room side. Then I'll have the sofa be free-standing, facing the front window with the easy chairs on either side of the window."

Michael stood up.

"Okay, got all that?" he asked Trey.

Trey finished his glass of milk.

"Yes, sir."

Katy stood in the opening between the kitchen and front room and spun around. None of Permelia's other eight children twirled like a top the way Katy did when she was excited. She'd done it since she was a child. Then again, with the exception of the red hair they all had, none of her kids were alike. Not even the twins, who were as different as night and day.

"Mom, this looks great."

Permelia surveyed the boxes and packing materials that covered every available space.

"It's a mess," she proclaimed. "But I agree, it shows promise."

"I didn't realize when we were here before that there's a stacked washer and dryer in one of the bathroom closets," Katy said.

Trey carried a box upstairs and into the front room.

"Where do you want this, Grandma?"

Permelia gestured to the end of the sofa, and Trey set it down.

"Hi, Aunt Katy, can I come to your house tonight?"

Katy smiled.

"Aunt Jennifer hasn't settled down, I take it."

"Nope."

Katy put her arm around his shoulders.

"Unfortunately, I'm behind on my work and will be working late tonight, and no, I can't do it with anyone else there.

He slumped his shoulders and frowned in an exaggerated manner.

"Come on, she's not that bad."

"Easy for you to say."

Michael and Trey awkwardly carried up a large blanket-covered wire cage.

"Where do you want him?" Michael asked.

"Let's take him into my bedroom," Permelia answered. "His litter-box and bed are already set up in there."

A loud yowl came from the cage at the sound of her voice.

Michael backed into the bedroom.

"Jen wouldn't let us bring him in the house, so he had to sleep in the truck."

"That's why we covered him with the blanket," Trey added. "He was yowling so loud we could hear him with the door shut."

Permelia followed them and lifted the blanket off the cage. Fenton, her Bengal cat, glared at her.

"I'm sure I'll be paying the price for this inconvenience for a few weeks."

Michael went back into the hallway.

"Jose made something for him that might help. Come on, Trey, help me carry them in."

Jose was one of the hands on the family's— now Michael's—wheat ranch. Jose's wife Graciela worked for the fiber co-op Permelia had formed on a twenty-acre piece of property that had been split from the main ranch as part of her divorce settlement. The wives of several ranch hands as well as women from neighboring ranches raised sheep and alpacas on the property and turned the fleeces into custom-dyed wool for spinning as well as finished yarns.

Michael and Trey returned, each carrying a climbing structure made from a thick tree branch. One had two carpet-covered platforms attached to horizontal branches off the main trunk. The other had a light at the top with a switch on the central trunk.

Trey set his down in front of Permelia, wrapping its cord around the base.

"Graciela told Jose how Fenton liked to turn on your light switches, so he decided to make him a light of his own. It's really cool."

"Okay, let's put that one in the front room and leave the other one in here," Permelia directed. "I don't need him turning on lights in the middle of the night when I'm trying to sleep."

Katy arrived as they plugged in the cat-tower lamp. She stood with her hands on her hips as her mother flipped the switch on and off.

"It's certainly a statement piece."

Permelia laughed.

"It's for the cat. Jose built a light switch into it in hopes Fenton will leave mine alone."

"That's a relief—I thought you bought it as a floor lamp."

Michael stepped over to his mother and gave her a hug.

"Trey and I need to hit the road." He looked at his son. "He wants us to drive home tonight, and I can't say I blame him. Call me if you need anything else."

Permelia kissed his cheek.

"And you call me when you're safely home."

He gave her a salute and stepped back to allow his son space to hug his grandmother. She hugged him and held on to him for a moment.

"You behave yourself and listen to your father."

"I always do, Grandma," he said with a grin.

Chapter 3

ould you like a cup of tea?" Katy asked her mother. "I'm going to make one."

"That sounds good. I need to sit a few minutes and put my feet up."

"Go ahead, I'll bring it in when it's ready."

Permelia sat in her overstuffed chair and pulled its matching ottoman closer. Fenton abandoned the empty packing box he was exploring and jumped onto her lap. She stroked his head.

"I know moving is hard," she crooned. "But it won't be so bad, you'll see."

"Is that how *you* feel?" Katy asked as she handed her mother a cup. "Do you think it won't be so bad? You know it's not too late. You could move back to the ranch. Michael said Tomás moved back to Mexico, so his house is available. I know he wouldn't mind."

Permelia took the cup and set it on a box beside her chair.

"I'm not going to pretend I'm thrilled about moving seven hours away from my family and the ranch, but you have to play the hand you're dealt. When your father decided to leave our marriage, I was hurt, but I was dealing with it. When he turned up with a little tart who is two years younger than our youngest child, I was mad. He wouldn't admit it, but I'm sure he'd been seeing her for months."

"But, Mom, you've always been a fighter. It's not your style to run away."

"Honey, if there was something to fight for, I'd be right there."

"I know I sound like a child, but is there really no hope for you and Daddy? Maybe he's just having a midlife crisis."

"Katy, your dad isn't having a midlife crisis; he and Heather are having a baby. I'm sorry to be the one to tell you, but it's going to become obvious real soon, and your dad clearly hasn't chosen to spread the happy news."

"I can't believe it." She buried her face in her hands. "Dad's having a baby! Aren't we enough for him?"

Permelia hated to upset her daughter. She'd always been so close to her father, but it was clear she'd had no clue about his new relationship.

"He should be the one who moves," Katy announced.

Permelia laughed.

"So, you'd rather have your dad and Heather and your new sibling live in your town instead of me?"

Katy sipped her tea and sat in the chair beside her mother.

"I see your point."

"In reality, I think the change will do me good."

"As long as Jennifer doesn't drive you crazy," Katy said and laughed. "Or put you in a home," she added.

Permelia shook her head.

"That's not going to happen."

"Does Michael know? Or for that matter, do any of the others know we're about to add to our numbers?"

Fenton head-butted Permelia's hand when she stopped petting him to reach for her tea.

"Michael knows. Your father asked him if he could stay in Tomás's house."

"You're kidding. Is Michael going to let him?"

"No, he isn't."

"How did Dad take that?"

"Your brother told him he was pretty sure the house had lead paint and maybe asbestos, and it wouldn't be a healthy place for Heather to live while she's pregnant, and it certainly wouldn't be safe for a new baby."

"That was clever of him."

"It's probably true, but your brother didn't want to appear to be taking sides."

Katy slumped back in her chair.

"Mom, I'm really sorry Dad is being such a jerk. I can't even imagine how betrayed you must feel."

Permelia sighed.

"When your dad and I got married we had great hopes and dreams for our future. And we agreed on what we wanted—the ranch, lots of kids, everything. As you-all grew up and left home, I started working with the fiber co-op. At the same time your dad started transferring the running of the ranch to your brother."

"Let me see if I understand where this is going," Katy said. "We left home leaving you guys with an empty nest. You filled your nest with helping the wives of the ranch workers start the fiber co-op. Dad filled his with starting another family with somebody young enough to be his daughter."

Once Permelia had gotten over the initial shock of finding out the only man she'd ever loved no longer loved her, she'd decided that, no matter how hurt she felt, and no matter how easy it would be, she wasn't going to be one of those women who poisoned their kids against their father. No matter what he did.

Katy got up and stood in front of the big window.

"I know he's my father, but you're my mother, and I can't stand the way he treated you."

"Sweetie, I know your father didn't handle things the best way he could have, but..." Permelia had to pause to choke back tears. She took a deep breath. "If your dad no longer loves me, we need to get on with our separate lives. We will always be your parents, and we both love you kids. That's what matters now."

Katy came to her mother's chair and leaned down to give her a hug. Fenton reached up and swatted her with his paw when she came in range. Permelia grabbed the paw before he could latch on.

"You stop that," she said and attempted a laugh.

Katy wrapped her arms around her mother and kissed her cheek before returning to her chair.

"I know you're taking the high road for us kids' sake, but Dad's acting like a jerk. I'm mad at him, and I think it's okay if you're mad at him, too."

"I'll admit, I was hurt when I found out, but staying mad at your dad and his new family only hurts me. He's moved on, and that's what I intend to do."

"You're a better person than I am."

Permelia reached over and patted Katy's hand.

"Not better, just older. I don't have time to stay mad at anyone."

Katy stood up again.

"I hate to leave you, but I've got to do some sketches for a new commission piece."

"Anything interesting?"

"Not really. A family wants a bust of their dearly departed grandfather for the foyer of their McMansion. Not my favorite thing, but it pays the bills."

Permelia stood up, lifting Fenton off her lap and setting him back in her chair.

"Fen and I have a lot of unpacking to keep us busy. We'll be just fine."

"Call if you need anything."

Chapter 4

I t was still light out when Permelia finished eating one of the sandwiches left over from lunch. Fenton sat on the chair opposite her at
the kitchen table.

"What do you think, Fen," she asked. "Would you like to take a short
walk around the block? I haven't scouted it out yet, so we might encounter
dogs."

Fenton meowed. Bengal cats were known to be chatty, and he was no
exception.

It took three tries before she found the box with his harness and leash.
She had worked with him and the harness since he was a kitten, and he
knew as soon as she pulled it out and untangled it that an adventure was
soon to follow. He paced by the door as she patted her pockets to make
sure she had her keys and phone, meowing to be sure she knew he was
ready to go.

"Allright, let's see what we can learn about our new neighborhood."

They circled their own block first to avoid having to cross a street until
she was sure how Fenton was going to deal with an urban environment.
He handled it as though he'd been born in the city. Emboldened by his con-
fidence, she picked him up and carried him across the street, setting him
back down when they were opposite their parking lot. They were almost
to the corner when a voice called out from behind a brick wall, "What sort
of cat is that?"

Permelia looked around, not sure where the voice had come from.

"Over here," the voice said, and she noticed a thick oak-plank door with
heavy iron hinges set into the wall. An iron grill covered a small speakeasy
door set at eye level. She stepped over to look through the opening.

The speaker was a woman with graying dreadlocks and dark brown eyes.

Permelia picked Fenton up so he wouldn't be squished when the door opened.

"He's a Bengal."

"Is that some sort of exotic?"

Permelia smiled. She got that question a lot.

"No, it's a domestic breed. They *were* created by crossing Asian cats, who are a wild breed, with domestic cats. But that's at least four generations back."

"Are you the new tenant at the morgue?" the woman asked.

"Yes, I am. I'm Permelia O'Brien, and I just moved in today. You are…?"

"I'm sorry, what must you think of me? I'm Wilma Granger, and I've lived here pretty much forever."

"Nice to meet you, Wilma."

"Was that a spinning wheel I saw your men carrying into your apartment?"

Permelia smiled.

"It was. I actually have two of them—three if you count the electric one."

"Would you like to come inside?" Wilma asked.

"Are there other animals?"

"Not in the garden. I have birds in the house, but nothing out here."

"In that case, we would love to come in."

⊬———⊣

The speakeasy grill closed, and Permelia heard the muffled clicking of locks before the heavy door opened. She stepped through the opening and stopped. Wilma was a tall woman, dressed in a bright green-and-purple-and-pink silk duster over wide-legged black pants. Dreadlocks ended in beads that matched the colors in the shirt. She had the sort of ageless face that suggested she could be in her forties or her sixties; Permelia couldn't tell.

Trying not to stare at Wilma, Permelia turned her attention to the courtyard she'd stepped into.

"This is…" Permelia was speechless.

Wilma smiled.

"My little world has that effect on people."

"It's breathtaking. I'm not sure if I'm more amazed by the exotic plants, the intricate tilework, or the sculptures. The outer wall doesn't give a hint of the beauty you've created in here."

"Come in and look around."

Permelia strolled along the stone path.

The tilework looked Italian, as did the sculptures. The plants were more Amazon jungle. The house was large, two stories or maybe three—she couldn't tell from this angle. The house and garden consumed an entire block and must have been built in an age when there was still room to have such space in the city.

"I can't take credit for most of it. My grandmother collected the artwork and some of the tiles in Italy. She was more into orchids, and had a special room built for them in the house. I killed off a number of them before I got the hang of keeping them alive, if not thriving." She made a sweeping gesture with her hand. "The rest of this stuff is mostly grocery-store variety plants gone wild."

"It's fantastic, in any case."

"Can I get you some iced tea?" Wilma asked when they arrived at a flagstone patio outside a leaded glass door. She gestured to a glass-topped bistro table and chair set, and Permelia sat.

"No, thank you, if I drink tea now, I'll be up all night. Water would be nice."

"I'll be right back."

She returned with two glasses, setting one in front of Permelia and sitting down as she took a sip out of the other.

"Tell me about those spinning wheels."

"I started a small women's co-op on our wheat ranch with some of the wives of the ranch hands. We have sheep and alpacas and a few angora goats. We collect the fiber and then spin it and dye it and sell it to a few yarn stores and online."

Wilma pulled back and gave Permelia a long look.

"Well, my, my, my, you're full of surprises. Here I'm thinking you're a sweet little retired lady and really you're a business mogul."

Permelia's cheeks turned pink.

"I'm hardly that. As my kids grew up and left home, I had a little time on my hands. We grow wheat on the family ranch; but there was a parcel that wasn't suitable for growing, so I got the idea that maybe we could get a few animals and play around. We had a group of ranch hands who had been with us for years, and their kids were leaving home, too. The wives and I and some of our daughters had been knitting together for years, and we'd always joked around about growing our own yarn. Then one day it wasn't a joke, and we sold our first skeins of yarn."

"I always wanted to learn to knit," Wilma said wistfully.

"It's not too late to start."

"I don't know about that."

Fenton jumped off Permelia's lap and strolled across a stone path to a small pool with a fountain in its center. He sniffed the water's surface.

"Oh. No, you don't, mister," she told him and started to reel in his leash. She was too late.

"He can't hurt anything," Wilma assured her, but Permelia stood up and grabbed for her cat.

Fenton was quicker, and jumped into the water before she could stop him. The water was deeper than he'd expected, and he submerged briefly before resurfacing, sputtering and shaking his head, his front feet paddling as Permelia lifted him out of the pool.

"I'm so sorry," she said and set him on the walk.

Wilma laughed.

"I've never seen such a thing. Let me go get him a towel."

"I don't want to trouble you. He'll be fine until we get home."

"Nonsense. I'll be right back."

"Now you've done it," she told the cat when Wilma was out of sight. "Just when we were getting to know the neighbors, you had to go and make a mess of things."

Wilma came back with a large towel and handed it to Permelia.

"I didn't know cats liked water," she said as she sat back down at the table.

Permelia put the towel in her lap and set Fenton in the middle of it, rubbing him with the ends.

"Some breeds do, and others don't. Bengal cats are in the do category."

"Well, I'm glad, because he's brought me a much-needed laugh."

Permelia waited to see if she would say anything else.

"I'm sorry. I've been a little tense lately. Someone has been...I'm not sure what you would call it. Trying to break in, I guess. This place is such a fortress someone would have to resort to serious methods to breach the wall, but I think someone's been trying."

"What makes you think that?"

"There are scratches on the outside lock, as if someone's been trying to pick it. Before she passed, my grandmother had state-of-the-art locks installed, so they're virtually pick-proof. The key resembles a piece of chain.

"The other night I heard a noise that sounded like a drill. I checked the security camera, and someone in dark clothing was attempting to drill around the lock. The door is made from ipe, which is a South American wood that's twice as dense as most woods and five times harder. A normal drill bit wouldn't make a dent. And the middle of the door has a steel plate, in any case."

"Have you talked to the police?"

"Unfortunately, my grandmother burned that bridge years ago. A few too many calls with nothing found put her on the crank caller list."

"I don't mean to be nosy, but all these defenses strike me as pretty extreme. Was your grandmother protecting something?"

"That's the crazy thing. Other than telling me never to let my guard down, she never explained. I have no idea why she made this place such a fortress. I've always thought she was just eccentric, but now that someone's been trying to get in, I'm starting to wonder."

"I wish I had an idea to offer," Permelia said.

They sat in silence while she finished toweling her cat off.

"I'd better get this scalawag home," she said and lifted him off the towel.

"You can take the towel. He might get a chill if he's not wrapped up."

"Oh, thank you. I'll have it back tomorrow."

"No rush."

Permelia stood up, wrapping Fenton as she did so. Wilma rose.

"You said it's not too late for me to learn to knit. Would you be willing to teach me?"

"After all the trouble we've been, it's the least I can do for you. My apartment is still a bit of a mess..."

"If you don't mind, could we do it here? I work from home, and people call at all hours. If we meet here, I can listen for the phone."

"I need to be home in the evenings for the morgue phone, but if we can do it during the day, that would work fine."

"It's a date, then. Just let me know when you're ready." Wilma pulled a card from a pocket hidden in the voluminous folds of fabric that made up her tunic. "Here's my phone number. Call, and I'll meet you at the gate."

Permelia pocketed the card.

"Speaking of the morgue phone, I'd better get back and check for messages. They told me I don't have to sit home all the time, but I don't want to miss anything if I can help it."

Wilma led her to the gate and pulled a ring with several strange-looking keys on it from her pocket. Permelia watched her new friend open a series of four locks like nothing she had ever seen before swinging the door open.

As she carried Fenton home, Permelia wondered if Wilma's grandmother had been merely eccentric, or if she had hidden something behind that wall that was worth going to such lengths to protect.

＊—＊

Permelia barely had time to remove Fenton's harness before he ran up the stairs to their apartment door. Her foot slipped as she started to follow, and she realized she'd stepped on a piece of paper lying on the entry floor. It was folded to fit through the mail slot in the door. She picked it up and blew out a breath as she read the four-word sentence.

YOU don't belong here!

Fenton paced in front of the door at the top of the stairs and meowed insistently. Permelia folded the piece of paper, stuffed it in her pants pocket, and climbed the stairs.

"Well, Mr. Cat, it would appear at least one person doesn't want us here."

Fenton meowed loudly and went into the kitchen, bumping his dish with his nose in case she wasn't reading his signals correctly.

"Okay, okay. I get it. You don't care about the letter, you're hungry after your swim in the neighbor's pond."

It took two tries to find his food and the scoop that went in the container, neither of which were in the box where his harness had been, but eventually she had his placemat situated on the kitchen floor with his bowl of food and water and he was able to eat his dinner.

She made a cup of herb tea for herself and took it to the chair by the window. She pulled the paper from her pocket and examined it. She hadn't expected a parade to welcome her to the neighborhood, but somehow, she hadn't expected something like this note, either.

Chapter 5

Dr. Grace had told Permelia night calls weren't a frequent occurrence and not to be surprised if days or even weeks passed before she got her first, so she was surprised when the phone rang while she was reading in bed that first night. She asked the questions on the checklist he'd given her and verified that the body in question was indeed going to come to the morgue that night. As they had prearranged, she called Dr. Grace as soon as she hung up.

"I'll be right in," he assured her; and true to his word, she saw his car pull into the parking lot fifteen minutes later. She went downstairs and met him at the morgue door.

He smiled when he saw her.

"I was hoping you'd have a few days to get settled in before you had to deal with any night calls, but our business is unpredictable."

"I don't mind. I just hope I did it right."

"I'm sure you did. I mean, someone being found in the middle of the night in the woods with head trauma isn't likely to have died from natural causes. Sure, people can have a branch fall and hit them on the head, but not usually in the middle of the night. It's important we secure any and all evidence."

"Will you do the autopsy tonight?"

He smiled.

"No, that's the great part of being a pathologist. In spite of what you might see on television, Tony will check him onsite and then bring him here, and we'll get him in the cooler, but his exam can wait until tomorrow."

<hr />

It took an hour, but finally an ambulance turned onto the street.

"We'll probably be done here in thirty minutes or less."

"I'll be on my way, then,"

Dr. Grace smiled at her.

"Congratulations on handling your first call."

Permelia walked back around to her entrance door and let herself in. The ambulance left soon after, and Dr. Grace was gone less than thirty minutes later. It would be several more hours, though, before Permelia managed to fall asleep.

⊷———⊶

Katy arrived early the next morning, a white bakery bag stamped with *Helen Bernhard Bakery* in her hand. She carried it to the kitchen table and then put the teakettle on.

"I have to visit a new client on this end of town this morning, so I thought I'd come by and see how you and Fenton did your first night in your new home."

Permelia told her about her first night call as Katy bustled around the kitchen and found teacups, saucers, and plates.

"Oh, and before that I took the cat for a walk, and we met our neighbor across the street. She lives in a bit of a fortress."

"A fortress? You're kidding, right?"

"Not really. The house is behind a solid stone wall a couple of feet thick and probably ten feet tall. And has a pretty sophisticated security system."

"That's strange."

"Not as strange as this," Permelia said and handed her the note that had been slipped through her mail slot.

"That's frightening. Have you called the police?"

"A prank note is not worthy of a call to the police, and I forgot to tell Dr. Grace about it last night. I will when I see him again. They never mentioned what happened to the previous tenant. Maybe they were asked to leave and aren't happy about it."

"Let me know what he says."

"Tell me about your new client," Permelia said, changing the subject.

They finished their tea and doughnuts, and Permelia walked Katy down to the parking lot. She watched as she pulled out and a Mercedes sedan pulled in. It was parked, and a pencil-thin woman in a gray wool suit got out and hurried to the front of the building. A boy of about twelve got out of the car and followed her, hurrying to keep up.

Permelia had put the note in her pocket, intending to speak to Dr. Grace right away, but she changed her mind, thinking the people might be the family of the dead man.

She spent the rest of the morning unpacking; and before she knew it, it was lunchtime and her kitchen was functional, but devoid of food.

"Fenton, you hold down the fort while I see if I can find the grocery store that's supposed to be three blocks from here."

She picked up her reusable grocery bag and headed out. As she started across the parking lot, she saw something colorful lying in front of the garbage cans. She walked over and picked up a knitted cap. Someone had apparently intended to throw it in the garbage but missed the can. She put it in her bag and continued on her way.

"Permelia," called Wilma as she passed the oak door. "How'd your first night go?"

The iron speakeasy grill was open, and Permelia could see Wilma's face behind the grate.

"Looks like you're headed for the grocery, do you have time for a cup of coffee?"

"I suppose I could stop for a little while."

Wilma opened the door and ushered her in, locking it behind her, before leading her along the path, across the patio, and through the back door into the kitchen.

"Is coffee okay? I can make tea if you'd prefer."

"Coffee is fine," Permelia answered as she took a seat at the kitchen table. "Your kitchen is beautiful."

Wilma glanced at the pumpkin-colored walls and the blue, orange, and yellow Italian tilework that covered the countertops, backsplash, and part of the floor.

"I read a memoir about a woman's love affair with Italy and decided to give my kitchen an Italian makeover."

"Did you do the work yourself?"

Wilma smiled.

"Why, yes, I did. What gave it away?"

"Your expression when you look at it. It was obviously a labor of love."

"I am pretty pleased with it. I spend a lot of time in this house, so it needs to please me."

Wilma handed Permelia a mug of coffee and set a small blue pitcher of cream on the table next to a matching sugar bowl.

"Did I hear a guest arrive at the morgue last night?"

Permelia stirred cream into her coffee.

"My first call. Dr. Grace had instructed me to call him the first few times no matter what, but this one was pretty clear. I'm not sure I can say anything about what happened."

"That's okay, I don't want you to get in trouble."

"Did you know the person or persons who lived in my apartment before me?"

Wilma sat down opposite her.

"I can't say that I did. I mean, I recognized the woman when she'd walked by, but that's it. Why do you ask?"

Permelia took a sip of her coffee to avoid answering. Wilma seemed friendly enough, but there was always the possibility *she* was the author of the note. But then she recalled the note was delivered while she was out walking, and Wilma would have had to hurry to slip it through the mail slot and return to her courtyard to be behind the big door when Permelia and Fenton walked by.

"Someone slipped a note through my mail slot while I was walking Fenton last night."

"By your expression, I assume it wasn't a 'welcome to the neighborhood' message?"

Permelia smiled.

"Quite the contrary. It said, "You don't belong here'."

Wilma covered her mouth with her hand and thought.

"I'm pretty sure the last occupant of your apartment was a student at the local seminary. The mailman said she had a lot of mail related to her graduation in the weeks before she moved."

"So, it doesn't sound like she'd have any reason to be trying to scare me off."

"I haven't heard of anyone having that sort of problem in the past, but not to state the obvious, you do live over a morgue. It could make anyone who lives there a target of pranksters."

Permelia leaned back in her chair.

"I suppose."

A kitchen timer rang, and Wilma got up and pulled a tray of biscotti from the oven.

"Perfect timing. Would you like a fresh-baked biscotti to go with your coffee?"

"That sounds lovely," Permelia said with a smile.

⊷——⊶

After a second cup of coffee and two biscotti, Permelia got up and carried her empty cup to the sink. She picked up her grocery bag and remembered the hat she'd found on her way over to Wilma's.

"I found a knitted cap by the dumpster when I was leaving. I stuffed it in my bag without looking at it." She pulled the hat out.

Wilma examined it.

"It looks handmade."

Permelia held it up and rubbed her hand over an area of textured knitting.

"Huh," she said, and stretched the hat to better display the textured area.

"What?"

"This blue tweedy fiber is *my* yarn."

"Your yarn? What do you mean? Does this have to do with that co-op you were telling me about?"

"Yes, this is yarn we make and sell. I'm pretty sure I spun this one."

"How can you tell?" Wilma asked her, clearly fascinated.

"I had a hard time getting the exact blue I wanted. I'd know it anywhere. We labeled it OOAC—one of a kind. It only went to one or two stores."

"That's quite a coincidence, don't you think? The yarn you spun in your coop in Washington ends up here?"

"My yarn is only sold in the Northwest, but you're right, it's still a coincidence."

"I don't mean to be nosey, but won't it be difficult to keep running your business from here?"

"There will be challenges, but I think it will work. Besides, I don't really have a choice." She glanced at her watch. She wasn't really in a hurry. She had nothing else but more unpacking to do this afternoon, but she wasn't ready to share the whole sordid tale of her divorce and her ex-husband's impending fatherhood just yet.

"I need to get to the store. I'll have to save that story for another time. Thank you so much for the coffee and biscotti. It was delicious."

Wilma walked her to the door and then the gate.

"I hope you'll come join me again."

Permelia stepped back out on the sidewalk and could hear the locks clicking into place as she walked away.

Chapter 6

enton was pacing in the entry hall when Permelia returned from the store, her grocery bag bulging.

"Cat, we're going to have to find the store where regular people shop." She made her way carefully to her new kitchen, Fenton winding between her legs the whole way. "I'm sure the organic foods are wonderful for us, but we can't afford the prices on a daily basis. Besides that, Katy's estimate of how far away it is was a little off. My bag was pretty heavy for me to carry that far."

She talked to the cat as she unloaded her groceries into the still-unfamiliar kitchen. When she reached the bottom of the bag, she pulled out the knitted cap. She looked down at her cat, who was now rubbing against her shin.

"I'll fill your treat ball if you'll quit rubbing on my leg," she told him. "Then I need to go see if Dr. Grace knows who this hat belongs to. It's much too nice to go in the dumpster."

Fenton arched his back and said, "Mrrooww."

Permelia took his plastic treat ball and separated the two halves, dropping a dozen kibble snacks into one side then screwing the other half onto it. She made sure the adjustable holes were the correct size to allow the kibble to fall out but only after the cat had batted it around a while.

She picked up the hat and set the ball on the floor, giving it a little push that sent it rolling.

"I'll be back in a few minutes," she said, but Fenton was too involved with trying to knock a treat out of the ball to even look up.

<hr />

Permelia climbed the front stairs to the porch; she could see Dr. Grace talking to a short, stout woman with steel-gray hair in the foyer. She decided not to interrupt and occupied herself deadheading the roses that filled the flowerbed at the base of the stairs, pinching the expired blooms off with her fingers and stacking them in a discrete pile under the end bush. She set the knitted cap on the edge of the sidewalk.

Fifteen minutes later, she heard the front door open. She dropped the dead flowers, brushed her hands together, and picked up the hand-knit hat.

"But he hasn't gone to any of the hospitals in the area," a woman said.

"It's a pretty big leap to assume he would be with us," Dr. Grace told her in a soft voice.

They came into view on the top step. The woman's face was tear-streaked, and she dabbed at her eyes with a crumpled tissue. Dr. Grace had a comforting hand on her shoulder.

"You said he's only been gone since dinnertime last night, right? You said a friend called him asking for help? Maybe the friend needed more help than expected. Maybe they had to leave town for some reason," Dr. Grace suggested.

"He wouldn't do that without telling me. He knows I worry. Besides, he left his cell phone charging on our dresser. He would have come back to get it. Something horrible has happened. I can feel it."

Permelia stood to the side of the landing, still clutching the hat, as Dr. Grace guided the woman down the stairs. The woman stopped halfway down.

"What are you doing with my husband's hat?" she demanded.

"I found it at our dumpster out back," Permelia said and held it out.

The color drained from the woman's face, and she fainted, tumbling down the two remaining steps and landing on Permelia, knocking her to the pavement.

<hr>

"I need some help out here," Dr. Grace yelled, and an office clerk immediately appeared in the doorway.

"Should I call nine-one-one?" the young man asked.

"Let's hold off for a minute. Get me a cool wash rag and a glass of water." He maneuvered the unconscious woman off Permelia. "Are you okay?" he asked her.

"I'm fine. How is she?" Permelia answered.

The woman was coming around as the clerk returned with the cool compress and water, and she attempted to sit up.

"Let's just lie still for a moment, shall we?" Dr. Grace said in a firm tone. He put the compress on her forehead and looked into her eyes, holding a finger up and directing her to follow it with her eyes. She did, and

Dr. Grace moved on to check for cuts or broken bones. When he finished, the visitor sat up, handing the compress to the doctor.

"I'm fine. I'm not sure what got into me. I'm not one of those women who faints when she hears bad news. I guess it was the shock of seeing my husband's hat." She looked at Permelia. "Why *do* you have my husband's hat?"

"As I said before, I found it at the dumpster in our parking lot."

"Are you sure it belongs to your husband?" Grace asked.

Both women turned to him.

"Yes, she's sure," Permelia said as the woman said, "I'm sure."

Dr. Grace stood up, and helped the woman to her feet.

"I'm *fine*," she repeated as he started to speak.

"I'm sorry," he said. "I wish I could help you, but your husband isn't here, and we haven't had any calls since last night."

"Why is his hat here, then?".

"I couldn't say." He looked toward the door. "If you're sure you're okay, I need to get back to work."

"I'm fine," the woman repeated a third time, and then watched him climb the stairs and disappear into the building, followed by his clerk. She held the hat to her face and inhaled. Her eyes filled with tears again.

Permelia waited a minute to let the woman recover her composure.

"Did you make the hat?" she asked finally.

"Yes, I did. I bought the blue yarn at a store not far from here." She held her hand out to Permelia. "I'm Betty Fitzandreu, and I'm very sorry I fell on you. Are you okay?"

Permelia smiled.

"I'm Permelia O'Brien, and no harm was done. Your hat is lovely, and if I'm not mistaken, the blue yarn was made by a cooperative I belong to."

Betty rubbed her hand over the blue yarn.

"This is Wheatfields yarn. I usually don't spend that much money on yarn, but the blue matches Eid's eyes."

"Wheatfields is our co-op name as well as the name of our yarn brand. What a coincidence."

Betty sighed.

"I just wish I knew why Eid's hat is here if he isn't."

"I suppose you've already talked to the police?"

She was silent so long, Permelia didn't think she was going to answer.

"They weren't much help," Betty finally said. "They said there wasn't any evidence of foul play at this point, and he hasn't been missing twenty-four hours yet."

Her shoulders slumped as she turned to leave.

"Say, would you like to come have a cup of tea?" Permelia asked her. "I live in the apartment over this place. I was just down to ask if they knew who the hat belonged to, and now, we've solved that little mystery."

"I would like that," Betty said.

◆─────◆

"Are you bothered by cats?" Permelia asked her guest before opening her apartment door. "I'm afraid mine is very curious. I can shut him in the bedroom, if you want."

Betty smiled.

"I love cats. I have a very chatty Siamese at home."

Permelia led her guest into the living room.

"I'll just put the kettle on," she said and went to the kitchen.

Betty stood looking out the front window as Permelia got the cups out of a cupboard and, after three tries, found her tray to set them on. She studied her guest through the open archway as she located teabags and waited for the water to boil. The woman twisted a damp tissue around her fingers before dabbing at her eyes again.

There was no doubt in Permelia's mind that Betty was genuinely upset about her husband's absence, and yet something about it troubled her. Granted, her own marriage was not a shining example of how long-married couples behaved, but even before she knew of Michael Senior's infidelity, and had still trusted him implicitly, she would not have showed up at the morgue looking for him after only a few hours. He had fallen asleep in a hay storage barn on the opposite end of the property more than once after a long day of cutting in the summer. And if the missing husband had left his phone at home, he simply might not have the means to contact Betty if he was delayed.

The water boiled, and Permelia filled the cups, set a dish with a selection of teabags on it beside the cups, then carried the tray to the living room.

"Here we go," she said and set the tray on her small living room table.

Betty snuffled as she selected a bag and dropped it into her cup of steaming water.

"What sort of work does your husband do?" Permelia asked as she assembled her own tea. She looked up at Betty. "We don't have to talk about him if it's too upsetting."

"Not at all. Eid is an accountant," she said with pride. "He has his own small business."

Permelia dunked her teabag up and down.

"Is there any chance he was out so late that he went to his office straight from his friend's emergency?"

"He doesn't have an office away from home. He goes to each place of business he does the books for, and he only does client billing from his home office. Quite a few of his clients are out of town."

"Have you tried calling any of them?"

"If he was going to one of his out-of-town clients, he would have taken his overnight bag, and it's still in the closet, and besides that, he wouldn't have taken his knitted cap on a work trip."

Permelia sipped her tea.

"So, there *are* occasions when your husband is gone overnight?"

"Well, yes," Betty said and set her cup down. "But that's when he's working. And he always tells me. Always. I iron his shirts and pack his ties. He always wears the green tie with a gold four-leaf-clover tie clasp when he's going to work out of town."

"Is he Irish?" Permelia asked.

"Oh, yes, very."

Two strikes against him, Permelia thought. Her husband Michael was Irish, and she knew she shouldn't paint all Irishmen with the same brush, but she couldn't help it. Her wounds were too raw.

"Do you have children?"

"We have one son. He's going to college in Ireland."

"Wow, that's a long way away."

"We're going to move there in another month. That's why Red decided to go to school there."

Chapter 7

The two women sipped their tea in companionable silence.

"Just to be clear, are you sure your husband was wearing his hat when he left your house?" Permelia asked thoughtfully after a few minutes had passed.

Betty sighed.

"I was sure he had it on. We have several hooks by our back door. We hang our outdoor jackets and hats on them. He always grabs that hat when he puts his jacket on, and his jacket is gone."

"Well, maybe he dropped it when he was helping his friend, and someone around here found it and put it in our dumpster."

"I just have a bad feeling about it. If his hat was found anywhere else, I would think what you just said, but the morgue? Is it really possible someone who found his hat accidentally disposed of it at the morgue?"

"Stranger things have happened, I suppose, but I agree, finding anything at the morgue has a bad connotation. It's too bad he didn't have that cell phone with him."

"He didn't tell me who he was going to help, either. He did seem somewhat irritated about it."

"Do you suppose the call would be on his cell phone?"

Betty straightened in her chair.

"I didn't even think of that. I'll check when I get home. I'll call the number and find out if he made it to wherever they were."

Permelia was relieved Betty had a plan. She didn't want to say out loud there was another possibility Betty wasn't considering. Maybe there wasn't a friend, and there had been no call. Hubby might have decided he didn't want to be married anymore, so he invented a reason to leave with no plan to ever return. Permelia acknowledged to herself this possibility was perhaps colored by her own recent experience. Not every Irish-bred husband was a jerk like her ex.

Permelia realized Betty was talking to her.

"I'm sorry," she said. "I was thinking of my ex-husband. He's also an Irishman."

"Oh, I'm sorry. Here I am dumping all my worries on you and you have your own troubles."

Permelia patted her hand.

"Don't you worry about me. I divorced my husband, and I just moved here to start over on my own. Two of my daughters live here, so I'm okay."

"Have you found anyone to knit with yet?"

Permelia smiled.

"I literally just moved in, so no. Do you know of a group around here?"

Betty's face pinked.

"No, I live on the other side of town, but I'd love to get together and knit until you find a local group."

"That sounds great. When are you available? My schedule is pretty flexible."

"How about the day after tomorrow? I'm sure my husband will be home by then."

"Perfect. I noticed a coffee shop down the block from here. Would that be okay? Say ten-thirty?"

"Ten-thirty works for me," Betty said. She picked up her empty cup, and set it on the tray. "Now I'd better get home and check that cell phone."

⊷——⊷

Permelia followed Betty downstairs and locked the outer door after watching her drive away. At the ranch, they'd only locked the door if they were leaving the property and even then only if their adult children were also going to be gone. Of course, there were ranch dogs who would put up a racket if anyone strange came on the property, she mused as she climbed back up to the apartment. She was sure Fenton saw himself as her great protector, capable of taking on anyone and anything. Unfortunately, in real life, at fifteen pounds, he wasn't going to be much use if a stranger wandered in.

She fetched a couple of kitty treats from a foil packet in the refrigerator. Calling him was unnecessary. He came running from wherever he'd been hiding when he heard the treat bag being opened. She put the treats on the floor, and he immediately began crunching them.

"What did you make of Betty?" she asked. "She doesn't seem like the unstable type," she went on as if he'd answered, "but I guess one cup of tea doesn't qualify as knowing her. Still, her concern seems real."

She was still trying to make sense out of Betty's story when her phone rang.

"Hey, Mom, there's a sale on at an art supply store on your side of town, and I was thinking about checking it out tomorrow. I need a new carving hammer. Would you like to come with? We could explore your neighborhood on our way back. You probably need a hairdresser and a pharmacy and stuff like that, right?"

Permelia unconsciously pulled on a lock of hair at the nape of her neck.

"Does my hair look bad?"

Katy laughed.

"Your hair looks fine, but don't you want to get oriented?"

"I'd like to find a normal grocery store. The one you suggested was lovely, but it was a bit expensive."

Katy laughed.

"Organic food is better for you, but I suppose we can find you a 'normal' supermarket."

"Thank you, honey."

"I'll be by around ten-thirty."

⊢——⊣

Permelia had eaten, washed her dishes, and was spinning some undyed blue-faced Leicester wool when Katy arrived.

"Behave yourself," Permelia instructed Fenton before locking the apartment door.

Katy's errands took them to the art store and the hardware store before she drove back to Permelia's neighborhood, where they located a hairdresser Katy had heard good things about and a pharmacy that delivered. Finally, she drove them to a grocery store.

"Here," she said and handed her mother a reusable plastic shopping bag. She'd parked in front of the grocery store. "In case you buy anything. You're not allowed single-use bags within the city limits."

Permelia took the colorful bag.

"I don't know what you think happened after you left home, but we've been using these for years."

Katy laughed as she got out of the car.

"Sorry, I forgot you were the original earth mother."

"I need to get some baking essentials," Permelia said, ignoring Katy's remark.

Katy pushed their shopping cart toward the baking supplies, several aisles away. Permelia noticed two boys in the canned goods row and was all but certain the taller of the two was the boy who had accompanied the woman to the morgue yesterday. She followed them to the display of beans,

31

She picked up a can of pinto beans, and feigned studying the nutritional data.

The boy who looked familiar picked up a large can of pork and beans.

"We have to eat these before my mom gets home. We're not allowed to eat regular food. It's not on our diet plan."

His friend rolled his eyes.

"I feel you. My mom's the same way. I'm afraid her plan is to stunt my growth."

"My mom is entertaining clients tonight, so we have plenty of time. Let's go get a bag of chips, too."

The boys exited the aisle, and Permelia put her can back on the shelf as Katy wheeled their cart into the aisle.

"I thought you needed flour and stuff."

"I do, but I recognized a young fellow who came to the morgue the morning after my first call. I know you'll think I'm crazy, but someone left a hand-knit hat at our dumpster, and it turns out it belongs to a man who is missing whose wife came looking for him at the morgue."

"What does that have to do with the kid?"

"He came with the woman I assumed was there to identify the body picked up the night before."

"And you thought what? The kid would say 'I left my newly dead father's hat at the morgue yesterday' while he was buying his beans? I think living over the morgue is making your imagination run wild."

"It sounds silly when you say it that way." Permelia said. "Now, where is the baking aisle?"

"So, what did he say?" Katy asked, pushing the cart to the desired aisle.

"He talked about having to hide the beans lest his mother find out he was cheating on his diet. He also said his mother was entertaining clients tonight. I guess the wake was a short one."

"It's possible her work obligation is such she can't get out of it."

"Even with her husband barely cold?"

"Assuming they're connected to *your* body, what does it all mean?"

Permelia put a bag of flour in the cart.

"I don't know, it's just curious."

Chapter 8

Permelia went to the coffee shop early the next morning. She had laid out three different outfits before settling on khaki pants, a blouse with a small floral print, and a navy-blue cotton cardigan. At the ranch, she'd have been in jeans and a teeshirt, as would most of her friends, adding a sweatshirt in the cold months. She had no idea how city people dressed for tea.

She habitually carried a small unlined notebook in her bag, and she pulled it out as soon as she was seated with her cup of Earl Grey tea. Shopping for groceries and then putting them away last night had driven home the point that she was going to have to learn how to cook for one. She was used to cooking for a crowd at the ranch—even after the kids were grown, there were always ranch hands, neighbors, and then grandkids stopping by and staying to eat. Cooking for one was going to take some planning.

She got out her pen and started making notes. She listed the various main dishes she made that could be divided into meals for one and then frozen. By the time she was done, she'd concluded she would need to buy a small freezer.

She closed her notebook and put it back in her bag just as Betty arrived, looking as though she hadn't slept since the previous day. She got a new cup of tea, Betty got coffee, and they sat at Permelia's table.

"Any news?" she asked when Betty was settled.

Betty slumped in her chair and shook her head.

"Nothing. It's like he vanished off the face of the earth. I looked at his cell phone and there was nothing useful on it. No calls anywhere near the time he said he got the call and left. In fact, most of the calls were to me, our house, or our son."

"Did he have another phone?"

"If he did, I never saw it. He worked from his home office, and we have a landline for that."

"I'm so sorry. I was hoping his cell phone would tell you something."

Betty sipped her coffee and gazed out the window.

"I guess I can go to the police station again and fill out a missing person's report."

Permelia pulled a sock she was knitting from her bag and held it up for Betty's inspection.

"I'm making socks for all my grandkids for this coming Christmas. I decided I needed to get an early start."

Betty opened a floral knitting bag and brought out a cable-patterned scarf.

"I'm making a hat and scarf out of Irish yarn my son sent me."

Permelia felt the scarf.

"That's wonderful. I love the tweed, and the stitch definition is perfect."

They made small talk while they knitted and sipped their drinks. An hour passed before either checked the time.

Betty rolled up her scarf and stuffed it into her bag.

"I'd better get going. I hope the police are ready to listen to me this time."

"Do you subscribe to the local paper?" Permelia asked.

"No, Eideard dislikes it. He says they're too politically biased."

"I saw they had them at the counter. I think I'll pick one up when I drop my cup off. Can I take yours?"

Betty held her cup out, and Permelia carried the white ceramic mugs back to the counter, purchased her paper, and brought it back to the table. She was about to fold it to put in her bag when she noticed a picture on the bottom half of the front page.

Local businessman found dead in forest, it said.

"This must be the person who came into the morgue my first night."

Betty looped her bag over her arm and glanced at the paper. The color drained from her face, and she collapsed unconscious, her face hitting the cement floor; blood from her nose began to pool.

Chapter 9

The coffee shop waitress raced around the counter and joined Permelia, one hand holding a cell phone to her ear, the other feeling for a
pulse on Betty's wrist. When she'd finished giving the particulars to the
911 operator, she turned Betty onto her back and held a napkin to her nose.
When she was done, she asked Permelia, "Has she been ill?"

"I have no idea—I've only just met her. She's been under a lot of
stress recently, I do know that."

"So, you don't know if she takes any medications."

Permelia shook her head.

"I'm sorry—I'm Tran, Tran Wilson," the waitress said. "I'm a nurse-
practitioner. This is my sister's shop. I'm covering for her while she's at
an appointment."

As she talked, Tran straightened Betty's legs and grabbed a stack of
newspapers from a nearby rack, using them to elevate Betty's feet.

Betty started to stir, and as she opened her eyes, she tried to sit up.
Tran gently pushed on her shoulder.

"Don't try to sit up yet. The paramedics are on their way."

This seemed to agitate Betty more. Tran spoke to her in soothing words
Permelia couldn't hear, and Betty stilled.

The fire truck and paramedics arrived, and Tran stepped back to let
them do their work. Permelia started to back away, and Betty tried to sit
up again.

"Don't leave me, please."

The color was beginning to return to Betty's face, but she still looked
gray. Permelia looked at the paramedic, who was setting an IV port in
her hand. He was a small wiry man with reddish hair and freckles.

"You can ride in the front," he told her. "It might help keep her calm."

The other paramedic, on her opposite side, a large dark-haired man, inflated a blood pressure cuff on Betty's arm. He read the number and then looked at her.

"Do you take medicine for your blood pressure?" he asked her.

"I take a water pill," Betty mumbled.

Permelia glanced at the reading on the machine. Betty's pill wasn't working now—her blood pressure was 220/150. Permelia was no doctor, but she knew that was *not* a good number.

The two men shifted Betty onto a gurney and wheeled her to the ambulance, the smaller man climbing into the back with her. The dark-haired man indicated that Permelia should get into the front passenger seat.

"Will my car be okay here?" she asked Tran.

"Sure, don't worry about it. And please, let us know how she is when you come back for it."

"I will," Permelia assured her, and climbed into the ambulance.

⊷————⊶

Permelia's sock was of the toe-up variety, and she was able to turn the heel and was on her way up the cuff when Betty's doctor came out to talk to her. Betty had given the hospital permission to talk to Permelia before they wheeled her away for a head scan. He explained that stroke was a concern when you fainted and were past a certain age.

She put the sock down and stood.

"Your friend seems okay except for her blood pressure. There were no signs of stroke. I gather she's been under a lot of stress lately?"

"I've only just met her, so I don't really know her background, but she is definitely very worried about her husband. She says he got a call and went out to help a friend several nights ago, and she hasn't seen him since."

"Do you think this was his way of leaving the marriage?"

"As I said, I don't really know them, but at least from her perspective, things were okay. In fact, they were about to move to Ireland, where their son lives."

"Her blood pressure is dangerously high, and given that and the bump on her head from hitting the floor in the coffee shop, I'm going to keep her overnight. We'll start her on stronger blood pressure medication and observe her for concussion."

"Can I see her? I'd like to find out if she has any friends or relatives who could come be with her."

"I think that would be fine."

⊷————⊶

"How are you feeling?" Permelia asked as she slipped through the door to Betty's room in the ER.

"Embarrassed…and confused. That picture of the businessman who was found in the woods is the spitting image of my Eideard. It makes no sense, but it was a shock, given that Eid is missing."

"Does your husband have a brother?"

"No, he's the only child of older parents. They moved back to Ireland when his dad retired, before we married. We talked to them once a month on Sundays."

"Could he have a cousin? Or maybe a brother he didn't know about?"

Betty sat up straighter in her bed.

"I suppose he could. He said his parents were both from large families." She pointed at a chair next to her bed. "Would you like to sit for a minute?"

Permelia put her bag next to the chair and sat down.

"Do you suppose your husband could have had a twin who was raised by someone else? You know, they did that sort of thing a generation ago. If a couple didn't have a lot of money, they'd give one of their children to a relative to raise. Maybe someone who couldn't have kids on their own."

"He's never mentioned anything like that, but I suppose his parents might not have told him."

"I don't suppose you two have done one of those DNA kits."

Betty brightened.

"We did. Eid's confirmed he's pure Irish. He said he wasn't notified of any relatives."

"Do you have access to his information?"

Betty's face clouded.

"I don't, I'm not very good with it, so Eid did all our computer work. He didn't want me to accidentally erase something important. He had a program where he kept all our passwords, but I don't have the password to that."

"Do you use a computer at all?" It was none of her business, but she found it hard to believe in this day and age that even a woman Betty's age would be completely computer illiterate.

"I know the basics, but Eid bought me an iPad, and I use that."

"I guess we'll just have to think of another way to figure out why Eid has a doppelganger," Permelia said.

"Isn't a doppelganger a ghostly twin?"

"Well, technically, I think it can be either ghostly or simply an unrelated look-alike, but I wouldn't ignore the possibility of an unknown twin just yet."

The nurse came in and peeked around the privacy curtain.

"Okay, Mrs. FitzAndreu, we need to take your vitals again."

Permelia stood up.

"I'd better get going. Do you have someone to take you home tomorrow?"

Betty smiled at her.

"Yes, I can call my neighbor—I need to have her check on Pan anyway. Thank you for coming here with me, it really has helped. I just wish I knew where Eideard was."

"I'm sure you'll figure it out soon enough."

Permelia picked up her knitting bag and purse and left. She was pretty sure she knew where Eideard was—he was in the morgue under her apartment, going by the name of businessman Edward Anderson.

Chapter 10

Permelia walked down the hall and to the elevator before she remembered she'd arrived in an ambulance and that her car was still at the coffee shop. She could take a cab but realized she didn't know the street address of the coffee shop she'd been at, only its proximity to her apartment.

She went down to the lobby and stepped outside before pulling her phone from her purse and dialing Katy. She explained her situation, and Katy assured her it was no problem to pick her up and take her to her car.

"What do you think is going on?" Katy asked when her mother was settled in the passenger seat.

"I'm not real sure, but I think it's too much of a coincidence that Betty's husband disappeared on the same night a businessman who looks just like him turned up dead."

"Do you think it's the same guy?" Katy asked as she guided her car out of the hospital parking lot and into traffic.

"The twin possibility takes us to a big coincidence. I suppose it could be a case of the twins discovering their connection and one killing the other and then taking off. But I don't know why someone would do that. The other possibility would be one man living two lives with two wives and two families, and that seems equally unlikely."

"You're right, either case is pretty awful, and the possibility of two men who look exactly alike being murdered and disappearing simultaneously sounds impossible."

"I guess we can just be glad we don't have to worry about it."

Katy glanced at her mother.

"Are you going to stay friends with this woman?"

Permelia thought for a moment.

"I suppose I am. She seemed nice, and she knits."

"Just don't let her drag you into her drama." Katy laughed. "Now I sound like Jennifer."

"You girls worry too much."

Katy pulled into the stripmall parking lot, and Permelia pointed to her car at the opposite end of the row.

"There I am," she said. "I promise you I will learn the public transportation system in case something like this comes up again."

"Don't worry, Mom. I'm out and about all the time, it's no problem."

"Still, it won't hurt me to learn how to ride the bus," she said, and got out of Katy's car and into her own.

＊＊＊＊

She could hear Fenton meowing from two doors away.

"I'm coming," she called to him as she unlocked the outer door. She stepped inside and put her foot on the first step, immediately noticing a familiar folded page. Her stomach clenched with dread as she picked it up.

leave or else

it read in cut-and-pasted letters in the middle of the page. She shook her head as she continued up the stairs.

"If you're trying to scare me, you're going to have to try a little harder than this," she muttered.

Fenton came out onto the landing as soon as she opened the door and began weaving around her ankles.

"I know you're anxious to explore your new neighborhood some more, but I think I need to show this to Doctor Grace," she said, waving the letter in the air.

＊＊＊＊

Permelia entered the morgue and was directed to Dr. Grace's office. She found him seated behind an antique oak desk, intently studying a printed page.

"Knock-knock," she said softly.

"Come in, come in," he said and stood up. "Would you like some coffee, or tea?"

"No, thank you. I don't mean to disrupt your work."

He smiled.

"I can use the distraction. Please, have a cup of tea with me and tell me what's on your mind. Believe me, you'll be doing me a favor. I've been working all day on a problem that's proved intractable so far. A break is just what I need."

Permelia smiled.

"Tea would be nice."

"I'll be right back."

He returned in a few minutes with two steaming cups of tea. He pulled a packet of sugar and a small container of creamer wrapped in a paper napkin with a stir stick from his lab coat pocket after he set Permelia's cup down. He smiled warmly.

"I didn't know if you needed these," he said and handed them to her.

She took the sugar packet and stirred it into her tea.

"Are you settling in okay? Is the apartment comfortable?"

"The apartment is fine." She handed him the note. "This is the second note of this sort I've gotten since I moved in."

He read it and leaned back in his chair. Permelia sipped her tea and watched him; his face was unreadable.

He handed the note back.

"I don't know what to say. We've never had this sort of problem before. Would you like me to call the police? I have some friends on the force."

Permelia shook her head.

"Thanks, but no. I suspect this is a simple prank. A 'welcome to the neighborhood' from the neighborhood kids. I just wanted to check and see if this was something you'd been dealing with before I came or it's only for me."

"This is normally a quiet neighborhood. We have the occasional prank on Halloween, but that's about it."

"As long as all I'm getting is notes, I think ignoring them is the best course of action."

Dr. Grace set his cup down and stared at her.

"Is there something you're not telling me? Do you have someone in your background who might be doing this?"

Permelia's cheeks pinked.

"My ex-husband's new wife is the sort who might indulge in childish pranks. It's not outside the realm of possibility she would have a friend here who would help her out."

"I see. Is there anything I can do to help?"

"No. If it's Heather, it will run its course. She's mad at me, but she'll forget about it after she has her baby."

Dr. Grace raised his eyebrows.

"I see."

Permelia grinned.

"Yeah, it's just as messy as it sounds, hence the real possibility Heather is behind the notes. I'm sorry I bothered you."

She stood up, and Doctor Grace did, too. He came around the desk and gently squeezed her arm.

"If there's anything I can do to help, please let me know. Maybe a letter to Heather from the Assistant Medical Examiner would deter her."

"Thank you for that, but I'm sure this will go away on its own. Heather, or whoever it is, probably hopes for some sort of reaction. Giving them none is probably the best option at this point."

He stood in his office doorway as she started down the hall toward the lobby.

"Let me know if anything else happens."

"I will," she promised.

Chapter 11

He was certainly friendly," Permelia said to Fenton when she'd returned to her apartment. "Now, are you ready for a walk?"

In reply, Fenton went to the door and sat under the hook that held his harness and leash.

"Let me get my walking shoes and hat." She replaced her loafers with her trainers before putting on her wide-brimmed sun hat and slipping the cat's harness on.

"Okay, I'm ready if you are. And I think we need to go around the back of the building to the next block and then return past our friend Wilma's fortress. I have a feeling she just might invite us in for a chat."

Fenton took thirty minutes to make his way around the block. He pounced every time a puff of wind moved a leaf, and he climbed three trees as far as his leash would let him go. As expected, Wilma's speakeasy door opened as they approached.

"Would you and his nibs like to come in for a refreshing beverage?"

"If by that you mean a glass of water, that sounds lovely."

Wilma opened the heavy oak door and let Permelia and Fenton into the courtyard.

"You two make yourselves comfortable, and I'll fetch the water."

She returned five minutes later with a tray bearing a pitcher of ice water with slices of lemon floating among the cubes, two glasses, and a bowl for Fenton. Permelia took a long drink from the glass Wilma handed her then set it on the table.

"Rough day?" Wilma asked as she scratched Fenton's ears.

Permelia blew out a breath.

"You could say that." She explained her meeting with Betty and the subsequent trip to the hospital.

"What are you thinking?"

"The idea of identical twins, one who is killed and the other who disappears at the exact same time, seems preposterous. I couldn't say this in front of Betty, but I'm wondering if her Eideard and the morgue's Edward Anderson are one and the same person, which is why Eideard's hat ended up in the morgue dumpster when Edward's family gathered his worldly possessions."

"You think that's more likely than the separated-at-birth twins routine?" Wilma asked and picked up her glass.

"I do. Think about it. Eideard has an accounting business he runs from home, but which takes him out of town 'visiting clients' on a regular basis. He was gone more than he was home."

"It would be interesting to know what Edward Anderson did."

Permelia sipped her water.

"According to the newspaper, he worked for a successful private company. He was the senior accountant."

"Think of the coordination that would take," Wilma said.

"Who better to pull off a detailed plan than an accountant?"

Wilma chuckled.

"Good point."

"The question is, how to prove it?"

"You could talk to the police," Wilma suggested.

"And say what? 'I met a lady who is married to a guy who looks just like your murder victim, and he's disappeared?' How do you think that would go over?"

Wilma leaned back in her chair.

"They might be skeptical. But they might listen, too."

"I'd like to find some piece of tangible evidence before I talk to anyone official."

"Any idea how you're going to get that?"

"I do, as a matter of fact."

"Hold that thought. This calls for a cookie from my batch that just came out of the oven."

"Do you always bake this much?" Permelia asked as she followed Wilma into the kitchen.

Wilma laughed.

"I love to bake, but I can't eat it all myself, so I ship them to service members overseas." She lifted a glass cake cover from a plate stacked with chocolate chip cookies and smiled. "I do save a few for myself."

She brought the plate to the kitchen table and then got a pitcher of iced tea from the refrigerator.

"Would you like a glass?"

"Sure."

She poured the tea and handed Permelia her glass with a napkin.

"Now, tell me the plan and how I can help."

"Hold on a minute. This isn't your problem."

Wilma picked up a cookie, took a bite, and chewed it slowly.

"I'm not trying to take over your operation, but whatever your plan is, you shouldn't try it on your own. Besides, you never know—you might find me useful."

"Why would you want to help me? You hardly know me. I don't mean to look a gift horse in the mouth, but I don't know what I might be sticking my nose into. I'm not sure *I* should even be trying to help Betty, much less dragging you into it."

"First of all, you're not dragging me into anything; and second, I might as well tell you now, I don't leave my property. Ever. I'm good with a computer, though, and I have some experience with tactical planning. That's all I'm offering."

Permelia's eyebrows raised when Wilma said *ever*, but she decided this wasn't the time to ask about that. She sipped her tea to give herself a moment to think. She *wasn't* sure she wanted to involve herself, much less someone who never left her property but had tactical experience. It was all one more reason to resent Michael for turning her life upside-down.

She looked up. Wilma was watching her expectantly.

"My plan isn't much, but I was thinking about the knitted hat."

"Of course, you were."

Permelia looked at her.

"Sorry, I just mean, if you knit all the time, you probably think of the knitted angle first. Continue."

"I gave the hat I found to Betty when she said she'd made it for her husband. The family of the deceased man had been to the morgue right before I found the hat by our dumpster. The main yarn used in the hat is one my co-op makes and sells. I happen to have brought a skein with me for a project. I can match the other colors well enough to pass casual inspection."

"You're going to knit a duplicate hat?" Wilma guessed. "Then what?"

"Then, I thought I'd pay a call on the not-so-grieving family to return the hat."

Wilma held her hand up.

"Why do you say not-so-grieving?"

"I ran into the boy who accompanied the woman to the morgue to identify the body that came in. I heard him say his mother was going to be late due to some work obligation or something. Clearly, they aren't gathering around in mourning. And, I'm guessing if they threw the hat away, they didn't pay enough attention to it to realize mine is a duplicate."

"If they recognize the hat as belonging to Edward, then Edward and Eideard are one and the same," Wilma said. "Simple but brilliant. How can I help?"

"If you could find the exact address of the recently deceased Edward Fenwick Anderson Jr., that would help."

"Consider it done."

Permelia sipped her tea and wondered what she was getting herself into.

Chapter 12

$\mathcal{W}$ here's my friend Fenton?" Wilma asked the next afternoon as she opened the oak door before Permelia rang the buzzer. She chuckled at Permelia's surprise. "I saw you on the security camera."

"Mr. Cat is home taking his afternoon nap," Permelia replied. "He's proven himself to be a less than helpful teaching assistant." She carried a large African basket filled with balls of yarn, knitting needles, and other knitting paraphernalia into the courtyard.

"I thought we'd sit at the kitchen table, if that's okay. I covered it with a white cloth."

Permelia set her basket beside a chair and sat down.

"That's a good idea. It will make it easier to inspect your work."

"Iced tea, hot tea, or water?"

Permelia selected iced tea, and while Wilma poured, she took two pairs of size-eight bamboo needles from her basket.

"I'm going to start you with bamboo needles, since the yarn doesn't slip off them quite as easily. In the beginning that will be good, I think. When you're a little more skilled, you may want your needles to be made from metal or a polished wood that's slicker and helps you knit faster."

Wilma smiled and sat down.

"I can't imagine I'll need those anytime soon."

"You can pick a ball of yarn from the basket. When you knit, you need to match the yarn thickness with the needle diameter, but I only put appropriate yarns in the basket today, so you don't need to worry about it. Pick a color you like. I've purposely not included black or any other dark colors that are difficult to see, for the obvious reason."

Wilma chose a light teal blue.

"I'm going to cast on for you. I've found if you master the knit stitch first, casting on is much easier." She quickly cast twenty-four stitches onto Wilma's needles. "I'm going to demonstrate, then hand it to you."

Permelia held the needle she'd cast onto in her left hand and slipped the tip of the right needle into the first stitch.

"Into the front, wrap around the back, pull the loop through the middle and push off the rest," she said as she made the motions. She repeated the phrase two more times as she did two more stitches then handed the needles to Wilma.

After a few initial struggles, Wilma began knitting her first row. Permelia cast on the same number of stitches in a lavender yarn and began knitting in the same style she'd just taught Wilma. She normally knit Continental style, which involved picking her new yarn from her left finger and scooping it through the stitch on her left needle in one smooth motion, but she found it was easier to teach new students the "throw" method before moving on to Continental.

Wilma glanced at Permelia's work.

"I thought you were going to make a hat like the one you found."

"I am, but not during your lesson. I find some students benefit from the visual of watching their teacher doing the same thing they're doing. It might help you pick up the rhythm more quickly. Don't worry—I can complete the hat in one or two days."

<hr />

Two hours passed quickly, with Permelia making sure to keep their conversation light so as to not distract Wilma from her new skill. She finished a row and dug in her bag of accessories to find a pair of rubber tips shaped like cat's heads to put on her needles. She handed Wilma a pair that looked like knitted socks for her needles.

"These will keep your knitting from sliding off the needle and your needle tips from creating mischief in the bag or basket you carry your work in."

"What a clever idea." Wilma held up the beginnings of her scarf. "I'm assuming my stitches will get more uniform as I go."

"They already are, if you look closely at what you've done." She tucked her own knitting in her basket and pulled a colorful book out. "Here's a visual guide to knitting. You can borrow it until you feel confident in your skills. I'm hoping you'll knit an inch or two before we meet again."

"I can do that," Wilma said and stood up. "I don't want to make a pest of myself, but I'm available whenever you have time."

"I'm going over to my daughter Katy's house tomorrow to see the new sculpture she's working on and have lunch, and then I'm going to see if I can check in on Betty. She should be back home. If late afternoon works, I'm game."

"What if we knit for a while, and then I make dinner for us? We could eat early enough that you'll be home for your phone calls."

"That sounds fantastic."

<hr/>

Permelia set her knitting basket down beside her chair when she returned to her apartment. She'd planned to call Betty and Katy as soon as she came in, but Fenton made such a pest of himself she decided to take him out for a walk first. She'd noticed on her map there was a park a few blocks away; and if there weren't too many dogs around, and if the park had the right sort of trees, she could put on his retractable leash and let him climb a little.

They approached the park on its uphill side, and she could see that several baseball games were taking place on the fields at the opposite side of the large park, leaving the tree-shaded picnic area empty. She chose a spot where she could sit on a tabletop and Fenton could reach the lower branches of a large maple tree.

She'd been sitting and watching her cat for thirty minutes when a scrawny girl in green cutoff shorts and a faded orange teeshirt approached her table. The girl's red hair was pulled back in a ponytail, but several strands had come loose and framed her freckled face.

"Is that a leopard? On your leash?"

Permelia chuckled. "No, honey, he's a house cat. He just looks like a wild cat."

Fenton recognized he was the subject of the conversation and jumped out of the tree and onto the table.

"Can I pet him?" the girl asked.

"What's your name?"

"Henri," the girl said. She paused, and when Permelia didn't say anything, she continued. "It's really Henrietta, but I hate that, so I go by Henri. What's the cat's name?"

"His name is Fenton."

"That's a weird name."

Fenton came over and rubbed his muzzle on her shoulder as if to prove *he* wasn't strange even if his name was.

"He was named when I got him, and the breeder didn't explain where the name came from."

Fenton started purring and continued rubbing on the girl. She giggled.

"He's a nice cat," she said, and stroked his head.

Permelia scanned around and didn't see any adults who might be with the girl. She looked like she was around nine, which seemed a little young to be at such a large park by herself; but when Permelia asked, she turned out to be eleven.

"Do you live around here?" she asked.

Henri continued petting Fenton but gestured with her free hand back toward Permelia's street. "I live around the corner from that creepy morgue house."

Permelia smiled to herself.

"Fenton and I live in the apartment at the top of that creepy morgue house."

Henri's eyes got big.

"Have you seen any ghosts? The ghosts of the dead people they bring there are all around the block. Especially the murderers."

"Have you seen any of the ghosts?" Permelia countered.

"I haven't, but River, a boy in my class, has, and he said the guy walks past my house every night with a big knife, dripping blood."

"Is there blood on your sidewalk when you go out to school in the morning?"

Henri thought for a moment.

"Nooo," she said slowly, drawing out the word.

"Then you probably don't have anything to worry about." She stood up. "Is anyone here at the park with you?"

"No, my mom's at home working."

"Would you like to walk home with Fenton and me?"

They walked in companionable silence. When they reached their mutual corner, Permelia watched until the child had gone inside her house and closed the door. She crossed the street and scanned the sidewalk. The only thing visible on its surface was a chalked hopscotch grid outlined in multiple colors. No blood.

Chapter 13

Permelia fed Fenton the next morning before digging through her tubs of yarn, choosing balls of brown and tan that coordinated with the colors Betty had used in her husband's hat. She knew the brown she had was a shade lighter than the one in the original but was pretty sure most people wouldn't notice unless they had the two hats side-by-side. She had time to cast onto her circular needle and knit the ribbed brim before she had to get dressed and drive to her daughter's apartment.

"You behave yourself," she told her cat before shutting the door and heading down the stairs. She kept an eye out for envelopes, but there were none.

<hr />

"Hi, Mom," Katy said. "How are things going in the dead zone?"

"That's not funny."

Katy gestured, encouraging her mother to continue.

"This is where you're supposed to say how wonderful everything is."

"You mean besides my first kaffee klatch ending with Betty being in the hospital?"

Katy smiled.

"Yeah, besides that."

"Things are good. I'm teaching my neighbor behind the wall how to knit. Oh, and I got another one of those prank notes."

"Are you sure they're prank notes?"

"No adult in this day and age cuts letters from a magazine to make a threatening note."

Katy led the way to the work area in her large living room.

"You're probably right. Magazines are becoming a thing of the past. Except the gossip rags, and who reads those?"

"So, what are you making here?"

"Can't you tell?"

Permelia slowly circled the block of stone.

"An animal of some sort?"

Katy looked disappointed.

Permelia rubbed her hand over a curve in the stone.

"It's beautiful, whatever it's going to be."

"Good recovery. It's a horse. It's for the lobby of a new upscale hotel in Kentucky."

"I'm sure they'll love it. I thought you were doing a man."

Katy pointed to a canvas-shrouded project across the room.

"I am, but he's in time-out right now. On an unrelated subject, and not to sound like my sister, but are you sure you should be getting involved with this Betty person? I mean, her husband is missing, and then when she sees the picture of a dead executive she faints and bonks her head."

"As near as I can tell, this 'Betty person' has no real friends, and right about now, I think she could use one."

"Just promise me you'll be careful, okay."

"I'm always careful. Now, can we get lunch?"

⊷——⊶

Lunch turned out to be a smorgasbord of food carts. The Vietnamese spring rolls were filled with fresh vegetables and a slice of tofu and served with a savory peanut sauce. The Korean spicy seafood soup was a little hot for Permelia's tastes, but the homemade ice cream they had for dessert cooled the heat nicely. Katy had a tight deadline for her sculpture, so Permelia left soon after and headed to Betty's house.

She entered the address Betty had given her into her phone and followed the directions across town to a neighborhood of pothole-riddled streets with no sidewalks. The houses were older, and the yards a mix of well-manicured grass and overgrown weed patches. Betty's was in the former category.

Permelia parked in Betty's driveway and stopped on her way to the porch to smell the lavender that lined the path. Betty stepped outside.

"Your lavender is really fragrant," Permelia said. "What variety is it?"

"It's called Lavandin. The man at the nursery told us it is supposed to be a hybrid created to be the most fragrant." Her shoulders slumped. "If Eideard was here, he could tell you more about it. He was the one who knew the scientific names of all the plants."

"Have you heard from him?" Permelia had to ask, even though she was certain Betty was never going to hear from him again.

"Where are my manners? Please, come on in." Betty held the screen door open for Permelia, ignoring her query.

"How are you feeling?"

"I'm fine, I just had a little shock. And my head is too hard to be affected by a little bump like that."

The front door opened into a tidy living room. The furniture was simple and neutral in color. The decor reflected the family's Irish heritage with a quilted wall hanging featuring a Celtic knot design in pale-green and gray on the wall over the sofa and several leprechaun figurines on the side tables. A large lilac-point Siamese cat lay curled in the center of the sofa; he raised his head and studied Permelia briefly, yawned, and went back to his nap.

"I made some tea," Betty said. "I hope that's okay."

A tray with a teapot covered in a knit cozy and two cups with saucers sat on the coffee table.

"That sounds wonderful. Your teacups are beautiful, are they Belleek?"

"You have a good eye. Eideard brings a few pieces home every time he goes to Ireland. He's been doing it ever since we got married."

Permelia held up the white cup with the delicate shamrock pattern on its side.

"I hate to use it, it's so pretty."

"Don't worry, it's strong."

"Have you heard from your husband's business clients or anything?" Permelia asked, and sat down on the sofa with her cup of tea.

"I haven't, and I don't know who they are."

"Have you looked in his office?"

"Eideard didn't like anyone to go in his office. He said if his papers got mixed up it could take him hours to straighten them out. He even vacuumed it himself."

"Did he lock it when he was out of town?"

"He always kept it locked. He said his clients' work was confidential, and he'd had to sign a contract saying their information would be secured in his office."

"Don't you think they'd make an exception under the circumstances?"

Betty sipped her tea, and Permelia was afraid she wasn't going to answer.

"I guess with him being gone this long, they wouldn't mind if we looked for their phone numbers. I mean, someone out of all his clients must be wondering why he hasn't been in contact."

Permelia sipped her tea and desperately hoped there *were* client names in his office. If Eideard had been leading the double life she suspected he had, he might have made all his money in his other life and not actually had any work he did at home. He might have kept Betty out so she wouldn't see his office was devoid of any paperwork.

Betty may not have gone into Eideard's office, but she'd allowed for the possibility. Years before, she'd seized an opportunity to have a copy made of his office key and several others from his keychain that she didn't recognize. Permelia didn't want to press her right now about how this had come about, but when things were calmer, she was going to ask. You don't copy a man's keys if you believe everything he's telling you. Something had made her suspicious.

"Do you think we need to wear disposable gloves like they do on television?" Betty asked.

Permelia smiled.

"Since this is your home, I think people would expect your fingerprints would be here. Besides, we're not investigating a crime, we're just trying to find your husband."

Betty handed her the key, and she slipped it into the lock, taking a deep breath as she pushed the door open.

She paused in the doorway, surveying the room. The office was neat and contained the sorts of things you expected to see in an office—a polished cherry desk set facing the door, and a matching credenza and filing cabinets behind that, under the window. A shredder sat atop a large black wastebasket to the right side of the desk. Several file folders lay on the desktop. She crossed the room and picked up the first in the stack.

The contents seemed to be financial documents for a fast food restaurant. At the top corner of each page was the logo for a company called Central Business Associates. She looked at the next folder and the next. They were each for a different business, but all done on Central Business Associates forms. She pulled open the top desk drawer and found the expected pencils, pens, and other office supplies. Her hand froze when she opened the right-hand drawer.

A partially-full box of business cards stared at her— cards for Edward Fenwick Anderson Jr. She slipped one into her palm and shut the drawer.

Edward Fenwick Anderson Jr. was the name of the dead guy in the morgue. If there had been any doubt that Eideard and Edward were the same person, this put an end to that thought. But how to tell Betty?

While Permelia searched the desk, Betty examined accounting textbooks on a shelf across from the desk that matched the rest of the office furniture.

"None of this is telling us where Eideard is," she complained.

Permelia was frantically trying to figure out the best way to tell her what she'd found when the telephone in the living room rang. Betty hustled out to answer it, and Permelia followed her, closing the door behind her.

Betty sat on the sofa with the phone to her ear, listening. Permelia could hear a male voice but couldn't tell what he was saying. Betty held her hand over the receiver and mouthed *Red*.

Permelia finished her tea and carried her cup and saucer to the kitchen sink. When she returned, she could tell Betty was trying to convince her son he didn't need to interrupt his studies to come home at this point and promising to let him know when she learned anything.

"Thank you so much for the tea," Permelia said, and gathered her purse and knitting bag. "I really must be on my way."

"Don't you want to search Eid's office some more?"

"Maybe we can do that the next time I come by," she said, realizing how lame it sounded as she spoke.

She didn't want to deal with another bout of hysterics and possible fainting from Betty until she knew more. She was pretty sure someone who started an office search with the accounting reference books instead of the files on the desk wasn't going to do any deep diving on her own. Whatever was going on, it seemed pretty clear—if Betty suspected anything, she didn't want to find evidence that would confirm her suspicions.

Chapter 14

Dr. Grace was fishing around in the trunk of his car when Permelia pulled into the morgue driveway. She was deep in thought about Betty and her situation. It seemed hard to believe the woman could be so naive that when she saw a picture of the man she'd been married to for twenty-five years on the front page of the paper, after first fainting from the shock of recognition she then could believe not that her husband was dead, but that he had a twin.

"Oh," she gasped as she came out of the garage and ran into Dr. Grace, stepping on his foot in the process. He had been waiting for her by the steps to her door.

He grabbed her to prevent her from falling. She felt her cheeks turn pink from embarrassment.

"I'm sorry. I was thinking about something, and I didn't see you standing there. Is your foot okay?"

"It's fine—I have my steel-toed shoes on today." Now his face turned red. "I don't mean to say you're heavy enough to have hurt me if I hadn't."

"Oh, no, I didn't take it that way," she said and looked away from his face, staring at his hands, still on her arms.

He saw where she was looking and released her.

"Sorry," he mumbled.

"*I'm* the one who ran into *you*."

He cleared his throat and regained his composure.

"What's got you so troubled?"

"It's a bit of a long story."

"When I saw you pull in, I was hoping you might want to have a cup of tea with me. I could use the break. I'm reviewing files from the field offices, and I can only look at so many in one sitting before I start going cross-eyed."

Permelia looked toward her door, thinking of Fenton.

"I suppose I could have one cup."

She walked with him around the building and up the steps into the medical examiner's offices.

"We have our own tea maker in town, and I've been working my way through his collection." He led her down the hall and into what turned out to be a comfortable break room. It had the usual countertop with a microwave oven, coffeemaker, and electric kettle as well as a sink and under-counter refrigerator.

What made this room different was that, in addition to a fifties-era dinette set, overstuffed chairs with matching ottomans, side tables with lamps, and a large coffee table took up half the remaining space. It felt more like someone's parlor than a company break room.

"After standing on our feet in the autopsy rooms, we find this set-up a little more restful," he explained. He gestured for her to sit in one of the comfortable chairs and set about filling the kettle then digging in the cabinet for his box of special tea.

"Here it is," he said and held up a dark-gray box. "This is a double bergamot. Will that be okay?"

"That's fine." It seemed strange to have a man making tea for her. At the ranch, the men would come in for meals in their overalls and boots, wash their hands, and sit down at the table, waiting for food and drink to appear before them. She'd worked hard to teach her boys that men sitting and women working was not the only way things could be in a house, but admittedly taught that lesson mainly when Michael Senior wasn't at the table. She was proud of the fact that all of her children knew how to wash a dish, fix a meal, and sew on a button.

"Thank you, Dr. Grace," she said when he handed her a steaming cup of tea.

"Can we let go of the formality? I'm Harold, Harry to my friends; and I hope I can consider you a friend."

Permelia blushed.

"Okay, Harry." The name felt weird on her tongue. Dropping the "Doctor" was going to be hard.

"Now, what was troubling you when you arrived home? You haven't gotten another threatening note, have you?"

"No, nothing like that," she said and sipped her tea before setting her cup on its saucer. "I've just been to see Betty FitzAndreu, the woman who fell on me the other day. I took her up to my apartment for tea that day, as she seemed so lost. She turns out to be a knitter, so we decided to get together for coffee and knitting at a local coffee shop. Things were going well until I bought a newspaper on the way out of the shop and she spotted a picture of the man who was brought in here the other night. She fainted and hit her head, and when the shop called an ambulance, she asked me to go with her. She doesn't seem to have any other friends."

"I can see how that would be upsetting."

"I just got back from visiting her at her home. I wanted to make sure she was okay. Her husband is still missing so she's very upset. Her husband did a lot of work from home, she said, but she never went into his office. In fact, he kept it locked."

"I think I can see where this is going." Dr. Grace said and leaned back in his chair. "Was the office empty?"

"Worse. It was filled with files and other paperwork from Central Business Associates."

"The company my dead guy was an executive of?"

"The very same."

"So, that dog had a second family stashed somewhere else in town?"

Permelia took a sip of her tea.

"Betty seems determined to avoid that conclusion. When we went into the office, she started looking at his accounting reference books on the opposite wall, away from the desk. What I was pondering when I ran into you was whether she really didn't know about the other family, or if she was trying to convince me she didn't know about them."

"Clearly, she had the foresight to have a key to his office."

"I didn't press her about that, but she said she'd noticed the strange key on his keyring one time, and when she had the opportunity, she made a duplicate and tried it on various locks around their house—toolboxes, cabinets in the garage, and, eventually, his office door."

Harry sipped his tea, a thoughtful look on his face.

"You have to wonder if he deliberately chose to marry someone who tended to not have friends, or if he made it a point to run off her friends. A lot of abusive men do that."

"It could be simpler than that. If she was involved in her son's school activities, *her* friends were probably the mothers of *his* friends. If they mainly had only that in common, when the kids went off to college, they didn't have a reason to get together. Plus, her son is going to school in Ireland, and Betty told me the family was going to relocate there when the son graduated."

"So, they have a son? I know my dead guy had at least one—he came with his mother when she identified the body. I wonder if they look alike."

"I don't remember seeing a lot of pictures in Betty's living room, but I have to admit I was distracted by her lovely Belleek china." She noticed his look of confusion. "It's a very fine and collectible china made in Ireland. Apparently, her husband would bring her several pieces each time he went there. His parents are Irish, according to her, so he has dual citizenship, and according to Betty, he did business over there on a fairly regular basis.

"You can see why I was pondering the situation. Betty seems pretty bright when you talk to her. I find it very hard to believe she's not a little curious about at least some of this stuff."

"Denial can be a pretty potent coping skill. She may like her life the way it is. Moving to Ireland means he chose her and their son. And she may not care what happens to his other family."

"A little voice in my head is saying 'What if Betty got tired of playing second fiddle and, now that her son is in his last year of college, decided to pay her husband back for putting her in that position all these years?'."

Harry leaned back in his chair.

"Wow, that's a hard thought."

"It could just be my overactive imagination. You know—too many late-night detective novels."

"Maybe, but it sounds like it could be possible."

"At this point, we don't even know for sure that it's a case of bigamy."

"As we also said, though, are there other options that are more plausible?"

Permelia sighed. "I guess the twins-separated-at-birth and both disappearing or being killed on the same day scenario isn't likely."

"The question now is what to do about it."

"I plan to take a duplicate hat to your dead guy's home. I'll tell them I found it in our parking lot. If they acknowledge it's Ed's hat, then we know they are the same guy."

"How so?"

"Betty made the hat for her husband. I realize he may have kept his lives separate enough his Ed family didn't know about the hat. But I have to try."

"I can't pretend I like the plan. We don't know where the danger lies. It could be Betty, but it could be Ed's other family, or he could have been into something entirely unrelated. If he was planning on leaving the country, he may have been running from something."

"All true, but I doubt anyone is going to pay attention to a little old lady trying to return a knitted hat."

He sighed.

"I have a friend on the police force. Maybe we should run this all by him."

"How about we wait until I do my hat test? Then we could have some real information for him."

"I know what you do is none of my business, but I don't like it."
A small smile crossed her lips.
"I'll be fine."

Chapter 15

Wilma was waiting at the gate at the time they'd agreed on.

"Enter," she said with a sweep of her arm. "I just put a pie in the oven. I thought we could knit while it bakes."

"That sounds wonderful," Permelia said and followed her into a cozy sitting room just off the kitchen.

"This is the best light," Wilma said, and turned on a brass table lamp that sat on a table between two comfortable-looking overstuffed chairs. Permelia set her knitting bag beside the chair that looked less used, assuming the other was Wilma's.

Wilma pulled her piece of knitting from her bag and held it up. A length of red string dangled from a stitch in the middle of the scarf.

"I realized a stitch had fallen off my needle two rows before, but I didn't know how to get it back, so I put a piece of string through it."

Permelia smiled.

"Not a problem. Learning how to pick up dropped stitches is a useful skill." She pulled a crochet hook from her bag and showed her how to work the stitch up the ladder to the current row. "Okay, you're ready to continue knitting."

They knitted in silence for a few minutes until Wilma had her rhythm going. "Any progress with your missing-husband situation?" she asked.

"It's pretty clear one guy had two families. I'm still going to do my duplicate-hat experiment."

"I've got the address for you. Are you sure you should be getting involved in this?"

"I don't know. I'm hoping if I can prove to Betty that she's wife number two, she'll at least stop waiting for him to come walking through the door. Assuming that's really what's troubling her."

"Assuming?"

"The more I'm around Betty, the more I think she knows what's going on, at least at some level. She may be trying to fool herself, but no one is that naive."

Wilma held up her scarf.

"Only…"

Whatever she was going to say was cut off by a loud whooshing noise. A bright flash lit up the room from the courtyard. Both women jumped up and ran to the kitchen. Wilma looked through the window beside the door before opening it.

Black soot stained the courtyard bricks in a circular pattern, brown glass shards were strewn across the stain.

"Looks like someone threw a Molotov cocktail into my patio." She picked up her phone and dialed.

"That was too many digits for nine-one-one," Permelia observed.

"So it was." She gave Permelia a look she couldn't decipher. "I'll understand if you want to cancel dinner."

"If that pie is for dessert, I'm staying."

Wilma smiled.

"As a matter of fact, it is."

"Count me in, then."

They returned to the sitting room. They'd barely finished a row on their respective projects when a tone sounded that turned out to be the gate bell.

"Would you mind waiting here?" Wilma asked in a voice that indicated it wasn't really a request. She slid a pocket door closed when she left the room, and a moment later, Permelia heard the kitchen door close. She slid her knitting needle into the next stitch and tried to ignore the deep male voice resonating through the closed door. Twenty minutes later she heard the kitchen door open and close again, and Wilma came into the sitting room.

"I'm sorry about that. The police took their time studying the situation."

"Unless you remotely detonated whatever blew up, it doesn't seem like you have anything to be sorry for."

"Are you hungry? All I need to do is cook the pasta, and we're ready."

"Can I do anything to help?"

"Can you butter garlic bread?"

Permelia smiled.

"That I can do."

Dinner was pasta tossed with grape tomatoes, artichoke hearts, Kalamata olives, parmesan cheese, and olive oil, fresh green salad, and garlic bread. They ate the still-warm blackberry pie with vanilla bean ice cream on top.

"This pie is fantastic," Permelia said as she finished eating hers.

"It's my grandmother's recipe. She was our family pie baker, and she designated me as the one who would take over from her in spite of the fact I didn't bake at all when she made her declaration."

"You've done her proud with this one."

"Do you have time for an after-dinner cup of tea?"

Permelia looked at her watch.

"I think I can manage one cup. Maybe we can knit another row or two while we sip."

Wilma smiled.

"Sounds like a plan."

＊――＊

Permelia carried her cup and saucer to the sink and set them down.

"Thank you so much for the delicious dinner. That pie was amazing."

"It was nice to have someone to dine with. And thank you for the knitting lessons."

Permelia picked up her bag and purse and headed for the door.

"I'll unlock the gate for you."

Wilma led the way, and Permelia noticed there was no trace of the broken glass, soot, or anything else to indicate that a bomb, small though it had been, had gone off in the courtyard. Someone had done an expert job of clean-up while she and her hostess had been knitting and dining.

She crossed the street, deep in thought. Her neighbor was an interesting woman.

＊――＊

Fenton curled into Permelia's lap as soon as she sat down in her chair by the window.

"Fenny, my boy, I had a lovely dinner that was finished off with fabulous pie." She scratched his ear. "It was a relaxing evening, apart from the minor explosion in the courtyard that was cleaned up by mysterious forces unseen by me."

She worked on her duplicate hat until she was too sleepy to see, then gathered up Fenton and went to bed, hoping for a good night's sleep after her busy day.

＊――＊

She was awakened at seven minutes after two by the morgue phone ringing. The person calling sounded bored. He gave her the pertinent information and told her they would be transporting the body to the morgue, and it would be after eight in the morning when they arrived.

Dr. Grace had told her to contact him immediately for the first few weeks until she got a feel for the routine.

"I'm sorry to disturb you," she said when he answered.

He chuckled.

"I'd have been disappointed if you hadn't called. Now, what do you have?"

"A body will be arriving after eight in the morning from Joseph."

"And the reason they are sending him to us?"

"A fifty-two-year-old male, fell out of bed and broke his neck."

"Good call. If he were ninety-two and falling out of bed, it might be different, but a fifty-two-year-old would need to be very sick to die falling out of bed. And I assume this guy wasn't."

"The man in Joseph didn't mention it," Permelia said, and made a mental note to remember to ask next time.

"Interesting though this case will be, with the body not arriving until after eight, this type call is one you can log in then inform us as soon as the office opens at seven. If the deceased were arriving before seven, you would contact whoever is on call that week to come receive the body."

"I've got it. And I'm sorry you're having to wake up in the middle of the night for my training."

"I was actually up reading journal articles. I've had difficulty sleeping for more than a few hours at a time since my wife died."

"I'm sorry."

"Well, hopefully, you can get back to sleep."

"That shouldn't be a problem," she assured him, knowing it was far from the truth. After everything that had gone on the last few days, she couldn't turn her mind off. She hung up the phone and put the tea kettle on to boil.

The kitchen window looked out over the morgue parking lot and across to Wilma's walled compound. Permelia was staring sightlessly out into the dark, listening to the sound of her kettle heating, when motion at Wilma's caught her attention. She leaned closer to the window. The gate in the wall had opened, and a black-clad figure came out. It stopped and looked both ways.

"Wilma?" Permelia said under her breath.

The distinctive silhouette of Wilma's dreadlocks was unmistakable. Permelia watched as she made the motions of a runner setting a watch and then took off running up the block into the dark night.

"Well, well, well, Wilma. I guess 'never leave my house, ever' doesn't include running around at night."

Permelia poured hot water into her cup over her chamomile teabag and carried it in to her comfortable chair in the living room.

Chapter 16

The following morning was hazy. Permelia put Fenton's harness on him and led him down the stairs. The cat needed his exercise, but the reality was she needed time to go over what she was going to say to Ed Anderson's family when she returned her duplicate hat.

She saw Henri sitting at a table through her kitchen window as she passed their house. The girl waved. Permelia smiled and waved back.

A red paramedic van was in the morgue parking lot when she returned home, backed up to an overhead door. Dr. Grace stood at the rear, watching as two attendants slid a black body bag onto a gurney and wheeled it into the morgue. He smiled at her as she and her cat approached.

"I hope we didn't disrupt your night too much."

"No, not too much," she lied.

"Good. Fortunately, we don't get too many night calls."

"At my age, I get up a few times a night so it's not much of a bother."

"That's quite a cat," he remarked.

"He is that."

Dr. Grace reached down to pet him, but Fenton reached up and batted at his hand.

"He's a feisty one."

"Yes, he is."

"Well, I'd better go inside and get our guest settled."

He turned to go and then stopped.

"I almost forgot," He pulled an envelope out of his lab coat pocket. "I found this in the parking lot this morning." He pointed to a spot near her door. "I think it blew off your porch."

She took it from him. It was unsealed, and she pulled the flap open, revealing a single page with the familiar cut-out letters. This one said

DOn't be foolish GO!

"Oh, for crying out loud," she said and stuffed the note back into the envelope.

"Another threat?" Dr. Grace asked.

"If you can call it that."

"Are you sure you shouldn't call the police and at least let them be aware you're receiving these letters?"

"I don't know how things work in the city, but where I'm from we don't have a large enough police force to bother with what is clearly some sort of prank."

Harold Grace shook his head.

"I think you're making a mistake. Let me know if you change your mind."

"I don't think I will, but thank you for your concern. Now, I better get this guy upstairs and feed him his after-walk snack."

<hr/>

Permelia hoped it would be one of the kids who answered the door when she went to present her duplicate hat. She looked up the local schools on her computer and discovered that classes generally got out around three o'clock. She'd busied herself doing paperwork related to the fiber co-op and then spun yarn for a couple of hours. She drove to Edward Anderson's home at twenty after three, practicing what she would say as she went.

I found this hat in the parking lot where I live, she thought, but that would leave them wondering how she knew who they were. *I work at the morgue, and found this hat in our parking lot last week after your visit.*

That was better, she thought, but was *I work at the morgue* stretching the truth too far? And did *visit* make it sound like she was making light of their tragedy?

She pulled up to the curb across from the address Wilma had given her. Could this be right? she wondered.

The grand house was as far from Betty's little cottage as a house could be. It sat back from the street behind a curved driveway with a black iron gate protecting it from the street. Thankfully, the gate was open. A large three-story structure was flanked on each side by smaller two-story additions connected at an angle, giving the house a curved appearance. Each of the smaller wings had a set of double garage doors on its end.

Permelia took a deep breath and let it out slowly.

"Well, here goes nothing," she said to herself.

She stepped out of her car. The air smelled like it did when Michael was burning debris on the ranch—faintly smoky. Her chest tightened. While she didn't miss Michael, she was beginning to realize how much she missed the ranch. The smells in the city weren't the same; not bad, just different.

A stone pathway led from the street along the side of the driveway to the front door. She stiffened her spine and touched the doorbell.

No one answered. She waited a moment then pressed it again. She started to turn away from the door but realized the smell of smoke had increased. It was too strong to be backyard burning, and she found it hard to imagine someone who lived in a house like this would burn their own trash, in any case.

She rapped on the door, first with her knuckles then her fist. The door didn't feel hot, and smoke wasn't seeping out from under it, but the smell *was* increasing.

She stepped off the porch and climbed through the shrubs to the first-floor window to the left of the entrance. The heavy drapes on it were open; sheers covered the space between them, but Permelia could see two things —the room was an office…and a stack of papers on the surface of the desk were on fire.

She dialed 911 as she made her way back onto the porch and to the windows on the opposite side. This looked like the formal living room. No one was in it, but she saw a flash of motion through an arch on the opposite side of the room. She pounded on the window, but no one responded.

Returning to the porch, she followed the stone path around the house to the back yard and stepped onto the patio. French doors led into an informal eating area and the kitchen. She could see the young man from the store standing in front of the six-burner gas stove, earphones clamped on his ears.

She pounded on the door, and when he didn't respond, she tried the latch. Locked. She looked around, and finding a garden gnome statue, she picked it up and lobbed it through the door. Hopefully, the family would forgive her.

By the time she entered the kitchen, flames were climbing the wall between it and the office. The boy looked up, saw the flames, and would have headed toward them if Permelia hadn't grabbed him by the arm.

She pulled the earphones from his head.

"We have to get out of here."

"We have to save my dog."

"Where is he?"

"It's not a he, it's a she."

"Where? Where?" Permelia demanded.

"I haven't let her out of the garage yet."

She pulled him to the broken door.

"The firemen are on their way, and they can break into the garage from the outside."

Flames had reached the kitchen, and Permelia guided the boy off the patio onto the grass.

"I should have let her in as soon as I got home." Tears ran down his cheeks.

"Is anyone else in the house?"

"I don't know what I'll do if she's dead," he cried.

Permelia shook him gently.

"Listen, honey, I need to know if anyone else is in the house."

"I don't think so," he finally said.

She let out a breath she didn't know she'd been holding.

"Let's go around to the front. Is there a way we can go that won't take us too close to the house? I can hear the fire trucks."

He led her in the opposite direction, past a koi pond and then around the end of the house that was not yet burning. Two red fire trucks pulled up, and firemen jumped off and immediately began unrolling hose, with two men dragging the end to a hydrant on the street.

A helmeted man led them back to the sidewalk.

"My dog is in the garage to the right," the boy told him. "You have to save her."

The man relayed the information to two of the other firefighters; they ran to the garage door and used an ax to cut a hole. A fluffy white dog bounded out and ran to the boy, jumping on his leg until he picked her up and buried his face in her fur.

"Is this your house, ma'am?" the man asked. "Can you tell me what happened?"

"The boy lives here. I came to visit and smelled smoke and then saw fire in the office to the left of the front door. When no one answered the door, I went around to the back and saw the boy in the kitchen with headphones on. He was cooking with the fan on over the stove, so he probably didn't hear or smell anything. I'm afraid I threw a yard ornament through the patio door."

"He's very lucky you did. Who knows how long it would have taken him to notice the house was on fire? Do you have contact information for his parents?"

If her face wasn't already flushed, she knew she'd be blushing as she related an abbreviated variation of the story she'd been practicing.

"I was returning a hat." She held out the knitted hat she'd been clutching throughout. "I work at the morgue. Unfortunately, this family lost their father recently, and I think they dropped this hat. I was attempting to return it."

"That's my dad's hat," the boy said and grabbed it from her. "My mom said she threw it away."

He teared up again, and Permelia put her arm around him and pulled him into a hug.

"I'm so sorry."

He clung to her until the dog in his arms began squirming. He smiled briefly and set her down.

The fireman had been waiting patiently while watching the fire crew. He held his radio up and called for more fire trucks.

"What's your name, son," he asked gently.

"Benton Anderson."

"I'm Joe. Can you tell us where your mother is and how to get hold of her?"

"She's a real estate broker." He pulled a cell phone from his pocket and pressed a button. He listened but clearly, no one was answering. "Mom, the house burned down," he said and started crying again. "She's going to be so mad." He put the phone back in his pocket. "She never wanted me to stay home alone after school, but I hurt my ankle, and the doctor said I had to miss the rest of spring soccer. She's going to be so mad that I let the house burn."

"Did you go into the office when you got home from school?" Permelia asked him.

He shook his head no.

"Then you couldn't have burned the house down. When I was at your front door, I could see papers on the desk burning. You were in the kitchen, so it couldn't have been your fault."

He leaned into her, and she hugged him again.

"Could you give me your mom's number and tell me where she works?" Joe asked in a soft voice.

Benton relayed the information, and Joe stepped away from them and spoke into his radio. Permelia assumed someone was being sent to the mother's office.

"Do you have brothers and sisters?" she asked Benton.

He nodded.

"My older brother and sister are out of college. Tiffany lives in New York, but she's in Africa right now, and Eddie has a condo downtown; so they're like grown-ups. My adopted sister Silver, she's sixteen, is in residential treatment. She'll be home at the end of the month unless Mom makes her stay longer."

"I'm sorry."

"It's okay, she likes it there."

"So, it's just you and your mom at home?"

"And my dad," he said, and then realized what he'd said. He hung his head. "Yeah, it's just me and my mom except for when she's gonna be out late. Then the housekeeper stays over."

"Does that happen often?"

He scraped his toe on the ash-covered pavement.

"It's okay, I like her. She has a cool accent. She came from Ireland, like my dad."

"My car is across the street. Would you like to sit there until your mom arrives, if it's okay with Joe?"

"That'd be great."

Fireman Joe also thought it was a good idea. Permelia looked up and down the street and saw nothing but firemen, so she led Benton to her car.

Chapter 17

Benton picked his dog up again.

"She's not supposed to be out of the yard without her leash."

"I think I have a spare leash in the trunk of my car."

"Do you have a dog?"

"No, I have a cat, but he walks outside with a leash and harness."

Benton laughed.

"That's weird." He looked at Permelia to check her reaction.

She smiled.

"It is unusual, but then, he's an unusual cat. He's a Bengal cat. He likes to walk outside on a leash, and he likes to get wet, and he's very active."

"Can I meet him?"

"If your mother says it's okay."

"Do you think it would be okay if I called my friend?"

"I think that would be fine."

Benton chatted with his friend, giving Permelia time to ponder how she was going to break it to Betty that there was now no doubt Edward Anderson and Eideard FitzAndreu were one and the same.

The implications were staggering. Permelia guessed that Betty had no inheritance rights, but surely Ed/Eideard would have been clever enough to have put joint property he held with Betty in her name. And if he had life insurance in Betty's name, that should not be impacted by the legality of their marriage, she hoped. She didn't even want to think about the possibilities of Ed's wife suing Betty for anything he may have given her. Betty was in for some tough times; they all were.

Benton ended his call.

"I have a couple of protein bars in my bag if you're hungry," Permelia offered.

He ducked his head.

"I am, a little."

She held up three choices, and he took one that had nuts and dried fruit.

They fell into silence, watching the firemen spray water onto the roof of the house. It appeared they were getting the fire under control. Thirty more minutes passed before the familiar Mercedes pulled up behind Permelia's car.

"Mom!" Benton shouted and opened the car door. The woman strode across the street as Permelia got out of her car.

"Who's in charge here?" Mrs. Anderson demanded.

Fireman Joe came over and spoke to her. Benton joined them, handing the dog's leash to Permelia. She felt sorry for the boy. She kept waiting to see some comforting gesture from the mother toward her traumatized son, but Mom was busy peppering Joe with questions. He finally shook his head and walked away.

Mrs. Anderson looked at Permelia.

"Who are you?" she demanded.

"I'm—"

"She saw through the front window that our house was on fire," Benton said. "I was in the kitchen, and I didn't know. She came around the back and saved me and called nine-one-one."

Mrs. Anderson looked Permelia up and down.

"Well, thank you for that," she said and turned toward her car. "Come on, Ben, I booked us a suite at the Vintage for the night."

He looked back at Permelia as he stuffed his father's hat into his pocket, then turned and followed his mom to her car.

Chapter 18

Permelia parked in the morgue garage. She'd thought all way home about whether she should tell Harold about the latest development. She assumed the information would cause him to call his friend the detective, but it wasn't obvious they needed police intervention; and she wasn't sure her conclusion was correct. Still, if wife one's house was set on fire, Betty might be in danger, depending on what the purpose of the arson was. She'd like to at least run it by him.

He again met her in the parking lot as she came around the building.

"I wanted to check on how you were after that letter this morning."

She blew at a strand of hair that was hanging over her eyes, and he reached out and hooked it over her ear. She felt the slightest flutter in her stomach but pushed any thought about it away for later contemplation. He pulled a handkerchief from his pocket and wiped a smudge of soot off her cheek.

"You look like you could use a cup of tea."

"Would you mind coming up to my place? Fenton's been home alone for hours, and I'd like to be sure he hasn't done anything mischievous. He's normally very good," she said quickly, not wanting him to think she wasn't a good tenant. "I'm trying not to leave him alone too long until I'm sure he's settled in properly."

"That sounds fine."

He followed her to the stairway and up to her apartment.

"You can sit in there," she said and gestured toward the living room. "I'll put the kettle on and see what Fenton's been up to."

"He's in here," Harold called.

She poured two mugs of tea when the water had boiled and brought them into the living room. Fenton was curled up on Harold's lap, and the doctor was gently stroking his ears.

"He seems to be doing well. He was curled up on his climbing thing when I came in."

"He's usually pretty good as long as I walk him regularly to burn off his energy and his curiosity."

Harold was in one of her side chairs, and she sat down in the other, sighing as she did.

"It's not my business, but you look like you've been to a barbecue," he said.

"That's part of what I wanted to talk to you about. Remember the experiment I told you about with the hat? Wilma across the street found the address of the dead man for me, and I took the hat over to return it. When I got there, no one answered the door, but I saw flames in what looked like an office. I went around the back of the house and there was a boy in the kitchen. He had headphones on and was cooking with the vent running, so he didn't know the house was burning."

"What did you do?"

She gave a half-smile.

"I broke the glass in the French door with a garden gnome and got the boy out, and then I called nine-one-one. The boy was worried about his dog in the garage, so we got a fireman to break her out and then they took care of the fire."

"Was the house a total loss?"

"I don't think so. I stayed with the boy until they finally found his mother, and she came home, then I left."

"I don't suppose she said thank you," he said dryly.

"You *have* met her," Permelia laughed. "She actually did say thank you. It was lacking in warmth and feeling, but she did it."

"I suppose you weren't able to resolve your question about the double families."

Permelia sipped her tea.

"Actually, I did. The boy, Ben, recognized the hat immediately. In fact, he kept it. And if I'm not mistaken, he secreted it away before his mother could see it."

"Are you ready for me to call my detective friend yet?"

"I believe I am."

<hr/>

Detective Liam James arrived thirty minutes later. Harold and Permelia were on their second cups of tea, and she was explaining the difference between acrylic yarn and natural fibers to him.

"Ah, Liam," Harold said when he'd let the detective in and showed him into the living room. "This is the friend I was telling you about."

The detective shook hands with Permelia and sat down on the sofa. He was tall, and had the build of a basketball player—all arms and legs, and hands big enough to palm a regulation ball.

"Harold told me you might have some information about the murder of Mr. Edward Anderson."

"I don't know who killed him, but quite by accident I've learned that Mr. Anderson had another life and another wife and son on the other side of town."

He scribbled in his notebook and settled back on the sofa.

"Did he really?"

"It would appear so," Harold said.

"His other wife, Betty, is very upset," Permelia added, "and she's not faced up to the possibility he's dead yet."

"I take it she's unaware of the other family?"

Permelia thought for a moment.

"I'm not sure how to say this, but my feeling is Betty has had suspicions and is working very hard not to let them be confirmed."

"You mentioned a son?"

"She says they have a son who is in college in Ireland. She told me they were planning on joining him there when her husband retired."

"That's interesting," Liam said. "And how do you know this other wife?"

Permelia and Harold took turns explaining Betty's appearance at the morgue and her reaction to the hat.

"After Harold revived her, she was still so shaky I invited her up for tea so she could recover a bit before she tried to drive home."

She explained how Betty had used yarn made by Permelia's co-op and their subsequent knitting date.

"When she saw Edward's picture on the front page of the newspaper, she once again fainted. The coffee shop called an ambulance and insisted she go to the hospital. She asked me to go with her, and I did. She doesn't seem to have a lot of friends."

"Was she injured when she fell?" Detective James asked.

Permelia pressed her lips together.

"She did have a knot on her head, but I've seen worse on the ranch. Her blood pressure was pretty high, so they decided to keep her overnight."

"Have you seen her since then?"

"I did go have tea with her," Permelia paused. "This is a little embarrassing, but I encouraged her to look in her husband's home office—which he always keeps locked."

"And?" James asked.

"There were business cards from Mr. Anderson's job. Like I said earlier, I think she's working very hard at not knowing her husband was up to something."

Fenton stretched a back leg up in the air and began licking his hindquarter. Harold adjusted the cat, who was still in his lap, moving the leg out of his face.

Permelia reached for Fenton.

"I'm sorry, he's not usually like this. He doesn't take to people quickly."

Harold brushed her hand away.

"He's fine. My wife was allergic to animal dander, so we were never able to have pets. I'm enjoying him." He stroked the cat's back. "I think you need to tell Liam what happened today. He needs the full picture."

Detective James turned to her.

"I know I should keep out of this, but Betty keeps refusing to see what's going on, so I thought if I could bring her proof beyond a doubt that her husband and Edward Anderson are one and the same, she could stop with the twins-separated-at-birth nonsense and start her grieving process."

Harold gave her an encouraging look. She twined her fingers together in her lap.

"I'd had a good look at the hat she'd made her husband—the one I subsequently found by our dumpster. Since I'd made the yarn she'd used, I was able to knit a reasonable facsimile in just a couple of days, and today I went to Edward Anderson's house. I thought I could say I'd found it in the parking lot and offer it to them. If they recognized the hat and took it, Betty would have to accept that Edward and her husband were the same person."

Liam James was leaning forward in his chair.

"Did they take it?"

"Only the younger son was home, and he did recognize it, but that was after I got him out of their burning house."

James leaned his head against the back of his chair and looked up at the ceiling. He flipped to a clean page in his notebook.

"You better start at the beginning of this story."

Permelia told him the whole story, stopping and adding detail as he asked questions. When she finished, he handed her his notebook and asked her to write down Betty's contact information.

"Do you think Betty is in any danger?"

"Let's not get ahead of ourselves. We don't know if the fire is arson or something more benign. I'll speak to the fire department. Even if it was purposefully set, it doesn't automatically mean it's connected to Mr. Anderson's murder."

Harold looked over the top of his glasses at him. James smiled.

"Okay, not likely, I agree, but we can't jump to conclusions until we have all the facts. If it turns out the fire is related to the murder, and it looks like your friend could be in danger, we'll send people over to talk to her and arrange for protection."

Permelia stood up.

"Thank you."

Detective James stood and returned his notebook to his jacket pocket.

"Thank *you*," he said and held his hand out to her. "You've given me a lot to look into."

Harold had remained seated, not wanting to disturb Fenton.

"You don't have to put up with that," Permelia said when she returned to the living room.

"He's fine. He needs to finish his bath."

"Would you like more tea?"

"No, thank you, I've had plenty. I *am* getting hungry, though. I was thinking of trying a new Japanese place that opened two blocks from here. Would you care to join me? It's walkable."

"I've not eaten Japanese food before, but it sounds lovely."

"When he's done," he said and looked down at Fenton, "I'll go downstairs and lock up, and then I'll be ready."

Fenton took another ten minutes to finish, at which point he jumped off Harold's lap and climbed onto his tree structure without a backward glance.

Chapter 19

Permelia hadn't been sure how she would like Japanese, but it turned out she loved it. She even tried some sushi, although she hadn't been brave enough to try the one with raw fish. Dr. Grace was easy to talk to and kept their conversation light, staying away from duel families, burning houses, or anything else stressful. He insisted on paying, since he'd been the one to suggest the outing.

"Thank you for dinner," Permelia said when they reached the parking lot.

"Thank you for joining me. It was nice to have someone to talk to. I hope I didn't bore you with all the stories about my grandkids."

"Believe me, I'll pay you back with stories of my gang next time."

"I'll look forward to it."

<hr />

Permelia's house phone was ringing as she climbed the stairs to her apartment.

"Hello?" she answered, out of breath.

"Mother, where have you been?" her daughter Jennifer demanded.

"Not that it's any of your business, but I went out to dinner with a friend."

"You don't have any friends here. You just moved."

"Give me some credit. I've made several friends, and this isn't my first dinner out."

"It isn't safe for you to be out at night. You're living in the city now."

"Was there a reason you called?"

"If your social schedule isn't too busy, Beatrice wants you to come to her piano recital next week. I'll email you the details. I can have a car come pick you up."

"Honey, I'm capable of driving myself. It doesn't get dark until nine this time of year."

"I'm sending a car. And wear something nice."

Permelia ignored the last comment and opted to change the subject rather than get into yet another argument with her eldest child.

"Do you know a real estate broker named Sylvia Anderson?"

"I know who she is. Everyone in real estate in the Pacific Northwest knows her, and she uses her own name—Everett. Sylvia Everett. Why?"

"I just wondered. Her husband came through here the other night, and I met her briefly earlier today. I was curious as to what sort of person she was."

"Oh, yeah, I heard her husband had been killed. Are you wondering because she was rude to you?"

Permelia smiled.

"Something like that."

"Don't take it personally. She's like that with everyone except prospective clients. She's an absolute barracuda around other brokers and agents. Competitive doesn't begin to describe the level of aggression with which she goes after accounts. She's not above stealing them out from under her own agents if it's a lucrative enough deal."

"Does she need the money?"

"Hardly. She's the only child of one of the founding families of this city. She works so she has somewhere to channel her need to dominate everyone around her."

"Was her husband like her?"

"Again, hardly. Everyone in the real estate community has a theory about how they ended up married. The most popular is they were married to settle a gambling debt between their fathers. Hers wanted grandchildren, and he could see that she was never going to get a man on her own. The stories suggest that any man who dared to date her ended up in shreds. Her dad arranged for his dad to get into gambling trouble and then offered a way out. Nobody knows why the son went along with it."

"That's very interesting."

"I don't know why you want to know, but you'd be well advised to stay away from that family."

"I'll take that under advisement."

"Have Katy take you shopping for something to wear," Jennifer said and hung up without waiting for her mother to reply.

Permelia looked at the phone receiver before setting it back in its base. She looked at Fenton.

"I know. I can't believe that child came out of these loins either."

Fenton was waiting in Permelia's chair when she returned to the living room after she'd changed into her pajamas, made a cup of tea, and found the pair of socks she'd been knitting on before her move.

Jennifer's information was interesting. It went a long way toward explaining why Edward Anderson had a second family. She didn't agree with his decision—after meeting Benton, she knew he deserved more than a part-time father. She supposed she'd never know the answers now.

+————+

Her sleep was restless when she finally went to bed, and she was up in the middle of the night again. She stood gazing out of the kitchen window as she drank a glass of water, but this night the big oak door in her neighbor's wall stayed firmly closed.

+————+

Permelia sat in the living room the next morning, sipping her tea and watching her neighborhood wake up out the front picture window. She was contemplating how to tell Betty the hat experiment proved without a doubt that her husband Eideard and Sylvia's husband Edward were one and the same. She was also debating whether it was her business to tell Betty anything at all.

Her quandary was solved for her when her phone rang.

"I hope I'm not bothering you," Betty said. "I was wondering if you would be interested in getting together for coffee and knitting? I know it was a bit of a disaster last time, but I promise I won't make you ride with me in an ambulance this time."

Permelia wasn't sure that was a promise Betty could keep, given how easily she seemed to faint; but her social calendar wasn't exactly overflowing with appointments, so she agreed.

"Shall we meet at the same place? If they'll let me in," Betty said with a chuckle.

Permelia hung up and turned to look at her cat.

"Fenton, my boy, this should be interesting."

+————+

Betty had a doctor's appointment in the morning, so they'd agreed to meet just after noon. Permelia had been craving spaghetti and meatballs, so she went to the store and bought fresh tomatoes and basil along with grass-fed ground meat and sausage. She had sauce cooking in her slow cooker and still had time to walk Fenton around the block before it was time to meet Betty.

She dug through her stash and finally pulled out a skein of variegated sock yarn in shades of orange, yellow, and brown with a touch of green thrown in. She added two pairs of size-one circulars from her needle box.

80

"Okay, Fenton, where is a sock-sized project bag?" she asked, but he was no help. He'd found a small ball of leftover yarn from another project and was batting it across the floor. She finally found a small flowered-print drawstring bag and stuffed yarn, needles, and a plastic box of knitting markers and other accessories into it.

◂──▸

The coffee shop smelled of cinnamon rolls and chocolate when she walked in. Betty was sitting at a table in the back. She waved, and Permelia stopped at the counter to order before joining her.

She set her cup of tea on the table and her purse and bag on the floor beside her chair.

"How're you doing?" she asked Betty.

Betty pulled her cabled scarf from her bag and arranged her ball of yarn in her bag.

"I'm taking things one day at a time, but I'll be fine."

Permelia got her yarn and needles out.

"I did the hat experiment, and—"

"And," Betty interrupted, "you confirmed that my Eideard is their Edward."

Permelia stared at her.

"What changed?"

"I realized I couldn't keep ignoring the obvious. I recognized my husband in the newspaper. I tried to convince myself Eid had a previously unknown identical twin, but come on. After twenty years you know the person you're married to. You knew I was kidding myself, right?"

"I knew you'd suffered a big shock."

Betty gave a rueful smile.

"You're being kind."

"You've had a lot to process."

Betty pulled a folded page from her knitting bag and handed it to Permelia. It was cream-colored linen with a gold-embossed letterhead.

"This came in the mail yesterday. It's from Edward/Eideard's lawyer. You can read it."

> I hope you are reading this on the porch of our house in Ireland, our grandchildren playing in the yard. If that's the case, then what I'm going to tell you won't matter much.

It went on to explain that he had found himself in a marriage his father had arranged with a business associate in order to erase a gambling debt. The associate wanted their less-than-legal dealings to be tied through marriage so neither of them would be tempted to back out. Eideard had tried to make it work, but his wife was uninterested. They produced the expected heirs and pretty much went their separate ways. They appeared in public when necessary.

Then he constructed his story of clients who lived out of town and began spending time away from home. He had established his identity as Eideard—his actual name when his family emigrated from Ireland when he was a child—and ultimately met and married Betty.

The letter went on to describe the financial arrangements he'd made to insure Betty's future.

Permelia looked up.

"Wow."

"I'd already accepted that I was married to a bigamist and would have no rights of inheritance before this letter came. Now I don't know."

"Have you called this lawyer?"

"I put a call in, but they haven't called me back. Thinking back, Eid was looking after me all along. Our house is in my name only. He had some story about making things easier in case he died, and I was left alone. I of course didn't realize the situation we were really dealing with. He said he wanted to be sure I had my own credit rating. When I worked, we kept separate bank accounts and our house and car payments came from my account. Groceries and utilities came from his accounts. He would make deposits in my account periodically, keeping it below the allowable gift value I now realize."

"That sounds clever."

Betty sighed.

"I worked as a teacher, so I have a state pension; and I'll have Social Security on my own, so Red and I will be okay."

"What a shock, though."

"I guess I've been really naive. I never questioned his need to 'work out of town'. Until he didn't come home, I never questioned our life."

"Why would you?"

"You said you took the hat to his other family?"

Permelia stopped knitting and looked up at her.

"I did. Before you ask, are you sure you want to know?"

"Yes...no...I don't know. I guess I already know he wasn't happy with his wife or there wouldn't be me. I do wonder about the children, though. Were they all born before Eid married me?" Her cheeks turned pink as she asked.

Permelia avoided making eye contact.

"I see," Betty said, wringing her hands. "He was still sleeping with her while we were married."

Permelia reached across the table and put her hand on Betty's, stilling them.

"Don't torture yourself. Two of the three children are out of college, I think. And at least one of the kids is adopted. You can't jump to any conclusions about the youngest."

Betty sighed and picked up her knitting again.

"I suppose it doesn't matter now."

"How's your scarf coming?" Permelia asked, changing the subject.

Betty held it up.

"Do you think the single cable up the center is too simple? I've been thinking of ripping it out and doing it again with three smaller cables that cross over every six inches or so."

"The three-cable scheme would help it lie flatter."

They debated patterns, and ultimately, Permelia helped Betty pull out her scarf and rewind the yarn.

Chapter 20

Permelia stopped and bought tofu, several cheeses, and lasagna noodles on her way home. Her tomatoes were going to yield so much sauce that she would have enough to make a pan of vegetarian lasagna for Katy. She knew her daughter had a tendency to skip meals when she was working on a commission piece.

She assembled her meatballs and Katy's dinner before settling in to spin yarn for the rest of the afternoon. She had just taken a full bobbin of yarn from the spindle of her wheel when she heard a soft knocking. She went downstairs and found Ben Anderson on her porch.

Ben held out the leash Permelia had loaned him.

"I brought your leash back," he said.

"Are you through using it?"

Ben hung his head.

"My mother sent Bobbi to the kennel. I don't even get to visit her."

"Does your mother know you're here?"

"No, but she won't be home for hours, and I left a note."

"I think you should call and make sure she knows where you are. You can tell her I'll bring you home."

"I have a bus pass," he protested.

"All the same. Call her and let her know I'll bring you home after you've had a snack."

He brightened at the suggestion of food and pulled his phone from his pants pocket. Permelia held the door open and stepped aside, allowing him to climb the stairs in front of her.

He stopped and pressed the speed dial button for his mom when he reached the landing.

"Mom, I went to the morgue to return the leash I borrowed from the lady who rescued me from the fire. She said she'll bring me home."

He walked through the office area and into the kitchen, collapsing to his knees in front of Fenton. He looked up at her.

"Is it okay if I pet him?"

"Sure. He'll let you know if it's not okay with him."

Fenton was fascinated by his new visitor. He was used to Permelia's grandchildren, so she wasn't worried about him scratching Ben.

"See that bamboo stick beside the chair in the living room? It has a feather on a string attached to it if you want to play with him."

Ben got up and went into the living room while Permelia took several cookies from her cookie jar and put them on a plate.

"Do you drink milk?" she asked.

"Yes, ma'am."

She poured him a glass and brought his snack to the coffee table. Fenton danced and jumped as Ben bobbed his toy up and down.

He set the toy down and sat on the floor next to the table, picking up a chocolate chip cookie as he sat.

"This is amazing." He finished the first and picked up another one. "And it smells really fantastic in here. What are you cooking?"

Permelia smiled. She loved the enthusiasm of a hungry boy. Her own sons only got picky about food after they'd quit growing.

"I've been making tomato sauce in the slow cooker, and then I made spaghetti and meatballs for myself and a vegetarian lasagna for my daughter."

"Whoa. My mother doesn't cook. She has dinner delivered. Except when she has a party, then she has people come cook."

"You were cooking when I found you, weren't you?"

His shoulders sagged.

"My dad taught me how to make grilled cheese sandwiches and tomato soup from a can."

Permelia smiled.

"That's useful."

He brightened at the compliment.

"I can make toast, too."

"Do you like to cook?"

"Yeah, except for the cleanup part. The dish soap itches my hands."

Ben ate another cookie and took a big drink of milk. Permelia handed him a paper towel, and he wiped his mouth.

"Do you think the police will figure out who killed my dad?"

Permelia pressed her lips together then lowered herself to the floor beside him.

"The police will try very hard to catch the person. They're working on it right now."

"What if they don't?"

"I don't think the police ever give up. It just might take them a little time to put all the puzzle pieces together."

"If they don't catch him, will he come back and kill my mom and me?"

Permelia put her arm around his shoulders and gave him a hug.

"Sweetie, I don't think you have to worry about that. Whoever killed your dad is probably far away from here. Does the hotel you're staying in have a doorman?"

"Yes."

"And the door to your suite has a lock, right."

He nodded.

"Well, there you go. No one will be able to bother you."

Ben sighed.

"I wish they would catch him."

"How would you like to be a taste-tester for me? I'm not sure I got the spaghetti sauce just right."

Ben's eyes got big.

"That would be great."

"Let me warm up some garlic bread."

She returned to the kitchen and unwrapped a loaf of French bread, splitting it down the middle and spreading it with garlic butter before putting it in the oven. Fenton sat in Ben's lap, his front paws on either side of the boy's neck, licking the side of his head.

She boiled water and cooked the pasta, then ladled meatballs and sauce onto a pile of pasta in each of two bowls. She had just set the basket of bread on the table when she heard the doorbell.

"Watch the table so Fenton doesn't try to eat the spaghetti," she said and went down to answer.

A young man bearing a strong resemblance to Ben stood on her porch. He was older and had black hair, where Ben's was auburn, but there was no doubt they were related. He smiled when Permelia opened the door.

"Hi, I'm Ed Anderson. Is my brother Ben here, by any chance?"

Permelia opened the door wider to let him in.

"He's upstairs." She turned and led the way.

Ben stood up, setting Fenton in his chair.

"Eddie, what are you doing here?"

"I went by the hotel. Mom asked me to take you out and feed you. I saw your note."

Ben glanced at his steaming bowl of spaghetti and meatballs on the dining table.

"Ben and I were just about to have some spaghetti and meatballs. Would you care to join us?"

"We couldn't impose on you."

"It's no trouble. I have eight children and a whole tribe of grandchildren, and I haven't gotten the hang of cooking smaller amounts yet. I've got plenty."

"If you're sure it's not a problem, I'd love to join you. It smells incredible in here."

Permelia set another place at the table and served another bowl of spaghetti and meatballs.

"What sort of work do you do?" she asked Ed when everyone had eaten their first bowl-full and Ed and Ben had started on their second.

Ed set his fork down.

"I'm learning real estate from my mom. I studied business in college and got my MBA from Stanford."

"Do you enjoy it?"

Ed glanced at Ben before answering.

"Honestly? I don't enjoy showing properties to individual buyers, but Mother wants me to experience all aspects of the business. She knows I'm more interested in commercial real estate. I've been working in our low-cost housing division, but I'm about to move into the high-end condo business for the next six months."

"That's nice your family has a business you can go in to."

"Mom does, anyway. My dad was an accountant, but the business he worked for didn't encourage nepotism."

"What's that?" Ben asked around a mouthful of garlic bread.

Ed turned to his brother.

"That's where someone hires their relatives just because they're related."

Ben looked confused.

"But Mom does it."

Ed smiled.

"It's not quite the same thing when your mother owns the business and plans on having you take it over when she retires."

"Mom's giving you the business?" Ben asked. "What about me and Tif and Silver?"

Ed looked uncomfortable.

"Look, can we talk about this at home? I'm sure Ms…"

"O'Brien," Permelia supplied.

"Ms. O'Brien," he continued, "doesn't want to hear about our family business."

"It's okay," she assured him. "I'm sure Ben is confused with everything that's gone on. He's just looking for reassurance."

"Ben, it's all going to be okay. I'm sure Mother is dividing her company among all of us. She's just teaching me to take care of it…" He glanced at Permelia, and she gave him a slight head shake. She could see he was about to say "in case she dies". He got her message. "…so she can retire eventually."

Ben relaxed and began eating again.

"I don't have anything special for dessert," Permelia said when everyone was finished eating. "I do have plenty of chocolate chip cookies."

"They're really good," Ben said.

She filled a plate with cookies and set it on the table. Ed stood and collected their dinner bowls, carrying them to the kitchen.

"You can just put those in the sink," Permelia told him.

"Thank you so much for feeding us," he said when he'd returned to the table. "Are you a professional chef or something?"

Permelia laughed.

"Not even close."

Chapter 21

Permelia cleaned up the dinner dishes and looked at the clock. It was still early enough that if Katy was home, she could deliver her dinner. She called Katy and let her know she would be doing so in a few minutes. As expected, her daughter confessed she'd been working all day without a food break and would greatly appreciate her mother's offering.

"Oh, Mom, you didn't need to do this," Katy said as she let Permelia into her apartment. "I'm glad you did, though." She peeked into the top of the shopping bag her mother handed her.

"The lasagna is vegetarian, made with tofu, and the bread is whole-wheat French." Permelia told her. "I didn't put garlic butter on it because I didn't know where you were on dairy products."

Katy smiled and turned her oven on.

"Butter is fine, but I have some. Will you join me?"

"I couldn't eat another bite. I had two gentlemen callers who shared my spaghetti and meatballs."

"Really? Two?"

"The younger one was returning a leash I loaned him, and the older brother was looking for the younger." She carefully avoided telling her daughter about the fire that led to the leash-lending.

"Speaking of callers, has my sister invited you to Bea's piano recital?"

"As a matter of fact, she has. She's pretty insistent about sending a car to pick me up. I tried to tell her I'm perfectly capable of driving myself."

"Don't tell her I told you, but it's a setup. She's inviting a stuffy old former business associate who lives in the senior living place she wants to put you in. He'll be in the car when it comes to get you. The whole car ride will be a hard sell to move to the place."

Permelia sank into the nearest chair.

"She doesn't give up, does she?"

"I'm afraid not."

"She told me Bea wanted me there. I wonder if Bea knows that?"

"I think Bea will be thrilled to have you there. She really likes to play piano, and she *is* talented at it."

Permelia thought for a moment.

"Is the recital open to the public? I mean, do you think I could bring a guest?"

"Like a date?" Katy asked, eyes opening wide. "Is there something I should know?"

Permelia laughed.

"No, but I think I can get a friend to help me out. If I have someone with me, we can drive ourselves, and Jennifer won't be able to corner me."

"Clever, Mom, clever. And yes, I'm sure you can bring a date. You better tell Jen, though, so she doesn't send the geezer and the car."

"Not to worry. I've got to be sure my friend will help me first."

"Are you sure you won't stay for dinner?"

"No, I should get home. Can I take a peek at the sculpture first?"

Katy laughed.

"Of course. Just don't tell anyone what you see, okay?"

"Scouts honor," Permelia said making the three-fingered salute.

<hr/>

Dr. Grace was sitting on the front porch when Permelia pulled into the parking lot. She took a deep breath. Her idea had seemed a lot better when she was standing in Katy's apartment. Now, she was going to have to pluck up her courage and speak to her potential recital date, and there was no time like the present.

She put the car in the garage and walked around to the front of the building.

"You're working late," she said when she'd arrived on the porch.

Dr. Grace stood up.

"Please, sit a minute."

She set her purse down and sat in the white metal chair opposite the doctor.

"Would you like some tea?" he asked.

"No, I'm fine, thanks."

"I've got a body arriving from down south. They were supposed to be here hours ago, but a tractor-trailer rolled over on the highway and dumped its load of chickens a hundred miles from here." He glanced at his watch. "They called a while ago and said they were underway again, so it shouldn't be too much longer.

"What brings you to my porch? Make no mistake, I'm happy to have the company, but you look like a woman on a mission."

Permelia picked up her purse and set it on her lap, fidgeting with the clasp.

"This is a little embarrassing, now that I'm here across from you. It sounded like a good plan, but maybe I'm overstepping..."

A warm smile creased his face.

"Why don't you let me decide. What can I do for you?"

"The first day I came here, I was with two of my daughters. You may remember."

Dr. Grace laughed.

"No offense, but your older daughter was rather unforgettable."

Permelia blushed. He reached over and patted her hand.

"I don't mean it in a negative way."

"Jennifer is and always has been a difficult child. She has very strong opinions. As you probably picked up on, she wasn't keen on me moving into the apartment here."

"She did make that pretty clear."

"Well, she called and invited me to my granddaughter's piano recital next week."

"That sounds nice."

"That's what I thought, too, until just now when I went to my younger daughter's to drop off some dinner. Katy told me that Jennifer plans to have a car pick me up, and waiting inside will be a gentleman who lives at the retirement community she wants me to move to. His job will be to sell me on the idea."

Harold sat back in his chair.

"And you're hoping I'll run interference?"

Permelia's face flamed red.

"Something like that. I hoped if you were willing to accompany me, we could drive ourselves, watch the recital, and escape without having to deal with Jen's fellow."

"I would be happy to accompany you to the recital, under one condition."

Permelia held her breath.

"Will you agree to go to dinner with me first? That way it will be quite natural that we would drive to the recital instead of you having to take the car she wants to send for you."

"Are you sure?"

"A piano recital sounds delightful. And thwarting a well-laid entrapment plan is a bonus."

"I don't want to impose. You would tell me if it's too much of an imposition, wouldn't you?"

"I would, but it's not. It will be fun. My children live on the East Coast, so I don't have many opportunities to attend recitals or anything else. I miss that. In fact, you're doing me a favor. I had actually looked into doing some volunteer jobs with young people because I do miss that interaction."

A panel van pulled into the driveway.

"Looks like my customer has arrived. Let's talk later about what time and where we'll go to dinner."

Permelia stood up.

"Thank you,"

He smiled at her.

"I'm happy to help."

⊬⸺⸺⊬

Permelia went upstairs; she picked up her knitting but put it down again after two rows. Fenton jumped onto her lap and back down again, wrapping his paws around her ankle and chewing on the top of her slipper. She batted at him, and he let go of her ankle and grabbed her hand, being careful to keep his claws sheathed.

"Okay, cat. You're right, we're aren't accomplishing anything here, and it is still light out. Let's get your leash."

This time of year, it was light until after nine o'clock; and it was not yet eight, so there was plenty of time for a good walk around the neighborhood. Permelia had chosen his extendable leash, giving the cat room to run; and Fenton zoomed down the stairs and stood on his hind legs, pawing at the doorknob.

They had barely gotten to the sidewalk when Wilma's big oak door opened and she leaned her head out, looking both ways before speaking.

"Would you and cat like to come in and have some iced tea?"

Permelia looked down at Fenton.

"Could I walk him around the block first?"

Wilma smiled.

"Sure, just use the knocker when you're back." She indicated the iron lion's head below the speakeasy door.

"I didn't realize that lion was a knocker. I thought he was part of the decorative grillwork."

"I'll go get the tea ready."

⊬⸺⸺⊬

Henri was jumping rope on the sidewalk in front of her house when Permelia and Fenton walked by.

"Who was that kid that came to your house?" she asked without missing a beat.

"Why? Do you think you know him?"

"Is his name Ben?"

"Yes, it is."

"I thought so. We take music classes at the same place."

"Do you play an instrument?"

Henri stopped jumping.

"We all have to play three. It's part of the deal. We all do piano and violin, and then we get to choose the third one."

"What's your third one?"

"I play the flute. Ben plays the drums, in case you were wondering."

"Is there a girl named Beatrice at your school?"

Henri started jumping again.

"Yeah, there is, not that she knows I'm alive. The older kids think they own the school."

"Have you tried standing up to them?"

"It's not worth it, believe me."

"I'm sorry."

"Yeah, sucks to be me."

<hr />

"How's your knitting going?" Permelia asked when she was seated with her glass of tea at Wilma's patio table.

Wilma reached into a basket by her feet and pulled her scarf out, holding it up for Permelia to inspect.

"This is looking really good."

Wilma had about six inches knitted. Permelia counted the stitches.

"You've got two extra stitches. But it looks like it just happened two rows ago. You have an option. You can knit two together two times or if you want, I can pull it out and fix it for you. It looks like you didn't finish taking the last part of the stitch off—twice."

"If you can take it out, I'd prefer that. I'd like to not get in the habit of compensating for boo-boos."

Permelia reached for the piece.

"How are things going with your friend Betty?"

Permelia recounted the activities of the two days since she and Wilma had last knitted.

"I don't have enough legal knowledge to know whether Ed's first family can challenge the financial arrangements he made for Betty and her son."

"It doesn't sound like the first family needs the money."

"That might not stop them from trying just to be vindictive. My daughter Jen knows the first wife from business. She says she's a real piece of work, and coming from my daughter that's saying something."

"You need to be careful. People like that are not to be trifled with. If she had anything to do with her husband's death, you could be in danger. Even if she didn't have anything to do with his death, you still could be putting yourself in danger messing around in a murder investigation."

"I don't think anyone is paying any attention to me."

"You don't know that. I was curious about our mister Ed with two families. The company he works for keeps a very low profile. They own a collection of franchise-type businesses—fast food, movie theaters, small groceries, that sort of thing."

"Does that sort of business make enough money to pay Ed enough to support two families?"

"It could. They own a lot of businesses. If even half of them are successful, they could have a pretty good money stream."

"I think his wife makes a lot of money, so maybe he used all his to support Betty and her son. She worked, too."

"Well, like I said—you need to be careful around all these people. Even Betty. Someone killed that man, and you only have Betty's word she was at home and he left. That could be pure fiction."

Permelia took a sip of her tea.

"I suppose. I feel sorry for Ed's youngest son, Ben. He came to see me earlier today. His excuse was to return a leash he'd borrowed at the fire, but I think he's a little lost with his father dead and his mother obsessed with work."

"I know you feel sorry for these people, and I will back you up any way I can; but please be careful."

"Ben is a child. There is no danger from a child." Permelia handed Wilma's scarf back to her. "It's a good idea to count your stitches every few rows to be sure you haven't gained or lost any."

"Thank you. I'll be more careful about making sure I clear off the stitches as I make them."

"On a lighter note, my eldest daughter asked me to come to my granddaughter's recital, but my younger daughter told me it's really a ploy to sic an elegant older gentleman who lives in the senior living residence on me who will try to convince me I should do the same."

"That's really cunning. If you don't go, you disappoint your granddaughter. If you do, you have to fend off some old guy all night."

"I've taken evasive measures. I'm not sure I've done the right thing, but I asked Dr. Grace if he'd go with me."

"Harold, the morgue guy?"

"Is that a problem?"

"No, not at all. He's nice. I just didn't know you were friends."

"We've had tea a few times. And I was desperate."

Wilma laughed.

"I'll need a full report. When does this happen?"

"Next Wednesday."

"How long have you lived here?"

Permelia smiled.

"Tomorrow it's been a week."

Wilma ticked off items on her fingers.

"Let's see. In a week, you've gotten involved in a murder, gotten threatened by someone as yet unknown, ridden in an ambulance with a woman you hardly know, saved a child from a fire, and arranged to go on a date. Not bad for a week's work."

Permelia grinned.

"As they say, idle hands are the devil's playthings."

Fenton grabbed the yarn trailing from Wilma's scarf.

"Speaking of idle hands, I'd better get this guy home."

"Thanks for fixing my knitting."

Wilma walked her to the gate and let them out. Permelia picked up her cat and carried him home.

Chapter 22

The next morning dawned sunny and clear. Permelia opened a window in the kitchen and another in the front room. It was early still, so she sat and knitted on her sock while she sipped her morning tea.

She thought about the last time she'd worked on it—at tea with Betty—and then thought about what Wilma had said. It didn't seem right to abandon Betty after all the trauma she'd had in the week Permelia had known her, but Wilma had a point. What did she really know about the woman? Maybe she'd gotten tired of sharing her husband with another family and decided to collect the money he'd left her. She did have a key to his office, even though she acted like she'd never been in it before.

Permelia had always thought she had good instincts when it came to judging people, but then, her instincts had failed her big-time when it came to her own husband. Maybe she was that far off on Betty, too.

She finished turning the heel on her sock and put it back in her bag.

"Do you feel like a walk?" she asked.

Fenton was lying on the highest sleeping platform of his climbing tree. He opened his eyes but didn't lift his head. He blinked and went back to sleep.

"You're no fun," she said to the unconscious feline.

When she was at home on the ranch on a Saturday morning, she would go to the farmer's market to buy vegetables and herbs. She remembered passing a sign on her way to Betty's advertising a local market. A quick check on her computer verified that, indeed, there was a farmer's market; and she was pretty sure she could find it.

With that in mind, she got dressed, gathered her purse and shopping bags, and headed out.

The market was busy when Permelia arrived. She had several bags with her and quickly filled them with rhubarb, asparagus, herbs, and various greens. She took them to her car so her hands would be free to carry a flat of strawberries.

She bought her strawberries and was carrying them back to the car when a bagel stand caught her eye. She could make a delicious strawberry cream cheese to spread on freshly toasted bagels. Wilma had served her with several treats, and bagels would be a nice snack to take to their next knitting session to reciprocate.

She set her berries on the counter while she purchased bagels and was struggling to carry both without squishing the berries when Betty approached her.

"Can I help you carry something?" she asked and grabbed the bag of bagels as it slipped from Permelia's hands.

"Thank you. I thought I was done except for the berries, but then I saw these homemade bagels."

"They *are* really good," Betty said. "We like the asiago cheese version."

"Do you have time for tea? I noticed a tea booth at the other end of the market. I just need to put my berries in the car."

"That sounds nice. I'll buy my bagels on our way back."

"What brings you to my neck of the woods?" Betty asked when they were settled with their cups of tea and frosted lemon biscotti.

"I wanted to get some fresh rhubarb and strawberries to make a cobbler and remembered seeing a sign advertising this market when I visited you. Since I'm not familiar with any other markets yet, I thought I'd try this one."

"I'm glad you did. I was going to call you and see if we could meet. There's something I wanted to run by you. If you don't mind being my sounding board, that is."

Permelia smiled and sipped her tea.

"As long as you're not planning to rob a bank or anything of that sort, I'm happy to listen."

Betty broke off a piece of her biscotti and set it down on her napkin.

"My son Red—that's Eideard Junior—is insisting on coming home for a visit, and he says we need to do some sort of memorial service. I'm worried it would be unseemly, given that we don't have a body." She dipped her head down. "And frankly, I haven't had the courage to tell our parish priest what has happened."

"I see," Permelia said.

"And I'm not sure who I could invite. I mean, we have friends from church, and neighbors, and there were several business cards from other people Eid worked with, plus he had two sets of business cards, one with each of his names, so I assume someone at his company knew about his dual identity." She sat back in her chair and ate her piece of biscotti. "This is just so complicated."

"Let's take it one step at a time. First, I don't see why you should avoid talking to your priest. You haven't done anything wrong. You didn't know Eid had another family when you met."

"Still, though, Red is the product of an invalid marriage."

"But only Eid knew that. You didn't. You married him in good faith. Besides, I suspect your priest won't be judgmental. I think you need to talk to him. Seek his advice. My guess is he'll support some sort of small memorial service to help you and your son."

Betty sighed.

"I've been avoiding the church, but I know you're right. What about the neighbors?"

"That's harder. Only you know your friends. I don't think I'd do a wholesale announcement. Rather, I'd carefully choose who to let in on the story. People who aren't going to gossip or judge, if there is anyone in your group like that."

"There are two couples like that. Both of them are Irish—like Eid. Connor and Erin Byrne both came here as young children and Padraig and Orlagh McCarthy came here right before Red was born. They've been very helpful in helping him get settled in college. They have relatives near his university."

"Okay, they sound like good options."

"I'd like to go talk to his boss at his workplace. Here comes the big ask. Would you come with me?"

"What are you hoping to gain from visiting them?"

Betty stalled, sipping her tea and nibbling on her biscotti before answering.

"I guess I'm seeking some sort of legitimacy. If people at his work knew him as Eid, maybe they knew about Red and I, and if that's the case, we're a little less like a hidden mistress with an illegitimate child."

"And if they did know him as Eid you would invite him or them to the private memorial service?"

"I suppose I would. Do you think I shouldn't?"

"I don't have an opinion either way. I think you have to meet his coworkers and see how they are. It's possible they won't be thrilled that their executive had a double life, if they didn't know."

"Oh, now I don't know what to do."

Permelia sipped her tea and thought.

"Today is Saturday, so you can't visit Eid's business, assuming it keeps normal hours. But you could visit the priest at your church. When you've had time to digest whatever advice he has for you, if the memorial service is still a go, you could consider contacting the two couples you mentioned. Meanwhile, if you'd like, I could give the names of Eid's bosses to my neighbor Wilma. She's very discreet and very good at computer research. Of course, I can't speak for her, but I think she'll be willing to check them out before we consider talking to them in person."

She decided not to mention that Wilma had already done some digging on the company Eid worked for.

"Does that mean that if your friend's research doesn't show anything scary you'll go with me to meet his boss?"

Permelia sighed.

"I guess it does."

Betty smiled.

"Thank you. I can't tell you how much your support means to me. I know we've only known each other for a week, but it feels like it's much longer."

Chapter 23

Fenton was still sprawled on his sleeping shelf when Permelia came home. He jumped down and ran into the kitchen as she put her bags on the counter. He immediately leaped up and began chewing on the ends of the rhubarb.

"Get down, you little scamp," she scolded. As she set the rhubarb in the sink to wash, she noticed Dr. Grace pull into the parking lot and get out of his car. She wondered if he was here to receive a body. She wasn't on duty during the daytime on the weekend, so her phone hadn't recorded a call.

She had enough fruit to make more than one dish, so she decided to make a pie to take to knitting with Wilma and a cobbler for herself. She'd divide it and put half of it in the freezer. When she'd finished with that, she still had plenty left, so decided to make a crisp she could take to the workers' downstairs.

She put on her apron and got to work.

+←——→+

The pie was out and the cobbler in the oven with the crisp waiting in line when Permelia heard the buzzer on her downstairs door. She wiped her hands and headed downstairs, surprised to find Dr. Grace on her doorstep.

He took a deep breath.

"Woman, what are you cooking? You're killing us downstairs."

"Well, they had rhubarb at the farmer's market I went to, so I bought a bunch, and now I'm making cobbler and crisp and pie."

"It smells wonderful."

"If you play your cards right, one of these will end up in your break room."

"Oh, you don't have to do that."

"It was already my plan, even before you came sniffing around."

"That's kind of you. Actually, I came calling for another reason. I realized no one has shown you the private patio off the bedroom on the back side of the building. I didn't think about it when I was taking you through the place because it was out of commission for several years, and we'd just had it rebuilt when you came to see the house."

"I noticed from the window there was some sort of structure, but I didn't see a connection from the house."

"When they decided to rent out this apartment years ago, they had to create a closet in that room to make it a legal bedroom. Since the patio was broken down even then, they built the closet where the access door was."

"So, how do you get to it?"

"I should have been more precise. The access door is still there. It's inside the closet."

"Show me," Permelia said, and stepped aside to let him in.

Fenton yowled at Dr. Grace as soon as he entered the apartment. Harold bent down and scratched the cat behind his ears before continuing on to the bedroom door.

Permelia had set the second bedroom up as a guest room, with an antique iron queen-sized bed centered on one wall and a single bed with a trundle, also of iron, against another wall in anticipation of visits from her grandchildren.

"I guess it's fortunate I haven't put anything in this closet yet," she said and opened the door.

Harold reached in, flipped a light switch to the right of the door, then stepped inside. It turned out the door to the outside wasn't obvious, as it was offset from the closet door. He turned the knob and swung it open, revealing a screen door.

"This is delightful," she said.

A metal bistro table with two matching chairs sat in the corner of the deck. Several large ceramic pots were in the opposite corner waiting for someone to plant them.

"Would anyone mind if I planted some herbs in these pots?"

"I think that would be fine. If I'm not mistaken, there are some planters that hang from the top rail in the storeroom."

"This is a really nice surprise."

"I'm glad you like it." He looked around the deck. "Everything seems to be in order, so I guess I'll be on my way."

"Are you in a hurry, or do you have time for a piece of pie?" She could always make another pie for Wilma. They weren't knitting until Sunday afternoon.

"Pie sounds wonderful. I was planning on watching a nature show tonight, but that's not until later."

"I have ulterior motives. I'd like to run something by you."

He laughed.

"If I get a piece of that wonderful-smelling pie, I don't care what your motives are."

She served two pieces of pie and poured iced tea for each of them.

"What's on your mind?" he asked after he'd savored several bites.

"I ran into Betty at the farmer's market. She had several things on her mind. She wants to have a memorial service for her husband. I understand that—she and her son need closure of some sort. I think she wants something formal, in the church maybe, but she hasn't talked to her priest about what happened. And of course, she doesn't have the body or ashes or anything."

"Seems like she needs to talk to the priest."

"That's what I told her. And if she's unwilling to do that, she can always have a private gathering in a home or some neutral space. The real problem is that she found some business cards from the place her husband worked—he had cards with both of his names from the same company. Betty thinks that means his company knew about his deceit."

"And what if they did?"

"She wants me to accompany her to the business so she can verify that they knew about her, and if they say they did, then she wants his boss to come to whatever the memorial service turns out to be."

Harold leaned back in his chair.

"Ooh, I'm not sure that's a good idea. Whether they knew all along or this is a surprise to them, she may not get the warm reception she's imagining."

"I think she's looking for some sort of acknowledgment of their marriage. Obviously, no matter how many people she finds that also thought her marriage was legally valid, it wasn't. It doesn't matter whether his boss thought it was or not."

"If I were you, I would avoid getting sucked any farther into her situation than you already are."

"That's what Wilma said."

"She's right. And don't forget—her non-husband was murdered by someone. Who knows what he was involved in, besides bigamy?"

"Wilma said that, too."

"She's a wise woman."

"Would you like another piece of pie?"

Harold smiled.

"Maybe a little sliver."

Permelia went to the kitchen, lost in her thoughts.

Chapter 24

It was dinnertime before Permelia got done baking. Her feet hurt, and she decided to have a cup of tea before contemplating eating. She'd just gotten settled in her chair, feet up on her ottoman, when her door buzzer sounded again. She sighed deeply and got up. She'd seen Harold drive out of the parking lot more than an hour ago, so she doubted it was him.

"Cat, it would be really helpful if you learned to look through the peephole and let me know who was there before I had to go down to the door," she told Fenton as she descended the stairs. She glanced out the peephole and quickly opened the door.

"Ben, honey, what's wrong?"

"Everything," he cried and tumbled into her arms, tears streaming down his cheeks.

"Come on upstairs, and let's see if we can sort this out."

"We can't," he said tearfully as he followed her up to her apartment.

She led him to the sofa and sat him down, handing him a tissue from a box on the end table.

"You stay here while I get you some water."

Ben leaned back, blowing his nose. Permelia returned with a glass of water and a chocolate chip cookie. He sipped the water and ate the cookie in silence. She handed him another tissue and waited while he dabbed at his tears. Fenton jumped onto the sofa and rubbed his head on Ben's arm.

"Now, tell me what's happened."

"It's my mom…" He started sobbing again. Permelia sat down on the sofa and took his hand.

"Ben," she said in a firm voice. "Has something happened to your mom? Do I need to call nine-one-one? Is she hurt?"

"No," he choked out. "Worse."

"Sip some more of your water and then try to tell me what's happened."

He obeyed then set the glass on the coffee table.

"Now, take a deep breath," she encouraged him.

"I was supposed to spend the night with Oliver—his mom works with my mom. Mom sent me in a taxi, but when I got there, they told me not to come in or even touch the door. Mrs. Shah barely opened the door and told me they were all throwing up, and she'd call my mom and tell her. She called another cab, and I went back to the hotel we're staying at."

Fresh tears ran down his face. Whatever had happened must have been at the hotel, and Permelia was beginning to suspect what that was going to be. Her heart went out to the boy.

"I didn't see her in the sitting room of the suite, but I heard noise coming from her bedroom, and I thought she was watching TV. I opened the door and...and..." He couldn't finish. He slumped over and buried his face in two sofa pillows, his sobbing renewed.

Permelia rubbed his back.

"There, there," she crooned. "We'll get this sorted out."

He finally sat back up.

"I'm not going back there. How could she do that?"

"Are you sure there's not some innocent explanation?"

He stared at Permelia.

"Do you really think there's an innocent explanation for two people who aren't married being naked in bed together?"

Permelia shook her head.

"No, I suppose not. I'm sorry you had to see that." She put her arm around his shoulders. "We'll figure this out, don't you worry."

Ben dabbed at his eyes with the wadded-up tissue he clutched in his fist, and Permelia handed him a new one.

"Could I have another cookie?" he asked.

Permelia smiled. You could always count on boys to have an appetite for cookies no matter how bad things got.

"Of course, you can," she said and went to the kitchen to fill a plate with cookies. "Would you like a glass of milk to go with them?" she called.

"Yes, please."

He stroked Fenton's head as he chewed a cookie. Fenton wrapped his paws around Ben's hand and pulled it to his mouth. He began licking the boy with his raspy tongue.

"Is he bothering you?" Permelia asked as she sat in her customary chair.

Ben freed his hand and began petting the cat's head again.

"No, I like him. Where am I going to go?" he asked in a strained voice. "I can't go back there."

"When you're ready, why don't we call your brother?"

"Will you tell him about Mom? I don't think I can say it without crying, and my brother will think I'm being a baby."

"I'll tell him, if that's what you want."

"Can I tell you something else before he gets here?"

"Honey, you can tell me anything you want to."

"It was the cologne," he said finally.

She waited for him to continue.

"I've smelled it before. At our house. It's really strong. I asked my mom about it, and she said it was my brother Eddie's, but Eddie has allergies. He always sneezes if anyone is around him wearing anything that smells. Our suite smelled like it when I opened the door." He looked up at her. "I think that same guy has been to our house before."

Oh, you poor, poor child, Permelia thought. *You are going to have to grow up much too quickly.*

"Everyone deals with grief in their own way," she began. "Your mother entertaining another man might not be the seemliest way, but it could be her sadness over your father's death that's caused her behavior."

"I smelled the cologne in our house *before* my dad died."

Permelia blew out a breath.

"Your mother was trying to shield you from her new relationship. She did arrange for you to be away. And she is still your mother. You may not like her behavior, but you still have to respect her."

"Please don't make me go back to the hotel."

"Let's call your brother and see what he advises."

"Do we have to right now?"

Permelia glanced at her watch.

"You can play with Fenton for fifteen minutes, then we call him. I'm setting a timer." She got up, went to the kitchen, and did just that.

⊷──⊶

"Ben, you can't stay with me. My apartment is a studio, and I work at home some days."

Ed had arrived thirty minutes after Permelia called him.

"I'm at school all day, so I wouldn't bother you," Ben whined. "I'd just eat dinner and sleep there."

"See? That's the problem. I don't keep food in the house, other than coffee, of course. I eat out, usually with clients."

Ben slumped back into the sofa, Fenton in his arms. Ed sat down beside him.

"I'm not trying to be mean here, Buddy, but if you give Mom too hard of a time, she might send you off to boarding school. Don't forget Silver."

"Yeah, but she used drugs," Ben argued.

"Did she? Or did Mom just get tired of her 'project'?"

Permelia caught Ed's attention.

"I'm not sure you're helping," she said in a firm but quiet voice.

He blushed and dipped his head.

"I'm sorry, you're right." He turned to Ben. "I'll take you to get something to eat, and you can go straight to your room when we get back to the hotel, and I'll talk to Mom."

Ben launched himself into Eddie's arms.

"You're the best."

"Thank you," Eddie said to Permelia and stood up. "And I'm sorry Ben dumped our drama into your lap."

Permelia stood up.

"I've raised eight children; I've seen a little drama in my day."

"Well, again, thank you. Now, we'll get out of your hair."

Ben hugged her.

"Thank you," he said.

She patted his back as she hugged him.

"You come back any time."

"Thanks again," Ed said as they went out the door and down the stairs.

Chapter 25

Permelia placed the second pie she'd made that day in her well-used pie carrier and headed across the street to Wilma's place. Her neighbor was waiting at the gate.

"Come in, come in. You must be wiped out after all that baking. The aroma of baked goods has been wafting into my upstairs windows for hours."

Permelia smiled.

"As I said on the phone…" She held up the pie carrier. "…this one has your name on it."

"I've got some vanilla ice cream, if you think that would go well with your pie."

"It would be perfect."

―――――

"How are things with your new friends? Any developments?" Wilma asked when they'd finished their pie.

"Betty is starting to come to terms with her situation. Her son came home from Ireland, and between the two of them, they've decided they want to have some sort of memorial service."

"That sounds reasonable."

"Unfortunately, Betty seems to be looking for some sort of acknowledgment. She wants to have the service at their church, and she wants to invite his co-workers. The problem is, she has no idea whether they knew about her and her son or not. She wants me to go with her to talk to them."

"You aren't going to go, are you?"

"Fortunately, it's the weekend, so I was able to put her off. I told her to go talk to her priest and approach their closest friends."

"The friends don't know about his other life, I assume. Are you sure they need to?"

"I think they have to be told. If she wants to keep them as friends, at any rate. If Betty recognized the picture of Ed on the front page of the paper, it's likely they've seen it, too. They're going to have questions."

"So, what about the business associates?"

Permelia was quiet for a moment.

"I was hoping you could do a background check on them. I know there's a limit to what you can tell about a person from the internet, but any information could be useful."

"I think this is a bad idea. No matter what sort of public face these people have, you have to remember—someone killed that man. Most people who are murdered aren't killed by strangers. The police will be looking at the people he worked with as potential suspects, and until they've done their job, you need to stay away from them."

"Betty's not going to like it."

"That woman is looking for answers she's never going to get. The only one who knows why her husband had two families is her husband, and he's done talking. She may want to risk her life trying to figure it out, but you don't need to."

Permelia sighed.

"What you're saying makes sense. I just feel so sorry for the woman."

"Bake her a pie," Wilma said.

Both of them laughed.

"How's your knitting going?" Permelia asked.

"Let me go get it, and you can tell me."

Wilma took both dessert plates and carried them to the kitchen.

⊢————⊣

Permelia was deep in thought as she crossed the street; she didn't notice the writing on her door until she started to unlock the outer door. LEAVE was written in red paint across it. The paint had dripped so it looked like blood.

She dropped her keys and reached in her pocket for her phone, only then realizing it was upstairs in her apartment. She thought about going to get it, but decided she shouldn't touch the door. The notes were one thing, but this was taking it up a notch. Whatever "it" was.

She hurried back across the street and knocked on Wilma's gate.

"Could I use your phone?" she asked when Wilma let her in.

"What's up?"

She explained about her door.

"You did the right thing not going in. I know you haven't wanted to take the letters you got seriously, but this is escalating. You need to call the police."

"I agree this seems to be a little more serious than I first thought, but it just doesn't feel like a lights-and-sirens emergency."

Wilma led her into the sitting room and fetched a cordless handset.

"I don't mean to sound patronizing, but things are different in the city. You don't know who did that or why, but you need to consider it a threat and let the police deal with it."

Permelia took the phone without saying anything and made her call.

"They were certainly more interested in who I was than in what happened," she said when she'd hung up.

Wilma handed her a cup of tea.

"What did they say?"

"They said they'd send someone out, and I shouldn't go inside until they come. I hope you don't mind, but I told them I'd be here and to call at the gate when they arrived." She took a sip of the strong black tea. "I hope they hurry. I don't like leaving Fenton by himself."

"He probably has no idea what happened," Wilma assured her.

"I suppose I should call Dr. Grace."

Before she could pick up the phone, Wilma's gate buzzer sounded, announcing the arrival of the police. Permelia stepped outside and gave them directions to her door at the back of the morgue. The officer instructed her to stay at Wilma's until he and his partner had investigated. He returned a few minutes later.

"There's no sign of a break-in but if you'd like, we can check your apartment."

"I would feel better if you did."

She returned home accompanied by a young dark-haired woman who could have been her partner's sister they looked so much alike.

"Give me your keys," the woman instructed.

Permelia did, and the two officers went up the staircase to the landing before signaling her to join them.

"My cat is inside, and is quite curious."

She'd no sooner gotten the words out of her mouth than the female officer opened the door and Fenton came rushing out onto the landing, yowling up a storm.

"There, there," Permelia soothed. Fenton put his front paws on either side of her neck so he could speak directly at her.

The man—Officer Yates, if his name badge was to be believed—stroked Fenton's head. His partner sneezed.

"Are there any other doors to the outside or down into the morgue?" he asked.

"No...oh, wait, there *is* a door onto a deck off one of the bedrooms. I'll show you."

She set Fenton down, and he meowed in protest.

"I only just learned of this door myself. Apparently, the deck was in disrepair for a number of years, so a closet was built over its entrance door."

She led them into the guest room and opened the closet, pointing to the door. Yates went out onto the patio, and Permelia started to follow.

"Wait there," he said and closed the door.

Permelia returned to the bedroom and picked Fenton up again, hugging him to her chest. Yates came back into the room a few minutes later.

"I'm afraid our graffiti artist has been busier than we first thought. The deck has been defaced, also. It's not likely they left any evidence, but I'm going to have the crime scene team come do their thing."

"Isn't that a bit extreme for painting on a couple of doors?"

"If you lived in a rough neighborhood, yes, but you live in a quiet, urban neighborhood in an apartment that happens to be part of our morgue building. That—"

Dr. Grace burst into the room,

"What's going on here?"

Yates held his hand out.

"Officer Yates, sir."

Dr. Grace shook his hand.

"Someone has defaced the downstairs door and the upstairs deck," Yates continued. "The messages seem to be targeted at your tenant."

Harold turned to Permelia and Fenton.

"Are you okay?"

"Oh, yes, I'm fine. I was across the street at Wilma's when it all happened. Whatever was done to the patio is a bit troubling, though. Someone had to be pretty nimble to get onto it."

"Which is one of the reasons I'm having the techs come and see if they can find anything," Yates said.

"I'm afraid it's going to be a long night," Harold said. "Is there somewhere else you can go?"

"I don't want to worry either of my daughters. I'll be fine here." They went to her kitchen. "Would you like anything?"

"A glass of water would be nice."

"I've got plenty of that."

Chapter 26

"The murder victim's sons visited here right before the graffiti happened?" Harold asked Permelia.

"Well, the younger son visited. I called the older one to come pick up his little brother when I'd gotten him settled."

"I'm thinking we need to call Liam and let him know what's going on."

"I got the first note before Ed's body came into the morgue," she reminded him.

Harold held his glass, about to take a sip, then paused.

"Curious timing, though."

"I don't know why or how anyone would connect me to the murder of a man I didn't know and had not yet heard of."

"Seems like they may have been prescient. You did become acquainted with both of our victim's families."

"Not on purpose."

"Yes, but the killer or killers may not know that. They may assume you know something."

"Again, I got the first note *before* he'd come to the morgue, and for all we know, it was before he'd even been killed."

"May I use your phone?" Harold asked.

Permelia frowned.

"It's *your* phone. Help yourself."

He went to the back entrance to call.

"Liam is coming over," he reported when he returned, and sat back down in the chair to Permelia's right. "He said he's getting nowhere on the murder, so anything might be helpful."

Ten minutes later, the detective arrived.

"As I've reminded Harold," Permelia told Det. James, "I got my first letter before Mr. Anderson's body came to the morgue."

"And as I've pointed out, he could have been dead, but not yet here when the first letter came." Harold countered.

"Either of you could be right, but we might as well consider the possibility this is connected, at least until we can prove otherwise. Tell me everything about the letters and this current event."

Permelia reviewed the times and exactly where she'd found the notes, then gave them to him. She set her teacup on the coffee table when she'd finished.

"I have a question for you."

"Okay," Liam said. "I'll answer if I can."

"Have you had occasion to meet with any of the people at Ed Anderson's workplace?"

"Why do you ask?"

"Betty—Ed's other wife—wants to have some sort of memorial service. She found business cards for a couple of the people he worked with and wants to talk to them to see if they knew about her and her son, and if they did, invite them to the service."

Liam leaned back in his chair.

"I've interviewed them all." He steepled his fingers under his chin. "I'd like to tell you to stay away from anyone remotely connected to Ed Anderson, but I understand your friend Betty is in a more complicated situation than most. I can't tell you whether they're safe to be around or they're not. Obviously, if we had evidence they were involved in Mr. Anderson's death, we'd have them in custody, but the fact we don't—yet—only means we don't have that evidence. And the most unassuming people can be cold-blooded killers, so don't let appearances fool you."

"What if Betty were to send them an invitation through the mail, inviting anyone who was a friend of Eideard to attend?"

"That sounds a lot better," Harold said at the same time Detective James said he liked that idea.

"Of course, I'd like to attend, too," Liam added.

"It's not just on TV that police attend funerals?" Permelia asked with a smile.

"Don't believe everything you see on TV, but in this case, yes."

Harold set his empty glass on the table.

"If it's okay with both of you, I'll call our handyman, Robert, and have him clean up the doors."

"We should be done here in another hour or so," Liam said.

"I think I'll have Robert put a motion detector on the deck light. The light flashing on should deter anyone who's trying to climb onto the patio."

+——+

A tap sounded on the apartment door forty-five minutes later. Liam answered, and after a quiet conversation he returned to the living room.

"Well, my people figured out how your graffiti artist got on the deck. The gardeners left their trailer around the back, and it has a ladder in it."

Harold shook his head.

"I didn't even think about that. They've been pruning the hedge around the perimeter of the property and asked if they could leave their trailer here until they were done. I told them as long as they parked it around the back, it would be fine, so this is my fault."

Permelia reached over and patted his hand.

"You couldn't have known someone was going to come by looking for an opportunity to create mischief."

"Why are you so sure this is 'mischief' and not a threat?" Harold asked her.

"My neighbor Wilma has been experiencing vandalism this week, too. Someone threw a Molotov cocktail over her fence the other night."

"Did she report it?" Liam asked.

"Yes, she did. I think she's had several incidents."

Liam made a note in the book he pulled from his pocket.

"I'll check with patrol for this area and see what they've got."

Harold blew out a breath.

"I'll sleep better if it turns out to be neighborhood kids and not someone targeting the morgue."

He looked at Permelia as he spoke, and they both knew it wasn't the morgue he was worried about.

+——+

Permelia had planned on checking out the Catholic church, the Madeleine, in her neighborhood the following morning with Katy. She called her daughter, explaining there had been vandalism at the morgue, and she needed to stay home to watch over the workmen. She didn't mention the nature of the incident, and as hoped, Katy was sufficiently distracted by her sculpture project she didn't ask.

That taken care of, she went downstairs to have a look at her door in daylight. Harold was parking his car, and got out dressed in jeans and a plaid workshirt.

"Good morning. Were you able to sleep after all the excitement last night?"

Permelia smiled at him.

113

"I'd like to say I tossed and turned all night, but in reality, I slept like a baby. All the baking yesterday wore me out." She shook her head. "When my kids were little, I got up with the chickens and baked twice that much before they woke up to do their chores before school. Those days are behind me, I guess."

"You baked an impressive amount yesterday, nonetheless. I'm sorry you've had to deal with this nonsense." He gestured toward the door.

"I'm sure it will all be fine. Your man will paint it over, and no one will be the wiser. The person who did it only wins if they can frighten me, and I assure you, I don't scare that easily."

Robert, Harold's handyman, arrived and parked his truck near Permelia's door.

"I hope it's okay," he said as he approached, "but I bought new locks for both this downstairs door and the deck door. They should be more secure than the old ones and claim to be 'pick-proof'."

"Good idea," Harold told him. "This is Permelia O'Brien, our tenant."

Robert was a small wiry man with an infectious smile. He was dressed in paint-spattered overalls and carried a plastic bucket and a scrub brush.

"Nice to meet you," he said. "I hope you won't let this little incident scare you off. This is normally a quiet neighborhood."

"I'm not worried," she assured him.

"I'm going to see if we're lucky enough I can scrub this off. If not, I have paint in my truck. I need to clean the doors in any case. Will it be okay if I go inside to access the deck when I'm finished with this door?"

"As long as you don't let my very curious cat out, it will be fine."

"I spoke to the gardeners, and they can't come by to move the trailer until tomorrow morning. I told them I was going to put their ladder into our garage."

"Seems like you gentlemen have everything in hand down here, so I'll go upstairs and get some work done. And, Robert, there's no need to knock when you're ready to do the deck. I'll leave the upstairs door unlocked."

With that, she turned and headed up the stairs.

Chapter 27

Permelia pulled a tub of wool roving from the armoire and pulled out a piece, separating pencil-sized strands, preparing them for spinning. She fussed with them for an hour, Fenton making a pest of himself grabbing at pieces and running with them, wrapping them around her ankles in the process. She finally gave up and went to the kitchen for his treat ball.

She rolled the ball, treats spilling out here and there, and he went off chasing and batting at it. With the cat occupied, she should have gone back to her spinning, but she was finding it hard to settle down. Her mind was churning, reviewing the previous day's activities. In the end, she went to the phone and called Betty.

"I'm so glad you called," Betty said when she answered. "I was going to call you to talk about visiting Eid's work but also to see if you wanted to get together to meet my son. He's arrived from Ireland."

"I'd like that. Listen, I spoke to a detective friend of Dr. Grace's, and he suggested that, rather than visit Ed's workplace, you write a letter to explain who you are and letting them know about the memorial service you're planning and inviting anyone who wants to attend."

"That does seem like a better idea. Would you be willing to help me write the letter? You can meet Red at the same time."

"I'd be happy to help, but I've got one problem. I need to...Let me rephrase, I *want* to stay around home while my apartment is having repair work done. There was some vandalism last night, and the handyman is cleaning it up and installing new locks. He'll be in and out of my place, and I'd like to make sure my cat doesn't make a pest of himself. So, if you and Red could come here, it would be easier."

"Are you okay? Did it happen when you were home?"

"I was at Wilma's, and cat and I are just fine."

"I'll double-check with Red, but I think that will work. We could be there in an hour."

"Perfect."

<hr>

With all the excitement, Permelia hadn't had time to freeze half the cobbler as planned, so she set it out on the dining table along with dessert plates, teacups and saucers, silverware, and napkins. She looked over at her worktable at the other end of the room to find Fenton tangling her roving into knots. She hurried over and picked him up, removing the wool that was stuck to his feet.

"You are not helping," she scolded him, but she couldn't help smiling as he looked up at her, his eyes round, a strand of roving draped rakishly across his face.

She shut him in her bedroom and returned to the wool. She gathered it into a ball and put it back in the appropriate tub in the armoire, then returned to the kitchen to fill the teakettle.

True to her word, Betty and her son arrived exactly an hour later. Permelia watched them drive into the parking lot, and she put the kettle on to boil before going downstairs to meet them. Robert held the door open.

"Be careful, the paint's wet," he warned.

She led her guests up the stairs.

"Would you both like tea?" she asked when she had them seated in the living room. They both did, and she poured, using the time she was fussing with the tea to examine Betty's son, Eideard Jr.

He was tall and broad-shouldered, with a full head of dark auburn hair, and looked like an age-progressed version of Ben Anderson. There was no mistaking that both boys had been fathered by the same man.

"Milk or sugar?" she asked.

"I'll have milk," Red replied.

Betty crossed over to the table and took the cup Permelia had poured for her.

"I'll have a little sugar." She doctored her tea and carried it to the coffee table, sitting back down beside her son. Permelia delivered his tea and sat in the chair to their left.

"As I'm sure you've guessed, this is my son, Eideard," Betty said.

Permelia set her teacup down.

"It's very nice to meet you. I just wish it could have been under happier circumstances. I'm very sorry for your loss."

"It's quite a shock," he said, his gaze a million miles away. "I can't believe someone murdered my father. Everyone liked him. And Mom says the police don't have any idea who killed him."

"I'm sure they're trying hard to figure it out," Permelia said, realizing how useless her reassurance was as soon as she said it. She picked up her teacup and took a sip. "Are you going to be staying with your mother for a while?"

He blew out a breath.

"I wish I could, but I'm taking a class in summer school. Due to the circumstances, my professor is letting me do this week and next week online, but then I need to be back. Plus, I've got some housing arrangements to attend to."

Permelia was sure Red's fellow students would find his accent very American, but she could hear a hint of the Irish creeping in, no doubt due to the years he'd spent there in school.

Fenton had been sleeping on his climbing perch since Permelia had let him out of her bedroom, no doubt aware that if he made mischief, he'd be locked up again. He suddenly jumped down and headed for the door to the stairs. A tapping sounded, followed by the door opening, and moments later Robert appeared.

"You have another guest," he announced. He stepped aside, and Ben stepped past him. His cheeks were red, and he was clearly upset.

Permelia got up and went to him.

"I didn't know you had company" Ben said. "Should I go home?"

"How did you get here?"

"I rode the light rail and then walked."

"Does anyone know you're here?"

"No," he said, his voice breaking. "That's why I came. I've been sitting in the hotel room for hours. When I woke up, Mom was gone, and she left me a note that said to order room service for breakfast and just sign the room number to pay for it."

"And did you?"

"Yes, but that was hours ago. There's nothing to do at the hotel. I came to see if I could play with Fenton."

Permelia glanced over her shoulder. She wasn't sure she should be the one to facilitate the family introduction between Ed/Eid's two sets of children.

Betty joined her in the kitchen.

"Is everything okay?" She looked past Permelia and saw Ben. She stared at the boy, the color leaving her face. "I'll just be...." She groped for words. "I'll be in the living room," she finally said, and retreated.

Permelia sighed.

"Oh, for crying out loud," she muttered.

"Did I do something wrong?" Ben asked.

Permelia put her hands on his shoulders and looked into his eyes.

"You did nothing wrong, but I'm afraid the actions of the adults around you are going to make things difficult for you. I shouldn't be the one to tell you this, but I'm afraid if I send you home, you'll be more confused, and you won't get any answers. Please remember, your parents and your brothers and sisters love you very much, and none of this mess is because of anything you did or didn't do. Do you understand?"

"I don't know what you're talking about."

She shook her head.

"Come with me."

She led him slowly into the living room. Betty and Red still sat beside each other, heads together, on the sofa. They looked up as Ben stopped. Permelia stood behind him, her hands on his shoulders.

"Betty, Red, I'd like you to meet Benton Anderson, Ed Anderson's youngest son. Ben, this is Mrs. FitzAndreu and her son Eideard."

Ben's mouth opened, but no words came out.

"Is this a joke?" he finally choked out.

Red looked confused.

"Who is this?"

"Why does he look like Eddie?" Ben continued.

"Who's Eddie?" Red asked.

"Come, sit down." Permelia guided Ben to the side chair opposite the one she'd been sitting in. "Honey, this might be a little hard to understand, and no one will be upset no matter how you feel about it. For reasons none of us know or understand, your dad, Edward Anderson Jr., decided to have another life using the name Eideard FitzAndreu."

"What does that mean?" Ben asked. "How do you have another life?"

"As I say, nobody except your father knew he had two lives. What that means is he had two families at the same time."

Ben looked at Red.

"Is he my brother?"

"We can't be one hundred-percent sure, but it appears he is your half-brother."

"How could you do that?" he accused Betty.

Her face turned bright red, but Permelia held her hand up to silence her before she could speak. Then, she knelt beside Ben and put her hand over his.

"Betty didn't know, sweetie. Your dad kept everyone a secret from everyone else, as far as we know."

"But...how?"

"My dad worked out of town on a regular basis. How about yours?" Red asked.

Ben's face turned redder.

"Yeah," Red said. "Think about it. How many times did your dad have to go back to work? And how many times did he miss important school events because of work? And did he ever go on a family vacation and stay the whole time? Or did he get called back to work, or join you after you'd been there a week?"

"He had to work." Ben said softly.

Red sat back in his chair and ran his hands through his hair, and Ben unconsciously mimicked the motion.

Betty and Permelia locked eyes.

"Eid's gesture," Betty said softly.

Permelia rubbed Ben's back.

"This is not the way you should have learned about this situation. Your mother should have told you."

Ben turned in his chair to face her.

"She knows?"

"None of us here has spoken to your mother about this, but Mrs. FitzAndreu got papers from the lawyer, and if your mother has seen the will, which she most certainly has by now, she knows."

"What am I supposed to do?" Ben said.

Red smiled a sad smile.

"There's nothing *to* do now. Dad's dead, and we're still here. We'll just have to make the best of it."

Ben stared at him.

"Are you Irish?" he asked finally.

Red's smile broadened.

"Our father was born in Ireland, and when it was time for me to go to college, he suggested I try the University of Dublin. We went to Ireland several times to visit relatives, so I already knew some aunts, uncles, and cousins, and our grandmother, of course. Wait, how did that work?" He looked at his mother when he said the last bit.

"We never went to Ireland," Ben said sadly. "We always spent the holidays and vacations with my mother's family on Cape Cod."

"Anyway," Red continued, "I've been going to University for five years now. I've gotten my bachelor's degree and am going for my master's. I guess I've picked up a wee bit of their accent."

"I know this is a lot to take in," Permelia said, and rubbed his back again. "Would you like some strawberry-rhubarb cobbler?"

"I don't know if I like rhubarb," he said.

Permelia smiled.

"How about I make you a dish, with some vanilla ice cream on top, and if you don't like it, I think I can find a few more chocolate chip cookies."

Ben smiled.

"I like your cookies."

"How about you two?" she asked Red and Betty.

"I never turn down food," Red said with a grin.

Betty stood.

"That sounds lovely, can I help?"

"You can start cutting the cobbler while I get the ice cream."

Chapter 28

Fenton decided to join the party as Red and Ben finished their second serving of cobbler. He reached up and patted Ben's leg, and then flopped onto Red's foot, untying his shoelace and chewing the plastic tip..

"Ben, honey, if you're done eating, could you get Fenton's pole toy and see if you can distract him?" Permelia asked. "I think it's behind my chair."

Ben smiled.

"Sure." He jumped up from the dining table, Fenton running behind him. Red followed them into the living room, watching his brother play with the cat.

Permelia waited until she was sure Ben was fully distracted.

"Shall we talk about the memorial service letter?"

Betty went to her purse and pulled out a folded piece of computer paper.

"Red wrote a draft, and I think it's pretty good, but I want to know what you think. He thinks we should email it."

Permelia read the message. Red had kept to the point, stating that there would be a memorial service for Eideard and telling the particulars, ending with an invitation to any interested parties. It was to the point and didn't address the issue of which identity they knew. If they only knew Ed, they could ignore the email and go about their business.

"Did you talk to the priest?" Permelia asked when she'd finished reading. "And this sounds fine," she added, handing the paper back.

Betty tucked it into her purse.

"Under the circumstances, Father thought we should do a service in the small side chapel. And he didn't think we should open it up to the whole congregation, even though Eid was a member of the church. He's worried that whoever killed Eid might show up at the service. Of course, he's assuming it's someone we wouldn't be inviting."

They sat in silence for a moment.

"I feel foolish," Betty finally said. She slumped in her chair. "I've been so wrapped up in my own feelings after discovering our life was a lie, I've lost sight of the fact that my husband, legal or not, was murdered. Someone out there killed him, and no one has a clue who or why."

"Have the police talked to you?"

"They came by when they found out about Eid's double life. I didn't have much to tell them. Obviously, Red and I have been kept in the dark for a very long time."

"Tell me this. What type of car did your Eid drive?"

"Why?"

"I was just wondering if he switched cars when he went from one family to another. If he did, he must have had a location where he left whichever car he wasn't using. I mean, somewhere like the airport or train station, although that would be expensive and public."

"He drove an older Ford Explorer. He kept it in mint condition." She gave a harsh laugh. "Or at least someone did. He used to go off to his 'car club' where they worked on their cars at one guy's garage. I guess he probably paid someone to work on it while he was living his other life."

"Try not to think about that part. Focus on the good times," Permelia advised her.

"I'd rather not ask Ben what car his dad drove," Betty said. "He's having a good time, and he and Red are getting to know each other. He seems like such a sad boy."

Permelia scraped her fork across the crumbs on her empty plate.

"His family doesn't seem to have time for him. Your Eid was probably the only one who paid any attention to him, and as we know, that was only half the time."

Betty hung her head. Permelia reached over and patted her hand.

"That's not on you. You didn't know Ben existed. And I'm guessing Eid did his best to raise his children with his other wife."

"I keep telling myself that, but I worry about that boy."

"Speaking of the other wife, are you sure *she's* the 'real' wife, and not you?"

"The fact that no one knew Eideard was lying in the morgue when I reported him missing says it all."

"That only says he had his Ed Anderson ID on him when he was found."

"He has dual citizenship, since he was born in Ireland. I've only ever seen his Irish passport and, of course, his driver's license."

"Does he have a US passport?"

"I've not seen one, but I believe as a minor child, when his parents moved to the US and became citizens, he automatically became one."

"Don't you have to give up your foreign citizenship when you become a citizen here?" Permelia asked.

"No, you can have more than one. Eideard helped Red get Irish citizenship before he enrolled in college there. He has two passports."

"I suppose they would have taken his fingerprints and verified his identification," Permelia said, more to herself than anyone.

Harold had been up and down the stairs several times while Permelia was entertaining her guests. Now, he joined them in the kitchen.

"I'm sorry to interrupt, but would you like to come inspect Robert's work on the deck?"

"Can I come?" Ben asked.

"Sure," Harold said. "You can all come look, if you want."

Permelia led the way through the guestroom closet and out onto the deck. Betty went to the rail and surveyed the view before sitting on the wooden bench-swing.

"This is really lovely. And private."

Permelia joined her.

"I only just found out about this deck."

"It had been disused for so long, I'd sort of forgotten it was here myself," Harold said. "The wood had rotted, and we only undertook repairs a few weeks before Permelia moved in."

Permelia stood up and crossed to look over the opposite rail.

"Fenton and I will enjoy this."

"Won't he jump off?" Ben asked.

She smiled. "I'll keep him on his leash. He's used to it."

Robert joined them on the deck.

"If Doc doesn't mind, I could screen in part of it and make him a regular catio. I've seen plans on the internet. Basically, it's just a screened patio that's covered so you could use it even when it rains."

Dr. Grace thought about it for a moment.

"We'll have to check with the historical people. I think we'll be able to get it by them, since it's on the back side and doesn't show from the street. Besides, we've already had a few exceptions because of our unique situation here."

"I'm sure Fenton would love it, if it isn't too much trouble," Permelia said.

Dr. Grace pulled a small ring of keys from his pocket and handed them to her.

"Here are your new keys—two for the downstairs and two for up here. The locksmith says no one can get past these locks."

Betty stood up.

"We should get out of your hair," she said. "Come on, Red."

"Shall we call your brother?" Permelia asked Ben.

Ben hung his head.

"He's not home. I called him before I came here. He has tickets to the soccer game, and no room for me. I can take the bus—it's how I got here."

Red smiled.

"We can take him. We're going out to do errands anyway."

"Is that okay?" Permelia asked.

Ben grinned.

"It would be great."

⊷⊶

The visitors left, leaving Permelia and Harold standing outside the downstairs door.

"Care for a cup of tea?" he asked.

"I think I need one. Shall we go upstairs so Fenton doesn't feel abandoned?"

She boiled water and set out teacups and bags.

"I've been dying to ask how the meeting of the brothers went."

She poured and brought the steaming mugs to the kitchen table.

"I think it went well. Red seems to be a well-adjusted young adult who was probably happy to find out he's not an only child. Ben, on the other hand, is clearly neglected by his mother and his siblings. He's grieving the loss of his father, and no one is trying to help him. They even took away his little dog. I think he was happy to meet Red."

"Hopefully, they won't end up disappointing him, too."

"Red is going to school in Ireland, so he's going to have to leave again, but hopefully Ben's mother won't object to the brothers keeping in touch." She sipped her tea in silence. "Betty is still moving ahead with her plan for the memorial service. The priest suggested a private ceremony in one of the small chapels. Red wrote a neutral email for her to send to her husband's workplace."

Harold sipped his tea.

"I'd feel better if Liam could figure out who killed the man. He always says the killer is usually someone the victim knew. That means you've possibly met the killer already. And that I don't like."

Chapter 29

Permelia watched out the kitchen window until she saw Harold drive out of the parking lot before cleaning up the dishes. She glanced at the armoire housing her roving to be spun, and then at Fenton, who was lying on the floor batting one of his small felt mice.

"You want to go for a walk before we spin?"

Fenton jumped up and headed for the door.

"I'll take that as a yes, then."

She pocketed her new keys, clipped him into his harness, and headed down the stairs.

Fenton was frisky after all the excitement of company, and he hopped down the sidewalk, pouncing on small sticks and rocks in the parking strips in front of the older homes in the neighborhood. She would have taken him to the park if it hadn't been a Sunday afternoon. Weekends tended to bring dogs to the parks, and an unfortunate number of people didn't obey the leash laws. She chose less-busy streets for their walk and ended up on the block that faced the back side of the morgue.

Her upstairs deck was barely visible. It seemed to her that you'd have to know it was there to find it. She mentally made a note to go to the nursery and look at potted trees to fill the corner of the deck she could see from the street.

The door in Wilma's wall opened as Fenton pulled even with it. His leash was extended to its full length, so he was inside the garden before Permelia reached the opening.

"I hope you were inviting Fenton in," she said with a smile.

"Indeed, I was," Wilma said.

Fenton reached his front paws up above her knees, and she picked him up, scratching his ears as she did so.

"After all the activity in your parking lot, I need a full report. Would you like some iced tea?"

"That sounds great."

⊷——⊶

"As you might imagine, the first wave of activity was Dr. Grace and his handyman Robert changing the locks and repainting the door downstairs and up on the deck, which had also been defaced. The gardeners had left a ladder out, and the graffiti artist made use of it to climb up and add to their vandalism.

"Then Betty called and wanted to get together to talk about her memorial service plan, and I didn't feel like I could leave with the work going on. She and her son came over."

"I thought that must be her son," Wilma interrupted. "I confess I watched them arrive from my upstairs window. How was he?"

"Red is a polite young man. I assume all of Ed/Eid's kids take after him, since they all look like they were created with a rubber stamp. Other than slightly different shades of hair, they look identical. It will be interesting to see the reaction if and when Ben's older brother meets Red. Next, Ben arrived on my doorstep after being left alone for a prolonged period at the hotel again. He's quite adept at public transportation."

"How did the boys get along?"

"They both seemed happy to have a brother. Red is an only child, and as I've said, Ben seems to be neglected. Red was good with him, too."

"And Betty is determined to go forward with her memorial service?"

"She is. Red wrote a very neutral email for her to send to his father's workplace. Not addressing the dual family issue at all, just stating there would be a service for Eid and leaving it up to the co-workers to acknowledge Eid's existence or not."

"I think it would be better if she had the service at her home. It would ensure all guests were invited."

"You think uninvited guests will show up?"

"I don't know. Edward, or Eideard, has been lying to a lot of people about who he is at any given point in time. You have no way of knowing who else is caught up in his deceits."

"Betty needs this service. She's mourning her husband and feels like she has to keep it a secret. I think it will help her to have a church service, even if it is small and in the side chapel."

"Will you be going?"

"I didn't know the man, of course, but I plan on volunteering to make food for the event. I assume there will be some sort of reception afterward."

"Just watch yourself."

Permelia smiled.

"Oh, I'll be safe enough with the police in attendance."

Wilma set Fenton down.

"Do you mind if he's off his leash?"

Permelia smiled.

"It's more a matter of whether you care."

Wilma unclipped the leash and handed it to Permelia, then poured the iced tea.

"Let's go sit in the parlor."

"While we're there, let's have a look at your knitting."

"It's not ready for prime time yet, but I think I'm getting better."

"Well, let's have a look."

◆━━◆

Just for good measure, Permelia decided to walk Fenton again on the way home from Wilma's. His breed was very active, and she knew after having company all day, he'd be wound up. A walk would ensure he didn't get into mischief while she attempted to spin the wool he'd "helped" with that morning.

"Can Fenton come see my tree fort?" Henrietta called from the tree in her front yard as they passed her house.

"If it's not too high. He needs to stay on his leash."

Fenton hadn't waited for Permelia to decide if it was okay; he climbed up the trunk and onto the thick branch Henri was sitting on. He rubbed his head on her arm, arching his back.

"Are you teaching Wilma to knit?"

Permelia craned her neck to look up at the girl and her cat.

"What makes you ask that?"

"She had her curtains downstairs open, and from my fort, I can see into her sitting room."

"You were spying on us?"

Henri's face turned red.

"Not on purpose. I was looking around to see what I could see from up here, and there you were."

"I *am* teaching Wilma to knit, but I'm sure she'd appreciate not being spied on."

"If you're not mad at me, I wanted to ask you if you could teach me to knit."

"I would be happy to teach you, with two conditions."

Henri sighed.

"What do I have to do?"

"First, you have to promise not to spy on Wilma anymore."

127

The girl's shoulders sagged.

"Who *can* I spy on? Having a tree fort isn't fun if you can't spy."

"You can watch the street and sidewalk to see if anyone litters or if people let their dogs make messes in your yard. If they do, tell your parents."

"Okay, I guess."

"The second condition is that I need to meet your parents, and they have to tell me it's okay for you to come to my place for knitting lessons."

"That's easy. They always want me to learn new activities that don't involve a screen or earphones."

"Are they home now?"

"Dad isn't, but Mom is."

"If you go get her, we can ask her now."

Henri climbed down, followed by Fenton. She raced into her house and returned a few minutes later with her mother, whose name turned out to be Eleanor.

Once the two women had introduced themselves, Permelia related Henri's request for knitting lessons.

"That would be very nice of you," Eleanor answered. "I'm a painter, and I've a gallery show coming up, so I'm afraid I've not been very entertaining lately."

"What sort of painting do you do?"

"This show is animal portraits. The gallery is donating a portion of the sales to a no-kill dog shelter."

"That sounds wonderful. One of my daughters here in town is a sculptor."

"What's her name?"

"Katy O'Brien."

"Small world—I know her. We've been at the same events several times."

"I have all the materials Henri will need for knitting—I belong to a fiber cooperative. If you have something to write with, I'll give you my phone number, and we can compare schedules and plan a time for her to start."

"Honey, go get me the pad and pencil from the kitchen desk," Eleanor told Henri. "If it's not too much of an imposition," she said to Permelia, "when I'm done with this group of paintings, I'd love to learn to knit, too. It would be something Henri and I can do together."

"That would be no problem. I taught all my children to knit, and after teaching my boys, I'm pretty sure I can teach anyone. I'll have to talk to her, but I'm teaching our neighbor Wilma also. Maybe we can all knit together."

"That sounds fantastic."

Henri returned, and Permelia wrote her cell phone number and name on the pad and returned it to Eleanor.

"Thank you, I'll be in touch. Now, I'd better get back to my painting."

Permelia called Fenton and headed for home.

Chapter 30

The next two days passed without incident. Permelia spun several skeins of yarn and spent some time figuring out how to set up her dye station. By late afternoon the following Tuesday she'd dyed half a dozen skeins and was pleased with the results. Her deck was an excellent place to dry newly-dyed yarn, at least as long as it wasn't raining or snowing. It was out of direct sunlight and there seemed to be a slight breeze every afternoon.

She was carrying an armload of used plastic wrap from the dye process to the dumpster in the parking lot when Dr. Grace came out of the building.

"Oh, I'm glad I ran into you. What time do you want to leave for the recital and dinner?"

"I think we may need to do the recital first and then dinner. They start at five so the youngest kids can go home after they perform."

"That's fine by me. I'm looking forward to it. I haven't been to a concert in years."

Permelia smiled.

"I'm not sure this rises to the level of a concert, but it's sure to be entertaining."

"Shall we leave at four-fifteen?"

"I'm not sure how traffic is around here, but that sounds like plenty of time. My phone said it's about fifteen minutes away."

"I will see you tomorrow afternoon, then."

"I'm looking forward to it," Permelia said with a smile, not sure if it was the prospect of dinner with Dr. Grace, or anticipation of the look on her daughter's face when she showed up with a date that pleased her more.

Permelia dressed in loose-fitting black linen pants and a purple silk blend short-sleeved blouse. She draped a purple print scarf over one shoulder and looked in the mirror. The scarf was large enough that if the auditorium was air conditioned, she could wrap it around her shoulders.

Fenton meowed.

"Is that approval or disgust?" she asked, but he remained silent.

"I'm wearing it either way."

At ten after four, she slipped her feet into a pair of black flats, grabbed her purse, and headed downstairs. Harold was in the parking lot, car doors open, wiping the seats and dash of his already immaculate car with a white cloth.

"You look lovely," he said as Permelia approached. She stopped and reached her hand out, resting it on his arm.

"This is your last chance to change your mind. I guarantee there will be some level of drama with my older daughter. It might be as minor as dirty looks for both of us, or she may say regrettable things."

"I am not afraid," he declared dramatically with a smile.

"Well, I apologize in advance."

"Tell me about your granddaughter," he said and held her door open.

"Beatrice is a gem. She's loved music since she was a baby and is lucky enough to be taking this particular music program. Due to the school's reputation, Jennifer put both her children on the waitlist as soon as they were out of diapers. Bea's brother, Malcolm, was less thrilled and did the minimum amount of work to get a first-level certificate then dropped music in favor of lacrosse."

They continued discussing their grandchildren until they reached the auditorium. Permelia slipped two tickets from her purse and handed one to Harold when they were out of the car. He looked at it.

"How did you get this without alerting your daughter you're bringing a guest?

She smiled.

"My daughter Katy was only too happy to help thwart her sister's manipulations. She told Jennifer *she* was bringing a date."

"I hope I didn't displace her real date."

"Not to worry. Her boyfriend is working on a museum installation in London right now."

Harold crooked his arm.

"Shall we do this?"

❧————❧

Katy, who must have been watching for them, joined them as soon as they were inside the auditorium lobby.

"You can relax for a while—Jennifer is going to get here after the little kids perform. She's working on a deal and asked me to bring Bea. I assume she'll bring her guest then, too." Katy reached her hand out to Harold. "I'm Katy. We met the first day."

Harold took her hand in both of his.

"It's nice to see you again. Your mother tells me you're a sculptor."

Permelia surveyed the assembled parents and other relatives waiting for the performance to begin. She spotted Eleanor and excused herself from Katy's and Harold's discussion of sculpting media.

"Eleanor, it's nice to see you again."

"Oh, hi. Thank you again for agreeing to put off knitting until Henri was finished with this recital. She likes her lessons well enough, but she'll use any excuse to avoid practice."

"We can knit anytime, and I wouldn't want to interfere with her music."

"I appreciate it."

"Do you know many of the other parents here?"

"Not a lot. Ben Anderson is in Henri's group." Eleanor's mouth tilted up on one side. "I wouldn't say I know his parents. I'm not sure how to say this, but we're not of the right social class to 'know' Sylvia Everett. Ed Anderson used to come to recitals, but I didn't see him pick up or drop off. Beatrice Fitzgerald is a sweetheart, although she's in a level or two above Henri. Her parents seem pretty busy, too."

Permelia beamed.

"She's my granddaughter."

"You must be very proud."

"We are."

Eleanor identified several families in Henri's class, but Permelia didn't recognize any names.

Katy and Harold joined them, and after the introductions, they went into the auditorium.

The first section of the recital was the usual mix of cute little kids who wielded instruments almost too big for them but managed to play their piece without flaw as well as the tots who were dazzled by the audience to the point that they couldn't play their instrument at all and waved to Mom and Dad instead.

Red Fitzandreu slipped into the seat next to Permelia during the break between the little kids and the group of students that included Ben and Henri.

"I hope it's okay I'm here. Ben invited me and arranged for the ticket. He hasn't gone on yet, has he? He told me not to come until everyone was seated and the first group had finished up."

"Don't worry, I don't think his mother has arrived."

Permelia looked around the hall and didn't see Sylvia or Eddie. She did, however, see her eldest daughter enter.

"Trouble is headed our way," she whispered to Harold, nodding in the direction of the back-lobby entrance as Jen led a white-haired gentleman who was at least fifteen years older than Permelia toward the empty chairs to Katy's left.

Jennifer settled in her seat and leaned forward to make eye contact with her mother. Permelia smiled, well aware her daughter hadn't connected the men on either side with her.

Ben and Henri played their violins in a group with three other children of a similar age, followed students playing piano one after the other. Finally, Beatrice's group came onto the stage. Each student played one or more instruments solo. Beatrice then played three solos—flute, cello, and piano. She was very accomplished, and received a standing ovation. Her father appeared from the wings and presented her with a bouquet of white roses.

"Bea was fantastic," Permelia said when Jennifer rose and stepped past her sister and Harold to greet her mother.

"Let's go to the lobby," Katy suggested as she pushed the purse looped over her sister's arm away from her face. "They have snacks, I think."

They all rose and stepped their way to the aisle.

"Can you join us?" Permelia asked Red as she passed him. "We're going to the lobby for refreshments."

He smiled gratefully and followed them to the main doors.

"Would you or Dr. Grace like some lemonade?" Katy asked as soon as they had reassembled. "Want to come with?" she asked Red.

Permelia and Harold both accepted, and the two young people left to stand in the drinks line.

"Smart girl," Harold said with a chuckle. "She's taking herself out of the fray."

Jennifer arrived with her guest in tow.

"Mother, I'd like to introduce you to Milford Dunn. He lives in that place I was telling you about." She looked over at Dr. Grace.

"Oh, Doctor…What was your name?"

Harold reached his hand to shake hers.

"Harold Grace."

"Are you here with a grandchild?"

"No, I'm here with—"

"Oh, here's Beatrice," Jennifer said, and pulled her child over to join them as soon as she was within reach.

Bea smiled.

"Hi, Grandma."

Permelia smiled.

"Beatrice, your solos were wonderful."

"I missed a chord in the first movement of the piano piece." She shook her head. "I've played it a hundred times, but my finger just slipped."

Permelia patted her back.

"I'm sure no one noticed except maybe your teacher. To us in the audience it sounded perfect. Now, sweetie, I'd like to introduce you to my friend Dr. Grace. He works in the morgue under my apartment."

"Very nice to meet you," she said.

"Dr. Grace is here with his grandchild," Jennifer said. "Isn't that right, Dr. Grace?"

Harold smiled.

"No, I don't believe I said that. I'm here with Permelia."

Jennifer smiled again, but it was more brittle this time.

"That was very nice of you to drive my mother here, but we can make sure she gets home."

"Jen," Katy warned as she and Red returned with the drinks.

"Jennifer, Dr. Grace and I are going to dinner when we're done here, and he'll see me home after that, so you don't need to worry."

"What about Milford? He's supposed to show you his residence."

Permelia smiled.

"Perhaps you can go see his residence with him."

Jennifer's face reddened, and she was about to speak when Ben joined them.

"Hi," he said, oblivious to the drama playing out in front of him. "Wasn't it great that Red got to come to the recital?"

Permelia put her hand on the boy's shoulder.

"It was very nice," she told Ben with a smile. "Red, do you play an instrument?"

"My mom made me take piano lessons, and my dad taught me to play the uillean pipes, which is the Irish version of bagpipes."

"I want to learn that," Ben said with enthusiasm.

"What's going on here?" Sylvia Everett demanded as she strode up to the group. "And who are you?" she asked Red, and moved closer, examining his face. "One of Ed's bastard children, I assume?"

"Mother," Ben cried, tugging on his mother's arm. "Please don't make a scene. People are staring."

"Look at him. He's the spitting image of you. There's no mistake where he came from." She glared at Red. "Leave my son alone."

Ben stepped closer to Red.

"Mother, I like him. He lives in Ireland."

"Well, he can just go back where he came from. In a few weeks it won't matter anyway. You'll be in Switzerland. You've been accepted at a music school there."

Sylvia's voice had grown louder, and other conversations stopped while people stopped to stare.

"Red, Permelia and I were about to go to dinner." Dr. Grace said. He looked at her as he spoke, and she nodded slightly. "Would you like to join us?"

"Yeah, that would be nice."

Permelia handed her partially emptied glass back to Katy, who reached for Harold's, too.

"We'll be on our way, then," Permelia said.

Chapter 31

"Does either of you care where we eat?" Harold asked when he, Permelia, and Red were seated in his car. "I know a place not far from here so we can come back and Red can pick up his car when we've finished.

"Sound's good," Permelia said.

Red agreed.

The restaurant was on a hill overlooking the river that dissected the city. It was decorated in Northwest Native American style, complete with a totem pole in the parking area. It offered a panoramic view of the south waterfront area and the river beyond.

Permelia smiled as their waiter led them to a table with a view.

"Harold, this is breathtaking."

Red looked uncomfortable.

"Am I making a *hames* of your dinner?"

Permelia and Harold looked confused.

"Sorry, am I messing things up for you two? This looks rather special."

The waiter held Permelia's chair, and she sat. Harold took the seat next to hers, and indicated the chair opposite.

"Not at all, sit down. I'm a bit of a regular here. A lot of our local restaurants seem to think exotic cuisine is the only sort. Sometimes, I just want nicely done seafood or beef."

Red looked out the window.

"This is a real treat. I grew up on the far east side of town. We never came into the city. My dad said he didn't like city life," he mused. "I guess we know why."

Permelia reached across the table and took his hand.

"Don't you go second-guessing your whole life. Your dad may very well have preferred living in a small suburban town. We have no idea at this point why your father chose the life he did."

Red gave a harsh laugh.

"After meeting Ben's mom, I can't imagine my father married to that witch."

"How about we don't ruin our dinner trying to figure out something we can only guess at," Harold suggested. "Why don't you tell us about yourself?"

"Well, I'm in graduate school in Ireland. My grandmother returned there when my grandfather died, so I see her on a regular basis. She went back because her sister lives there as well as various nieces and nephews and their families, so Dad's cousins and their children are there. So, even though I grew up an only child and had no family around, I've got loads of relatives in Ireland, so it's nice."

Permelia opened her napkin onto her lap.

"Do you think your mother will still be moving to Ireland, now that your dad has passed away?" she asked.

"That was the plan," Red replied. "Dad already bought a house from one of his cousins—I'm living there this year. Mom has visited before, and she seems to like it. She gets on well with Dad's family."

They paused their conversation while the waiter took their orders. Red went last and handed him his menu.

"Mom tells me you're new to the city," he said to Permelia.

"It's true. My family is having its own drama, and rather than being confronted with my ex-husband's young pregnant girlfriend on the streets of our small town, I chose to move seven hours away, where I have two lovely daughters and several talented grandchildren."

Red chuckled.

"I guess no one gets a free pass where family is concerned."

Dr. Grace took a sip of his water.

"My life has been relatively drama-free. I was married to the same woman for forty years and most of them were good. Unfortunately, she suffered early-onset dementia and eventually succumbed to it."

"Oh, Harold, I'm so sorry."

He toyed with his napkin.

"This might sound a little harsh, but when she finally died, it was a blessing. It was like somewhere over the last years her spirit slipped out the window like a wisp of smoke and went away, leaving an empty shell that none of us could recognize."

He looked down at his lap, and Permelia reached over and took his hand. They sat in silence for a few minutes, watching boats on the river negotiate the channels. The waiter delivered bread, and Red tore off a piece, chewing thoughtfully.

"What I don't understand is how my father afforded all of us. I mean, he was an accountant, basically. The company wasn't all that big. Mom worked as a teacher, so her salary was modest. How could he afford two families?

"By the looks of things, the other family is a lot more upscale than Mom and I are. According to Ben, Dad paid for two of the other kids to go to college, plus the adopted one goes in and out of an exclusive-sounding rehab. Now the mother says she's sending Ben to boarding school in Switzerland."

"My daughter Jennifer says Sylvia is a successful real estate agent. And if the rumors about Ed's marriage to Sylvia are true, her father was loaded."

"There *is* a lot of old money rattling around this city." Harold added. "More than one family made a fortune in the steel business after the war, for example."

"Still," Red said. "It's curious. Most people can't afford one family, much less two. Especially paying for all that college tuition."

The waiter arrived with their dinners, and the discussion turned to food and other trivial matters.

<hr />

"Red brought up a good point," Harold said after they'd dropped him back at his car and headed for the morgue. "I have to admit I was wondering myself how Ed/Eideard afforded his double life. Sylvia drives an expensive car and was loaded down with jewelry. Then there's all that college tuition. And I'm with Red—what sort of accountant was he to pull in that sort of money?"

Permelia chuckled.

"You didn't see the Andersons' house, either. That cost a penny or two, even for a Realtor with an inside track. If her father really did blackmail Ed into marrying Sylvia, it's hard to imagine he'd let Ed have access to enough money to support Betty and Red. Unless that was part of the marriage agreement."

"I wonder if the old man is still alive?" Harold mused.

"I think I know how I can find out. Our neighbor has offered to help Betty and says she's better than average at computer research. I'll see what she can find out about Sylvia and her parents."

Harold pulled into the parking lot, stopping outside Permelia's apartment entrance. He got out and opened her car door.

"Thank you," she said with a smile. "And thank you for dinner. I know it wasn't quite what either of us expected."

He took her hand, squeezing it.

"It was wonderful, drama and all." He smiled. "Will I see you tomorrow? Perhaps afternoon tea, to further analyze our evening."

"That sounds lovely," Permelia said, returning the smile.

Her second week living in the city had proved very interesting indeed.

Chapter 32

Permelia called Wilma the next morning to see if she was receiving visitors and she was, so after breakfast she buckled Fenton into his harness, took a brisk walk around the block, and then tapped on her neighbor's gate.

"Hot tea or iced?" Wilma asked when Permelia was seated in the kitchen and Fenton was exploring off his leash.

"Hot tea sounds lovely."

Wilma filled her kettle and put it on the stove to heat.

"What can I help you with?" she asked.

"You mentioned you were pretty good at computer research. I'm not sure what I'm going to ask you is something you can find on the internet, but I figured it was worth a try."

"Almost everything is on the internet if you know where to look," Wilma said with a grin. "And I do know a lot of places to look."

"Well, Harold and I took Betty's son Red out to dinner last night, and we were all talking about our families. Red talked about his in Ireland, which is where he's living right now, and he was saying how he wondered how his dad—the chief financial officer of the business he works for, who in the grand scheme of things is a sort of mid-level accountant working for a private business—could be making enough money to support not only him and his mom, but a whole other family living in a higher end neighborhood.

"That led to us speculating about whether his dad's other wife might come from family money. She's a Realtor. My daughter is also in real estate and knows her. Jennifer characterizes her as a shark. I could be wrong, but she seems to be scrambling too hard to be a multi-millionaire in her field.

"I'd like to see if you can confirm the reason Ed and Sylvia got married. Apparently, people believe her father blackmailed his into marrying Ed to her to settle a gambling debt he'd maneuvered Ed's dad into. Her father is said to be 'loaded'. I'd like to know if he really is or was, and if Sylvia has access to that money. It would also be interesting to see how he made the money if he *is* rich."

"You never know what's going to turn up, but I should be able to find some answers for you."

"Anything would help. You can imagine poor Red is trying to make sense of this whole double-family mess."

"It is hard to imagine what circumstance would lead someone to the conclusion that having two families was the best option."

"On a lighter note, I met the woman across the corner—Eleanor, Henri's mother—and she wants to learn to knit with her daughter. I suggested I could ask you if they could come here while you're learning. I'll completely understand if you don't want them to, but it might be fun if you all could learn together."

"I think that would be nice. I haven't met Henri's father, but her mother seems like an interesting person. I've looked up her artwork on the internet."

"Is she any good?"

"Indeed, she is."

"She's working on a show for the near term, so it will be a little while before she's available. Maybe Henri can come get started with us until then."

"Let me know when. Also..." She handed a card to Permelia. "Here are my contact numbers, email and text info. Only use the one at the bottom of the list in case of emergency."

Permelia raised an eyebrow.

"Don't ask. Just trust me. Only in case of emergency."

"Thank you," Permelia replied and tucked the card into her pocket.

"I'll let you know what I find out about Edward Anderson."

Permelia sipped her tea.

"I appreciate you doing this."

"Just be careful. I hate to keep repeating myself, but a man was murdered, and until they arrest someone, you could be in danger from your proximity to Betty."

"Thanks for the reminder," Permelia said and stared into her teacup.

"Would you like a refill?"

"I guess I could put off my work for a few more minutes."

Wilma smiled.

"That's the spirit."

Permelia spent the rest of the morning spinning more wool and then the early afternoon plying what she'd spun. She'd just gotten up to stretch her back when the intercom buzzed on her work phone.

"Can you come down for afternoon tea?" Harold asked when she picked up her receiver.

"That sounds wonderful. I'll be right down."

She met him in the morgue lobby moments later. He held up a white paper bag.

"After last night, I figured we might need something sweet to fuel our postmortem."

"Good idea, although I'm not sure there's much more to say about our evening. I asked Wilma to check out Ed's finances, and she said she should be able to find something."

Harold led her into the break room where he already had water heated and cups set out.

"I had a thought last night. How would you feel if I came with you to the memorial service Betty is planning? I'd really like to see if anyone from Edward Anderson's employer shows up."

Permelia fussed with her tea a moment to give her time to think. She was pretty sure Harold wanted to come because of a misguided sense of chivalry, but in the end decided she wouldn't mind another excuse to go somewhere with the good doctor.

"I don't think Betty would mind, and it wouldn't hurt to have another set of eyes on whatever happens."

Harold smiled.

"Like me, it sounds like you're expecting some sort of incident."

"I really hope not, for Betty's sake."

Harold opened his white bag and removed four large white sugar cookies frosted with pastel icing, which he put on a plate in front of Permelia.

"What did you make of Red?"

"He seems to be a nice young man," Permelia said. "And smart."

"Do you think he really didn't know about his father's other family?"

"Betty was clearly shocked. I'm not sure I know Red well enough to think anything other than it was a shock to him, too."

Harold picked up a cookie and took a bite.

"He's such a smart kid, you'd think he'd have noticed something."

"I hear what you're saying, but I've known several women, myself included, who had clear evidence their husbands were cheating on them but gave them the benefit of the doubt long after they should have figured it out."

"I suppose. I guess if your father wasn't home as much as your friend's dad was, your first thought probably wouldn't be *He must have another family*."

"I'm not sure that would be your fourth or fifth thought," Permelia said and laughed.

"I suppose. And maybe Edward was that good at keeping his lives separate."

Permelia sipped her tea.

"From what we've seen so far, I'm guessing Edward was the invisible man at the Anderson house. And just the opposite at the FitzAndreus'. It would be helpful to find out how he ended up married to Sylvia in the first place. I mean, it seems like he found Betty pretty close to when he married Sylvia. My daughter says there were rumors it was an arranged marriage to settle a gambling debt, but I find that hard to believe in this day and age."

Harold leaned back in his chair.

"You do realize we may never know the answer to any of this."

"I guess. I just hope the police can figure out who killed the man. I'm not sure Sylvia cares, but Betty will be devastated if she never finds out."

Harold reached across the table and squeezed Permelia's hand. His was soft and clean, the opposite of a farmer's hands. Not better or worse—just different. He held her hand in both of his.

"This must be a lot to deal with on top of moving to a new place away from everyone you know."

"I'm not entirely alone. I do have my two daughters here."

Harold smiled but said nothing.

"Okay, so maybe Jennifer has been less than helpful with my transition, but at least she's familiar. Betty's the one I feel sorry for. She seems to be pretty alone with Eid gone."

He patted her hand before letting it go.

"She does have a mess to deal with. I just hope her problems don't end up spilling over onto you."

"You sound like Wilma."

"She's a wise woman."

Permelia took another cookie.

"After raising eight children, I feel like I'm pretty well prepared for whatever life has to throw at me."

"Still, it doesn't hurt to be careful."

Chapter 33

Permelia got up early the next morning to walk Fenton. Clouds had moved in, and while it wasn't raining, there was moisture in the air. It would surely be raining by afternoon. She sighed. It was like the weather was mourning Eid along with Betty. Fenton felt it, too. He walked quietly along beside her, his tail up with a little bend in the end.

"Are you ready to head back home?" she asked him. He looked up at her and meowed, and she turned around to start back home.

Her mind began wandering as she walked along. When she thought about it, her situation and Betty's weren't entirely different. Both had husbands who were unfaithful, hers for a short period of time and Betty's of longer duration; but in her own case, her husband didn't love her anymore. If she were honest with herself, he hadn't done so for a long time. Betty at least had the consolation of knowing Eid loved her, even if she'd had to share him.

Permelia reached down and scratched Fenton's head. They had reached their own parking lot.

"At least you still love me," she said in a quiet voice. He arched his back and rubbed his head on her leg. "Come on, then, let's go upstairs."

A warm bath and an hour of knitting had Permelia in better spirits by the time she had to get ready for Eid's memorial service. She and Harold had agreed to arrive a half-hour before the eleven o'clock start time.

"You look nice," Harold said when she came down to the parking area at the appointed time. She had decided on a gray knit dress with a gray-and-black knitted shawl around her shoulders.

"As do you." He was wearing a charcoal suit with a white shirt and maroon club tie.

"Are you ready for this?" he asked as he opened the passenger side door.

"I'm hoping it's going to be a quiet, sad memorial and nothing more."

"I'm hoping for that, too. Hoping but not expecting. There are too many wild cards."

"Maybe it will give Betty some peace, at least, no matter what happens."

⊷⎯⎯⟶

Betty and Red were standing in the narthex of the church when Harold and Permelia entered. Permelia hugged Betty.

"I'm so very sorry for your loss."

Betty dabbed at the corner of her eye with a well-used tissue.

"This is all such a mess. What if no one else comes?"

"Then you will still have us here to mourn with you." Permelia said. "Now, is there anything we can do?"

Betty looked around.

"No, the church has a volunteer group that helps. All we had to do was have the cards printed and pay for the flowers."

"Would you like to follow me to the chapel?" Red asked and headed for the interior door without waiting for a reply. "It's not obvious," he added and led them into a hallway that skirted the main sanctuary.

Harold reached for Permelia's hand as they followed him down the dark hallway. Finally, Red opened a door to a beautiful little chapel.

"Is this an apse chapel?" Permelia asked him.

He smiled.

"You know your architecture. It is, indeed, a modern take on an apse chapel. And it is where we're having our service. Now, if you don't mind, I'd better go help my mother."

"You'd think they'd have a more direct way to access this space," Harold said quietly when the door was closed. It opened again before Permelia could comment. This couple had found the chapel on their own.

They joined Harold and Permelia in the aisle. The woman was tall and slender. She wore a cotton print dress and sensible black shoes. Her husband was of a similar height but broader. He wore a dark flannel shirt and neatly pressed jeans.

The woman held her hand out.

"Hi, I'm Betty's friend Orlagh. Are you the woman she's knitting with? She told me she fainted on you when she found out about Eid."

Permelia shook her hand.

"I guess I am the woman she fainted on. I'm Permelia O'Brien, and this is my friend, Dr. Harold Grace."

"And this is my husband, Padraig McCarthy."

145

"It was such a shock to hear about Eideard. He was a fine fellow, this latest revelation notwithstanding." Padraig said.

"And you never had any suspicion about Eideard?" Permelia asked.

Orlagh sighed.

"Padraig and I have discussed that ever since Betty told us. We've thought a lot about it, and neither one of us ever noticed anything out of place. He said he had to work out of town auditing the various businesses his employers owned. Nothing he did or didn't do made us suspect he was doing anything but just that."

"Hard to believe," Padraig added. He looked up as the door opened again. "Oh, here are the Byrnes."

The Byrneses, both a good six inches shorter than the McCarthys, joined them. Padraig stepped aside to make room.

"Connor, Erin, meet Permelia and Harold. Permelia here is the one that helped Betty when she found out about Eid."

"That was very kind of you," Erin said, her Irish accent apparent. "We'd gone to see our grandchildren in California, and Orlagh had gone to take care of her husband's aunt in Arizona. We didn't know Betty was going to need us here."

Permelia smiled.

"Who could have guessed what was going to happen here?"

"That's for sure," Erin said.

Harold put his hand on Permelia's elbow. A few more people had entered the chapel.

"Shall we sit down?"

She followed him to the third pew and sat. When she was settled, she leaned forward and ran her hand over the upholstered kneeler.

"This is hand-done tapestry," she whispered. "And a beautiful job."

"I read about this in the newspaper. Some members of the church undertook the project to redo all the tapestry in the church. It's taken them something like two decades to complete it all."

"The detail is amazing."

She looked up as Ben came rushing down the aisle and slid in beside her.

"Has anything happened yet?" he asked, out of breath.

"No," Permelia told him. "Does anyone know you're here?"

"I told Eddie I was going to be at a friend's house and asked him to drop me off. I had him leave me two blocks from here."

"Did it occur to you he might wait to see where you went and follow you?"

"He's not interested enough," Ben said and settled back in the pew. "Besides, he's on his way to the airport."

"Oh?" Permelia said.

"Yeah, he has to go to San Francisco on business."

"Any news on your house repairs?"

Ben sighed.

"I heard Mom talking on her phone. The fire people haven't finished their investigation. They won't let the repairs start until they figure out about the arson."

Permelia patted his hand.

"I'm sure it'll all be sorted soon enough."

Harold nudged her arm. Three men had come through the chapel door. The smell of expensive aftershave wafted through the air as they made their way to the pews in front of Permelia and Harold.

Permelia leaned into his shoulder.

"These fellows must be Eid's co-workers," she whispered.

"Business must be good," he whispered back. "Those are bespoke suits, if I'm not mistaken."

"Good eye," she whispered with a grin, turning her face to his shoulder to avoid onlookers.

Finally, Betty and Red came in and sat in the front pew, Red winking at Ben before sitting.

A pianist and three vocalists appeared, followed by a guitarist and a violinist. Permelia noticed Detective Liam James enter just behind the musicians, slipping into a back pew.

They began playing soft music, and the service began.

The vocalists sang beautiful songs, and several bible passages were read. The priest spoke about Eid, avoiding any mention of his family or his children. He focused on his community activities and participation at the church. More music was played, and then Red got up and delivered a heartfelt eulogy. No mention was made of Eid's other family.

Ben hung his head and whispered to Permelia, "It's like I don't exist."

She took his hand.

"Honey, this is a difficult situation. Red knows you're his brother," she said in a quiet voice.

At the conclusion, Red stepped from behind the dais.

"You are all invited to a reception in the assembly hall downstairs," he announced before taking his mother's arm and leading her out the door.

⊷⊶

Betty came over to Permelia and Harold, who were standing at the back of the room, coffee cups in hand.

"Thank you so much for coming. It meant a lot."

"It was a lovely service," Harold told her.

"And Red's eulogy was very moving," Permelia added. She noticed Detective James by himself at the coffee service area. He nodded to her, and she could tell by his expression he wanted to be left alone to do his job.

The three men in suits were seated at a table, coffee and cookies in front of them. One of the three, a slightly overweight, dark-haired man, got up and came over to speak to Betty.

"I'm Mark Murphy," he said. "Edward Anderson worked for me."

Betty looked him up and down.

"Did you know about us?" she asked bluntly, emboldened by her grief.

He put his hand over his mouth and hesitated for a moment, as if considering how to answer.

"First, let me say, Ed was very good at his job. As long as he did his work effectively, I didn't need to know anything else. I did know that he had business cards both as Edward Anderson and Eideard FitzAndreu. He said he chose to use his original Irish name with some of our Irish-American franchise owners. He told us they were more cooperative with his audits when he emphasized his Irish heritage. We probably should have questioned it, but he got results, so we had no reason to.

"We contacted our lawyers as soon as we got your notice about this gathering. I'm afraid I don't know how the insurance and pension issues will play out. None of us has any experience with this sort of situation."

"I have my own pension, so we'll be fine," Betty said. Her tone said she didn't think the life insurance Ed left her was any of his business. "Thank you for coming today, it means a lot to Red and me."

"I'm sorry for your loss," he said.

Chapter 34

Betty moved on to the table where her neighbors sat, leaving an awkward silence in her wake.

"Are you friends of Ed's?" Mark Murphy finally asked. "Or should I say Eideard."

Harold smiled.

"I met him after he died—I did his postmortem."

Mark started to speak then closed his mouth, frowning.

"I'm a friend of Betty's," Permelia said. "I met her at the morgue."

"How very odd," Mark said after another awkward pause, a puzzled look on his face. "I'd better go join my associates."

Harold and Permelia looked at each other once he'd gone back to his friends and laughed.

"I hope he and Ed/Eid weren't close friends," Permelia said. "I couldn't resist, though."

"I wouldn't have said anything if I thought that were the case. He doesn't seem very grief stricken."

Permelia watched as the trio of businessmen got up to leave, stopping briefly at the neighbors' table to speak to Betty before they exited the hall.

Ben stepped into the space between Permelia and Harold, his paper plate filled with cookies, cakes, and other desserts.

"Perhaps we should find a table," Harold suggested.

Permelia looked around, then led them to one that had three places at the back of the room.

"Those guys from my dad's work sure like their perfume," Ben said around a mouthful of snickerdoodle.

Harold chuckled.

"I think it's aftershave or cologne when you're talking about men."

Permelia was about to reply when the door flew open, banging on its stop. Sylvia Anderson stood, hands on hips, just inside the room.

"What is going on here?" she demanded.

Ben hunched his shoulders and ducked his head, and Detective James strode across the room toward Sylvia, but she was already on the move, weaving between the tables until she was in the middle of the room.

"What do you people think you're doing?" she shouted. "My husband Edward Anderson already had his funeral, with his real family and his real friends—" She was cut off as Detective James stepped in front of her then herded her back toward the door.

"I will not stand for this," she continued shouting over Liam's shoulder. "You people have no right to do this."

"Come on, Mrs. Anderson," Permelia heard Liam say in a soothing voice. "This isn't going to help anyone."

Everyone had fallen silent when Sylvia started shouting, but as soon as the door closed behind her the room began buzzing.

"Should I go out there?" Ben asked Permelia.

"I think you should give your mother a little time to calm down."

Red came over and crouched beside Ben, putting an arm across the back of his chair.

"Are you okay, laddie?"

Ben fought tears.

"Why does my mom have to be so crazy?"

"We don't get to choose our family," Red told him. "We just have to make the best of the one we get."

A tear escaped and rolled down Ben's cheek.

"Easy for you to say, you got the good family."

"That I did. But you know, now that we know about each other, *we* can be the good family."

"Do you really mean that?" Ben asked.

"Of course. Now we know we're brothers, we can't unknow it. When everything calms down, we'll see if your mum will let you come visit me in Ireland. Until then, we can talk on the phone and video chat. Don't worry. I'm not going to abandon you."

Permelia looked at Harold, and he had the same worried look she was sure was on her face. Red was too young to realize that you can't promise things to children lightly. If he was making promises to Ben, he'd better keep them. The poor child couldn't take much more disappointment.

Betty rejoined them and pulled a chair from the next table so she could sit down.

"When I got over the shock of Eid having another family," she chuckled, "at least I got over the initial shock, I'd had a fleeting hope that our two families could have some sort of relationship. I mean, our children *are* half-siblings."

"Can I get you some coffee, or anything?" Harold asked.

"I think I'll go splash some water on my face, but a glass of water would be nice when I get back."

Liam James returned and signaled to Permelia. She glanced at Ben and then back to Liam.

"Don't worry, we'll stay here," Red said, catching the exchange.

When she reached Liam, he ushered her out into the hall, nodding across the room at Harold before closing the door.

"I left Sylvia in her car. I told her to take a few minutes to settle down before she tried driving. She was still there when I came back in.

"The problem is her son. I asked if I should come in and get him, and she said something to the effect that if the little traitor liked his father's other family so much, they could have him."

"That's terrible!"

"What's terrible?" Harold asked as he joined them.

Liam brought him up to speed.

"We can make sure he gets back to the hotel," Permelia said, "But is that the right thing to do?"

"Unfortunately, without evidence of abuse, you can't just snatch him," Liam said. "Doesn't he have older siblings?"

"He says his older sister lives back East and is currently in Africa, and his adopted sister is in rehab. His brother who lives locally is currently on his way to San Francisco for business. In any case, he says he lives in a small studio and can't keep Ben there," Permelia said.

"For now, he'll have to go back to the hotel," Liam said. "I can talk to our people, but I'm sure you've read about how overworked our social services are. If there's no evidence of abuse, there isn't much to be done."

Permelia's face turned red.

Harold put his hand in the small of her back.

"We should get back inside. Ben is a resourceful kid. Besides, Sylvia is guilty of neglect and maybe emotional, but not physical, abuse."

Liam followed them back into the reception, scanning the room, probably looking for Betty to say goodbye. She herself planned on giving Sylvia plenty of time to leave to avoid any further unpleasantness.

"Who needs another cookie?" Harold asked when they reached the table.

When Ben didn't speak up, Red answered for them both.

"I think we could both use one more, wouldn't you say, Ben?"

"I guess so," Ben said softly.

Liam remained standing as the rest of the group sat back down.

"I'd better get going, I've got paperwork to do at the station before I go home."

Betty returned as he started to leave.

"Thank you for coming. I know it sounds silly, but somehow having people attend Eid's funeral makes our life and our family more real. I mean, I know we're real, and it's pathetic of me, but I guess I'm grasping at any signs of legitimacy I can."

Liam put his arm around her shoulders.

"No matter what the legal papers say, you, Eid, and your son are a family; and for my money, you were the real family if Sylvia is any indication of the other one. I personally think you had every right to mourn your loss in the church you attended all these years."

Betty swiped at her eyes with a tissue.

"Thank you for saying that."

"Now I really do have to go," Liam said and left the room.

"He's a nice man," Betty said as she sat down. Harriet couldn't help noticing that her hair was disheveled, as if she'd been out in a windstorm or pulling on her hair in frustration. Her trip to the ladies' room hadn't had the expected calming effect.

Chapter 35

Permelia was discussing dates to meet for knitting with Betty a few minutes later when the hall door opened, and Liam leaned in, signaled to Harold, and went back out.

Harold stood. He raised his eyebrows and shrugged. He seemed surprised to see his friend again, since he presumably had gone back to work.

"I'll be right back. His car battery probably died again. I keep telling him he needs to replace it, but he keeps recharging the old one."

Betty got up to refill her water glass.

"I wonder if Ben would like to learn to knit?" she whispered when she returned. He was at the next table talking to a gray-haired woman who had brought in a fresh plate of cookies before sitting down. "Assuming his mother doesn't send him to Switzerland before we start."

Harold came back and started hurrying through the maze of tables.

"Something's wrong," Permelia said. "I don't think that's a dead-battery face."

He signaled for her to join him when he was halfway across the room.

"I'll be right back," she said to Betty and went to him. "What's wrong?"

He put a hand on her arm.

"When Liam got to the parking lot, he found Sylvia still sitting in her car. She's dead."

"*What?* How can she be dead? We just saw her," Permelia said in a shocked whisper.

"I don't know any more than that."

"What do you need me to do?"

"I've got to stay with Liam and work the scene—I've got work clothes and a kit in the trunk of my car. Have Red and Betty take Ben home with them. Liam is trying to reach Ben's brother, but he's probably still in the air.

"Everyone else has to stay here to be questioned, but you can take my car back to the morgue once I retrieve my gear. Then, I need you to call whoever is on tonight—Tony I think, but double-check. Tell him what's happened and to come in."

"I could take a bus."

"My car will be faster. I'll ride back with Sylvia. I'm really sorry about all this."

"It's not *your* fault."

"I've got to go back out. Are you okay with all this?"

Permelia smiled at him. "I'm fine. I'll see you later?"

"I'll come get the keys when I'm done."

<hr/>

"Ben, could you go get me a cookie?"

"Sure. Do you want something to drink, too?"

Permelia took his hand.

"Water would be nice."

Red watched until Ben was out of earshot.

"What's going on?"

"Someone killed Sylvia Anderson in the parking lot. Harold has to work the scene, and Liam would like you to take Ben home with you until he can get hold of Eddie and get him back here. Can you do that?"

"Yes," Betty and Red said at the same time.

"Okay, I have to get back to the morgue and make a call for Harold."

<hr/>

Fenton wove around Permelia's legs, meowing as she confirmed Tony was at the top of the on-call list. She called downstairs and broke the news to him.

"He must not think the body is going to be transported for a while if he's having you call me," Tony told her when she'd repeated Dr. Grace's message.

"I don't know how these things work, but the detective had just found the body. Dr. Grace said he would work the scene, whatever that means."

"That means I have time to race home and have an early dinner with my wife before he gets back. Normally, we wait until the next morning for the autopsy when a guest arrives at the close of business hours, so there must be something special about this one."

Permelia smiled to herself. Tony was fishing, but she wasn't biting.

"I don't know any more than what I told you."

"Okay, thanks for the message," he said, his disappointment evident.

She hung up and went into her bedroom to change clothes. Fenton followed her and jumped onto her bed.

"Yes, cat, a nap would be nice, but after today's events I'd never get to sleep." She glanced at the fitness watch on her wrist. "If Tony has time to go eat dinner, I think we have time to go visit Wilma and update her on the latest developments."

At the mention of Wilma's name, Fenton stood up. He was very clever, as cats went.

Permelia knew she shouldn't be talking about police business, but Wilma's reclusiveness meant she was unlikely to share anything said. Besides, she didn't seem like the type to talk out of turn in any case.

"Let's give her a call, and if she's receiving visitors, we'll go across."

⊷——⊶

Wilma was, indeed, interested in visitors, so Permelia snapped Fenton's harness on and carried him across the street.

"I was hoping I'd see you today," Wilma said as she opened the big oak door and ushered them inside the wall. "I've dug up a little information on your suspects."

"I have news, too. Betty's memorial service was quite the event."

"Do tell," Wilma said. "Hot or cold tea?"

"Definitely hot."

"I can listen while I make it. Come on in."

"The first news is that Sylvia Anderson came to the reception after the service."

"Did she really?"

"Indeed, and she made quite a spectacle of herself. She was ranting about how her husband had already had a memorial service, and she called Ben a traitor, which upset him, especially when she refused to take him home with her. Finally, the detective who came to the service had to escort her out and suggest she sit and calm down before driving anywhere. He came back in and talked to us for a few minutes, and when he went to leave, he found her dead in her car."

Wilma carried mugs, spoons, and sugar to the table and sat down to wait for the water to boil.

"That is big. Any idea who killed her?"

"Not even a hint."

"I guess you know who *didn't* do it," Wilma said. "I mean, whoever was still inside with you couldn't have done it."

Permelia looked at the ceiling as she thought. "Ed's coworkers had left. Of course, we only saw them leave the room. They may have still been in the parking lot. The neighbors were still at their table. Betty and Red were still…" She paused. "Now that I think of it, Betty left to go splash water on her face after Sylvia's little sideshow."

"Was she gone long enough to have killed Sylvia?"

Permelia thought further.

"Maybe. She was gone quite a little while, and her hair was a mess, but not wet. I wonder how Sylvia was killed. For Betty to have done it, she'd have to have used her bare hands, or a weapon of opportunity.

"The coworkers could have had a concealed weapon on them. And like I said, they could have been in the parking lot. For all we know, they may have been the ones who let Sylvia know there was a memorial service. They could have been waiting for her to arrive."

"There's always the possibility it was someone from a different part of Sylvia's life who followed her to the church and had nothing to do with the husband drama." Wilma suggested. "From what I've learned, a number of people have sued her over real-estate deals that have gone sour. One of them may have decided to take revenge."

"That's interesting."

"I *haven't* found anything to indicate why Mr. and Mrs. Anderson chose to marry, other than the rumor you mentioned that Mr. Anderson senior had amassed some sort of debt to Sylvia's father and it went away when the kids married. Sylvia was a little long in the tooth for a debutante of that era when the marriage took place, which lends credence to the idea her dad arranged the circumstances in order to ensure an heir."

Wilma got up to retrieve the steaming kettle and pour their water.

"Did you find out anything about Ed's boss?" Permelia asked.

"Nothing specific yet. He keeps a very low profile. I've been looking at each of his businesses one-by-one, and somehow, *his* franchises seem to be less profitable than their fellow franchisees. For example, if he has a McDonald's, it clears less profit, to the degree I can find numbers and business journal references, than other similar-sized McDonald's in this area. And that holds true for all of his businesses so far."

"Does he build in less-prosperous neighborhoods?"

"On the contrary, his locations are prime. He should be at the top of the heap."

"That *is* curious. I wonder what it means?"

"It's too early to tell yet, but I'll keep after it."

"Have you turned up any enemies for him?"

"Not really. And a cursory glance at Eid's and Betty's neighbors didn't turn up anything, either."

Permelia sipped her tea and set her cup down.

"It's all such a mess. I hope Betty didn't have anything to do with it."

"Don't let the fact you like her dull your powers of observation."

"I won't, but I worry she may be in danger. I mean, first Ed, then Sylvia."

Wilma got up and took a plate from her cupboard, placing several cookies from a gallon-sized glass jar on it and bringing it to the table.

"Have a cookie," she said and set the plate between them. "It appears no one in the Anderson's circle knew about the FitzAndreus, which could lead us to believe they are not involved in any of this."

"Yet," Permelia said. "I just wish Detective James had some idea what was going on."

"He may have more of an idea than you think. He can't share everything he knows."

"I guess..."

Wilma took a bite of her cookie then looked at the remains.

"These could have used a little more butter. What do you think."

"They aren't bad," Permelia said and took another bite of hers.

"But...?"

Permelia smiled.

"Okay, they would have benefited from a little more butter."

"Do you have time to stay and knit? I assume you have a project in your bag."

"Always," Permelia said with a grin.

Chapter 36

"Your scarf is really coming along nicely," Permelia said when they had put in an hour of knitting.

"I can't believe how fast you're churning out socks."

Permelia held up the nearly finished yellow one she was working on.

"I have three pairs going at the same time. One is always in my purse, one in my car, and one in the house. I work on them whenever I have a delay or wait-time anywhere. I have a lot of children and grandchildren who wear them out with alarming regularity. Once they start wearing home-made socks, they don't like anything else, especially when it's cold out."

"How many children did you say you have?" Wilma asked her.

Permelia sat back in her chair.

"I tell people I have eight. In reality, I've given birth to nine babies. The youngest, Baby Robert, was stolen from the hospital when he was a day old. In my dreams, a couple desperate for a child took him and have been raising him, giving him a wonderful life. The truth is, we may never know."

"How old would he be?"

"He's thirty-two now."

"That's really hard. I'm sorry I asked."

"Don't worry. I've had a lot of time to learn to live with it. I've put my DNA out there and hope someday he'll have his tested, too. He probably doesn't know the circumstances of his birth, so he may not be as anxious to be tested as we were."

"Again, I'm sorry." Wilma said and began working on her scarf again.

<hr />

Permelia had just started the ribbing on her sock when her cell phone rang.

"Betty, slow down, I can't tell what you're saying." She held the phone away from her ear and pressed the speaker button so Wilma could hear.

They could hear Betty crying and then a scraping noise.

"Hi, this is Red. We took Ben out for a late lunch after the memorial service, and when we got back, we found our house had been broken into. The police are here. Mom is all flustered because we're supposed to be taking care of Ben, and the police won't let us into the house."

"No problem—you can come to my apartment. You don't even need to ask."

"I was hoping you would say that. I need to check with the police and make sure that's okay, and then we'll be right over."

"I have a suggestion," Wilma said when Permelia pressed the end button and pocketed her phone. "I know you have a guestroom, but it might be a little tight quarters, having all three of them. Why don't you suggest the boys stay here? I've got a bedroom with twin beds and its own bath."

"Thank you. Assuming they agree, that will be very helpful."

"They should feel safe here, at least. That's probably pretty important for Ben at this point."

"You're right. I wonder if they've been able to reach to his brother yet. He was just leaving for San Francisco when he dropped Ben at the memorial service."

" I should go open the window in the spare rooms so they can air out a little. You can join me if you wish."

Permelia texted Betty, instructing her to come to the big oak door in her neighbor's wall and ring the buzzer when they arrived. Betty texted back acknowledgment.

⟊──⟊

"Wow, your grandmother was an amazing decorator," Permelia said as they returned downstairs. "Those bedrooms decorated as storybook worlds are delightful."

Wilma grinned.

"When she gave me the house, I didn't have the heart to change them. Our visits here when we were kids were magical."

Fenton came bounding into the room after them, a dust bunny clinging to his whiskers on the left side. Permelia picked him up and wiped his face with a tissue Wilma handed her.

"If he lived here, he'd spend all his time running up and down the stairs."

"Would you like more tea?"

"I probably don't need any more, but yes, I'd love some. Maybe herbal this time."

Wilma fixed the tea, and they were seated in the kitchen staring at the door buzzer panel when it finally rang.

"And they say a watched pot never boils," Wilma said and got up to open the gate. She returned a few minutes later followed by a wide-eyed Ben and a frazzled-looking Betty. Red was the only one who looked half-way normal, but even he was red-faced.

"Coffee or tea?" Wilma asked. "Or hot chocolate or lemonade," she added with a glance at Ben.

"I'm Betty's son Red, and I'd like coffee," Red said.

"I'm Permelia's neighbor Wilma, and I'm very sorry about your dad."

"I'll have coffee," Betty said in a dull voice.

"Do you have marshmallows?" Ben asked.

"It wouldn't be hot chocolate without marshmallows, now, would it?"

That got a weak smile from Ben.

Permelia was anxious to grill Betty about the break-in, but she kept quiet, giving them all a chance to recover a bit. Wilma refilled the cookie plate and set a stack of napkins on the table.

"Permelia and I were talking after you called," she said. "I've invited some or all of you to stay here tonight, if you'd like. Permelia has one guest room, and I have several. We were thinking the boys could stay here, at least. I've got a room with twin beds and its own bathroom."

"Betty," Permelia said, "I thought maybe you'd prefer to stay with me."

"Thank you both for your generosity. I hate to trouble you. We could get a hotel room."

"I'd like to stay," Ben piped up. "I'm tired of living in a hotel. People are noisy on the weekends, even in nice ones."

Red reached over and took his mom's hand.

"I know you don't want to be a bother, but staying with people we know feels safer right now. Permelia is over the morgue, and Wilma…" He looked around, blushing a bit. "…lives in a fortress. Given everything, I think it's a good plan."

Permelia picked up her teacup.

"I'm guessing the police will do some extra patrols around here if Detective James asks them to."

Betty set her half-eaten cookie on her napkin.

"I can't imagine why anyone would break into our house. I don't have anything worth stealing."

"I'm sure the police will figure it out," Permelia said, thinking of Sheriff Miller in the county the ranch was in. He always got his man or woman. She wasn't sure if that was as true in the city when crime went beyond the petty vandalism and drunken brawls most common in her former town.

Betty ran a hand through her hair.

"Do you think I could lie down for a little while? I'd just like to close my eyes for a few minutes."

Permelia crumpled her napkin and put it on the table.

"Sure, let me capture my cat, and we can walk across to my place."

Betty turned her attention to Red and Ben.

"Will you two be okay for an hour or so?"

Red grinned.

"Mom, I live an ocean away most of the time, and I manage." He ruffled Ben's hair. "And I can keep an eye on this wee laddie. It probably wouldn't hurt for us to have a little down time, too."

"I want to talk to the police," Ben protested. "I need to know what happened to my mom."

Permelia put her hand on his shoulder.

"Honey, the police are going to want to talk to you, too, but they're busy investigating right now. Don't worry, they'll be in touch when they're ready."

Fenton was under Ben's chair, and Permelia picked him up and attached his leash to his harness. Wilma rose and accompanied them to the back door.

"I'll show the boys upstairs after I get you two out of the gate. Let me know what the good doctor says when he's done doing his thing."

"Will do," Permelia promised.

Chapter 37

Permelia was sitting in her chair in the living room knitting a sock, Fenton curled up in her lap, when she heard the EMT vehicle drive into the parking lot. She got up and went to the kitchen to watch. Harold climbed out of the boxy vehicle, and Tony emerged through the open double morgue doors. She waved when he looked up at her window.

"You stay here," she said in a quiet voice to her cat.

She slipped her slippers off and her shoes on at the door and went downstairs, hoping the noise wouldn't wake Betty. She could hear rhythmic snoring through the closed guestroom door as she softly opened the apartment door and slipped out, closing it silently behind her.

Harold was talking to the EMT driver as Tony wheeled Sylvia into the morgue. Permelia waited a discrete few feet away while they finished their conversation. When he came over to her, she pulled his car keys from her sweater pocket and returned them.

"Thanks for getting Tony lined up for me," he said. "And bringing my car home." His hair still had a ridge from the hat he'd worn while working the crime scene. He was dressed in green scrubs and looked tired.

"Thank you for letting me use it."

"Do you have time for a cup of tea before I go home?" he asked.

She put a hand on his arm.

"I do, but can we do it in your break room? There have been a few developments here."

He raised an eyebrow.

"Let's go make that tea first. This will take a few minutes to explain."

They went past his office, and he ducked in to drop off his notebook and pen.

"I'll cook," Permelia said. "You sit and put your feet up."

She put on the water to boil then got out mugs and teabags. Harold was leaning back with his eyes closed when she set the mugs on the end table and sat down.

"Do I really want to hear this?" he said without opening his eyes.

Permelia smiled.

"Probably not, but I'm going to tell you anyway, because you need to know."

She sipped her tea and waited while he slowly sat upright and then picked up his cup.

"Okay."

"When last we spoke," she began, "Betty and Red were taking Ben home, and I was returning here, which I did. Shortly thereafter, I went across to knit with Wilma. I'd been there about an hour when Betty called to tell me her house had been broken into while they were out eating." She told him the rest of the story of their arrival, the splitting up of the group, and ended with the fact that Betty was asleep upstairs in her guest room.

Harold looked up at the ceiling and finally blew out a breath.

"I'm not at all happy that you have Betty in your apartment."

The color drained from her face.

"I never considered that there might be restrictions on my having company in the apartment. I'm so sorry."

He reached over and patted her hand.

"There aren't. You misunderstand. You can have whoever you want to stay with you. I'm concerned for *you*. As far as I can see, Betty is a person of interest in two murders. Hopefully, she's not a danger to you in any case, but still it's a concern."

"How could Betty be a person of interest in Sylvia's murder?"

"It seems she went out to splash her face with water during the window of time when Sylvia was killed."

"You can't possibly think that poor woman, who just lost the love of her life, could race out and kill her son's half-brother's mother," Permelia said, her face flushing.

"I know she's your friend, but it wouldn't take much time to go out to the parking lot, kill Sylvia and come back in."

"She wouldn't do that, not to Red and especially not to Ben."

"If I were the detective, she wouldn't be on the top of my suspect list, but she would have to be on it."

Permelia sipped her tea.

"Just be careful. Keep your eyes and ears open."

She smiled.

"Thank you for your concern. I will be careful."

Permelia sat with Harold for another half-hour before returning to her apartment. Betty had gotten up and was sitting in the living room with Fenton in her lap.

"He didn't wake you, did he?" Permelia asked.

"No, he was sleeping out here when I got up. I have to say, I feel a little better after the rest."

"You've had a hard couple of weeks."

"At least they didn't break my Belleek. Red opened the door and saw what had happened, but I got to the doorway. I couldn't see much, but I did see my ceramics safely on their shelf."

"Well, that's something, I guess. Hopefully, the police will be done with your house by tomorrow, and we can get in there and clean it up."

"You've done so much for us, I don't expect you to help clean on top of it all."

"Where I come from, when something bad happens, everyone pitches in to help put things right."

"I confess the company would be nice. I just feel like the world is falling in on me, and it won't stop."

"I'm sure the police will get this all sorted before you know it."

"I worry about that Ben. I think it would do him good to go back to school for the last week. Being around kids his own age might help him feel more normal. But only if he's ready for it. I'm sure Eid gave him attention when he was there. It's just I know I've only seen Sylvia briefly and only at her worst, but I didn't detect any maternal warmth from her."

"You were a teacher, right?"

Betty's cheeks pinked.

"Once a teacher, always a teacher, I guess. I don't know what Sylvia's been through, but I do know the signs of a neglected child."

"I wonder if his brother is back from San Francisco yet?" Permelia said.

"You'd think that if he's back, he'd have called his little brother to make sure he's okay."

"That family isn't normal. None of them seem to care about Ben. Now, I know you folks ate before all this began, but I was thinking I might take my leftover spaghetti and meatballs over to Wilma's for supper."

"That sounds good. Do I have time to freshen up a little?"

"Indeed, you do. I'll give Wilma a call so she knows we're coming."

"Is there a reason she lives in such a fortress?"

Permelia took a breath and blew it out.

"I think there is, but it hasn't been revealed to me. I'm sure she'll tell me if she wants me to know."

"It's nice of her to take the boys in, fortress or not."

⊬⊶⊶⊣

Wilma had a loaf of French bread split and spread with garlic butter, ready to go in the oven, when Permelia and Betty arrived. Red and Ben circled the kitchen table placing silverware, napkins, and plates.

"What can we do to help?" Permelia asked.

Wilma opened the refrigerator and took out a large bowl of green salad.

"You can put this on the table."

"My spaghetti can pop in the microwave right before we eat."

Ben settled in his chair at the table.

"Why hasn't Eddie called?" he asked the room at large.

The adults looked at each other. Permelia went to him and put a hand on his shoulder.

"Honey, I'm sure your brother will call you as soon as the police find him and let him know what's happened. They probably have to wait until he gets to his hotel before they can reach him."

"If it's okay with you ladies, I was thinking to take my little brother here to the zoo tomorrow, if the police say it's okay, I can do whatever heavy lifting you need done at the house either before or after our trip."

"I think that's a marvelous idea," Permelia told him with a smile. "Perhaps you could go to the house first and set big things right, then I'll go with your mother, and we'll do the cleaning and repairing while you're gone."

Red nodded agreement and sat down beside Ben.

"Did I ever tell you about my adventures doing volunteer work at the zoo?"

Of course, they all knew he hadn't, as he and Ben barely knew each other, but Red was a good storyteller.

"Well, laddie, my task was to keep the little goats in their pen, and they were determined to get out and explore the zoo..."

He entertained Ben until dinner was over and the kitchen had been cleaned up again.

Chapter 38

Permelia fixed toasted bagels and strawberry cream cheese and set them on the kitchen table. By the time Betty came out of the guest room in her borrowed bathrobe, Permelia had made a pot of tea.

"I thought we could have a little breakfast out on the patio before we start our clean-up."

Betty stretched her arms out and yawned.

"That sounds wonderful."

"Strangely, the door to the patio is in the closet in your room."

"Really?"

Permelia picked up the tray of food and tea and led the way back into the guest room.

"It seems this was not originally a bedroom, and to be legally declared one, it needed a closet. The patio was out of commission at the time, and well…" She opened the closet and stepped in. Betty followed her.

"What a wonderful spot. No one would know it was here if they didn't already know."

Permelia spread her bagel with cream cheese and took a bite.

"Now, how bad are things at your house? Be honest. Do we need to buy any storage tubs or garbage bags or brooms and dustpans on our way there?"

Betty thought for a moment.

"Definitely garbage bags. I have brooms and a dustpan." She was silent again, looking off in the distance. "I didn't take a good look, but my sense is that they didn't break a lot. Things were mostly tossed around. Lots of books were on the floor, but then, we have lots of books."

"That doesn't sound as bad as it could have been."

"Thank heaven for careful crooks," Betty said and laughed.

"I'm just glad you were out when it happened. On the other hand, the fact that you were might mean someone has been watching your movements."

"That's an awful thought."

"Given what's been going on, if anyone is watching, and that's a big if, it could just as easily be Ben they're watching as you and Red."

"Still, it's our house that got broken into."

"It makes you wonder which man was killed—Ed or Eid?"

Betty stopped mid-bite.

"I hadn't thought about that. Since I didn't know about his other life, I just assumed it was Eid who was murdered, but you're right. Now that Sylvia has been killed, maybe it was *Ed* they were after, just because he was Sylvia's husband."

Permelia sipped her tea.

"Let's hope Detective James gets it figured out sooner rather than later."

Betty picked up her cup.

"I just want things to return to some sort of normal so I can figure out what's next for me. I mean, Red will go back to school and finish his degree and find a job just like he was going to, but I need to figure out what I'm going to do."

"I hear you. I'm still trying to figure my life out, and it's been months now since I got divorced."

Betty sighed.

"This might sound terrible but, in some ways, I think it's better that Eid died. I'm not sure how I would have handled finding out he'd been sleeping with another woman all these years." She laughed. "I might have killed him myself."

"Maybe he would have had a really good reason, though."

"Yeah, maybe. But clearly, he didn't feign impotence when he was with Sylvia. Ben's existence attests to that."

"Try not to dwell on that part."

Betty gave her a wry smile.

"I guess I've moved into the anger part of grief."

Permelia reached over and patted her hand.

<hr />

Thirty minutes later, they stood inside Betty's front door, garbage bags in hand, surveying the wreckage. Good to his word, Red had already been by. Several bookcases stood upright, although empty, against the walls, thanks no doubt to his efforts.

"Let's start in the kitchen," Permelia suggested. "That way, the dishwasher can be running while we put books back on the shelves in the living room."

They worked for three hours before they took a break. The living room, kitchen, and downstairs bathroom were back to normal, and three large garbage bags were stuffed and lined up at the door. Betty blew at a strand of hair that was hanging in her face and finally swept it back with her rubber-gloved hand.

"This is certainly the deepest spring cleaning I've done in years."

"There *is* a silver lining to all this," Permelia said, and they laughed.

"The good news is, I've found a box of tea cookies," Betty said.

"The kettle is washed and on the stove, and if I'm not mistaken, the mugs just finished in the dishwasher."

Betty tossed her cleaning rag toward the sink.

"Clearly, it's break time."

Minutes later, they were sitting at the kitchen table, tea and cookies in front of them.

"I wonder what they were searching for," Permelia said thoughtfully and looked around. "It was smaller than a breadbox, judging by what they've emptied and opened. Do you have any valuable collections? Jewelry? Watches?"

Betty shook her head.

"We don't have anything like that. My Belleek china is the only thing of value, and whoever broke in clearly wasn't after that. There isn't a piece missing or broken. Eid tied fishing flies for a hobby. I can't imagine anyone coming after them."

Permelia finished her tea and carried her mug to the kitchen sink.

"How about I take the office and you tackle the bedrooms?"

Betty stood up.

"Sounds like a plan."

"Do you have any furniture polish? I might as well give the desk and shelves a good dusting before I put the books back."

"Under the sink." Betty said.

Permelia fetched it and headed into Eid's office.

She gave the large bookcase opposite Eid's desk a good polish with the lemon-scented spray and gathered the books that were scattered around the floor, replacing them on the shelves.

The robbers had been very thorough with the desk. There wasn't a book, a pen, or a scrap of paper on it or in it. Permelia refolded her cloth and began wiping. She sprayed the polish on the top of the desk and slid her cloth across the surface in a circular motion, making larger circles with each swipe, reviewing in her mind who or why someone would search Betty's house. She swept the cloth over the left side as she struggled to come up with something, given the small amount of information she had. She was so deep in thought she almost missed the slight movement of the wooden surface as she pressed the cloth across it.

She swiped her cloth over the spot again, pressing more firmly. It really had moved. The third time was, indeed, the charm as she applied a firmer hand and the front left strip above the row of drawers popped forward an inch. Permelia gently pulled the panel toward her and discovered it was a shallow drawer.

She glanced toward the door, thinking she should call Betty, but decided to look herself first in case it was something that might cause another fainting spell. It did occur to her that perhaps Detective James was the appropriate person to look into the secret drawer of a murder victim, but she rejected that idea as a waste of valuable detecting time.

In the end, she pushed aside all concerns and reached in, removing the contents and laying them on the surface of the desk. They were anticlimactic—three sets of keys and two passports, an Irish one in the name of Eideard FitzAndreu and a US passport for Edward Anderson Junior.

"Betty," she called. A moment later, her friend appeared from the hallway. "I've found something interesting. I was polishing the desktop, and I discovered a hidden drawer. The thieves missed it."

Betty examined the collection on the desk.

"I recognize two of the sets of keys." She turned the key tags around to display addresses neatly written in block letters. "These two are rental houses we have. One is a condo at the beach, and the other is a cabin in the mountains. We rent them out through an agency most of the year. While Red was growing up, we'd go to each for a week or two each year. We haven't gone since Red went to Ireland. We talked of selling one or both of them when we moved there."

"Do you know what this other set of keys is for?"

"I've no idea."

Permelia picked them up and examined the tag.

"There's an address written on here. It looks like it's in town. Maybe we can drive by on our way back to my place."

"I have to admit, I'm curious about what other secrets Eid has been keeping from me."

"We'll know soon enough."

Chapter 39

Permelia wiped the desk down with her polish cloth twice, lest any additional secrets be revealed, but none were. She went back over the bookcase and credenza also, but if they had any hidden drawers or compartments, she didn't trigger them. She felt fortunate that Eid had not chosen to keep much in the way of files in this office, or her task could have been much more time-consuming. As it was, after another hour, the office was clean and orderly again and smelled of lemon polish.

"I'm finished with the bedrooms," Betty said from the office doorway. "Should we call it a day? I know the garage still needs to be put back together, and I haven't done the bathroom upstairs, but I'm pooped. And I *would* like to check up on Red and Ben."

Permelia carried her polishing cloth and furniture polish back to the kitchen.

"I wonder if the police have reached Ben's brother?"

"Who can we call to find out?"

"I could check in with Harold. I assume one of the adult children will have to make arrangements for Sylvia at some point."

"I'll go pack a few things while you call him." Betty said.

Permelia pulled her cell phone from her bag.

"Good idea. You're not going to be able to come back here for at least another day or two."

Betty went upstairs, and Permelia dialed the morgue.

"I was just thinking about you," Harold said when he answered his phone. "I noticed your car's been gone all day. Not that I'm spying on you, but with everything that's been going on, I was concerned."

"That's nice of you to worry, but Betty and I have been at her house all day cleaning up after the break-in."

He sighed audibly.

"I was afraid you'd say that."

"Harold, it's broad daylight. The neighbors are home. And Red was over first to set the heavy furniture back in place. Besides, while I was cleaning the desk, I found a secret drawer."

"And?" he prompted. "What was in it? The answer to this whole mess?"

"Nothing that exciting. There were three sets of keys. Two were rental properties they own, and the third Betty didn't recognize. There's an address on the key fob, and it's in town, so we're going to drive by on our way home just to see what sort of property it is."

"If it looks dodgy, please tell me you'll keep on driving."

Permelia smiled to herself. Harold's concern was sort of charming.

"What I actually called you for was to see if you'd heard whether the police have been able to get in touch with either of Sylvia's adult children. Red is distracting Ben for now, but at some point, a more permanent arrangement needs to be made for the boy."

"I saw Liam today—he came by to ask a few questions about Sylvia's autopsy. He mentioned that the daughter is out of the country. She apparently does some sort of work with infectious diseases and currently is in Africa dealing with Ebola. The son, Eddie, will be returning from the Bay area tonight."

"Ben will be happy to hear that. Eddie's place is apparently too small for both of them, but I'm sure he'll work something out."

Permelia said her goodbyes as Harold admonished her to be careful one more time, and they rang off.

Betty came downstairs wearing a different outfit and with a tote bag over her shoulder.

"Did you find anything out?"

Permelia related the news from Harold.

"Ben will be happy to hear that," Betty said.

"That's what I said. I guess the sister is in Africa saving the world, so she won't be reachable for a while." She looked around Betty's living room. "Shall we be on our way?"

"I'm ready," Betty replied.

⊷——⊶

Permelia unlocked her car and got in.

"I wonder how the crooks got in the house?" she said as she tapped the address from the key fob into her phone.

Betty slid into the passenger seat.

"I checked the windows and doors, and for the life of me, I can't see that anything was broken. And we didn't leave anything unlocked. I know we didn't."

"I guess that leaves two options—they either picked the lock, or they got a key somehow."

"I can't imagine how they would get a key. We don't hand them out at the corner."

Permelia looked over her shoulder as she backed out of the driveway.

"They must have picked them. I think you need to call a locksmith and have your locks replaced with something more secure. Wilma says she has locks that can't be picked, so she might be able to recommend someone who could help you."

"Okay. Now, let's see what we find at Seventy-two-thirty NW Ramsay Drive."

The map took them up into the forested hills on the west side of the city. The roads got narrower and went from pavement to gravel. Finally, they reached a drive that led to a garage at the base of a steep hill. Permelia turned off the car and got out.

The two women looked at the garage and then up the hill, where between the trees they could just make out a house.

"I'm guessing this…" Permelia pointed at the garage. "…belongs to that house up there." She held up the key fob and looked at the black numbers painted on a white background on the side of the building.

"This is definitely the place."

The weathered blue garage had an overhead door and a white-painted regular one on the side. Permelia walked to the side door and slid the key into the lock. The door opened into a dark, damp space dominated by a ten-year-old Volvo station wagon.

Betty gasped and covered her mouth with her hand. Tears threatened to spill from her eyes.

"It's Eid's car."

Permelia put her hand on Betty's shoulder. Finally, Betty took a deep breath and entered the dark garage.

"That answers our question about which man was killed. If Eid's car is here, his switching station, as it were, then he was driving Ed's car when he was killed."

The women peered into the empty car.

"I don't care what he called himself," said a masculine voice from the door. "I want my book." He closed the door.

"What book?" Permelia asked.

"That doesn't really matter. What matters is whether you're going to try and stop us from looking for our book."

"If you're asking for our permission to tear apart this car and this garage, you don't have it," Betty said.

"I think you'd better leave," Permelia said. She pulled her cell phone from her pocket.

"I was afraid you were going to say that." Mark Murphy knocked her phone from her hand and grabbed her wrist, wrenching her arm behind her back.

"Stop that," Betty said, and hit him from behind.

Mark ignored Betty and pulled a length of cord from his pocket, tying Permelia's wrists behind her back. Another man came in and grabbed Betty. Permelia recognized him as one of the men-in-suits who'd come to Eid's funeral. He efficiently bound Betty's hands then roughly pulled her to the front of the garage and pushed her down onto the floor. Mark shoved Permelia down beside her. The other man quickly bound their feet with duct tape.

"What book are you talking about?" Permelia asked.

Mark went to a set of built-in cabinets at the back of the garage and began pulling cans of oil, tubes of caulking, and boxes of various-sized nails onto the floor. A stack of mailing boxes leaned up against the wall. Mark went through them one by one, feeling in each box.

"Clearly, your book isn't here." Permelia said. "Why don't you let us loose, and we can all go our own way."

Mark's associate looked at him with a grim smile.

"We haven't even started looking in this garage," Mark told them. "And you aren't going anywhere."

"You're an upstanding businessman—Eid's boss, if I'm not mistaken—and you're acting like some television villain," Permelia said. "Nobody really ties up two senior citizens so they can tear apart the garage of the recently widowed one. Just ask us for what you want, and if we have it, we'll give it to you."

Mark looked at the thug-in-a-suit he'd brought with him.

"Why didn't I think of that? Just ask them, she says. Okay, I think that's where we started, but okay." He turned to Betty. "Where is my financial journal?"

Tears filled Betty's eyes.

"I don't know about any journal. You've torn through his office, and we've gone through it all again as we cleaned up. There isn't any journal."

"Which is why we're here," Mark said in exasperation. "He took it home with him every night."

"Maybe it's in his other car, since that's the one he was found in," Betty said. "Or his other house."

"We looked in his other house," Mark said. "My brilliant associate decided to set the office there on fire just in case when he didn't find it. Once the police finally left, we went back and searched the house again. It's not there."

Permelia squirmed, trying to find a more comfortable position.

"Is that why you killed Sylvia?"

Mark stiffened.

"I did not kill Sylvia," he said emphatically, enunciating every word.

"We're supposed to believe you didn't kill Sylvia, but you're willing to tie us up and do…what?…with us?" Permelia pressed.

"I don't know, I just know I need that book."

Mark continued opening storage cabinets, tossing their contents to the floor.

"Can't we consider this a misunderstanding and go our separate ways?" Permelia asked.

He stopped.

"Would you please stop talking?"

Everyone stopped talking as the door opened and Red walked in, Ben following him.

"What's going on here?"

Mark nodded to his companion, and the man approached Red.

"I just want my journal ledger," Mark said.

If his intent was to distract Red from the approaching menace, it didn't work. When his minion got within arm's reach, Red executed a series of martial arts moves that ended with the thug flat on his back on the floor, a blue welt appearing on the side of his neck.

Red dusted his hands off on each other and looked at Mark.

"Next?"

Mark held his hands up, palms forward.

"Let's just wait a minute. Maybe you're right. Perhaps we should all just walk away and chalk this up to a misunderstanding."

Permelia shook her head.

"You had your chance, but I think it expired when Red arrived."

Red pulled a knife from his pocket and opened it, cutting first his mother's bindings and then Permelia's. He held his hand out to each woman in turn, helping them stand up and brush the dirt off their slacks.

He turned to Mark, still holding the knife.

"Now, what to do with you."

They all froze as the sound of sirens was heard in the distance, growing louder as they approached.

Ben had stayed behind Red while he dealt with Mark's minion.

"I called nine-one-one while you were busy," he told Red. "Is that okay?"

Red grinned.

"That's perfect."

Chapter 40

R ed and Ben left the garage and headed for Wilma's, while Permelia and Betty followed the police to the station to give their statements.

It was three hours later by the time Permelia and Betty finished and were in the car headed back to the morgue.

Permelia wasn't surprised to see Detective James's car in the parking lot, and there was a note stuck to the downstairs apartment door when she unlocked it. She opened it and scanned the message as she opened the door and headed up the stairs. She could hear Fenton yowling through the closed door.

"We're invited to Wilma's for dinner," she told Betty. "Apparently, Harold and the detective are over there already."

"Do we have time to freshen up?" Betty asked. "I'd like to wash the grime from those two jerks off my hands."

Permelia smiled.

"Me, too."

Fenton threw himself at Permelia when she opened the door.

"Apparently, I also need to spend a few minutes with this one. Let's say we'll head over there in fifteen or twenty minutes."

Betty opened her bedroom door.

"Sounds good."

⊷──⊷

Pizza boxes were stacked on Wilma's kitchen counter when Permelia, Betty, and Fenton arrived. Harold got up from the table and came over to stand in front of Permelia. He started to spread his arms as if to hug her and then stepped aside and patted her awkwardly on the back.

"I'm so glad you're okay." He stepped further back to include Betty. "You two could have been killed."

Tears filled Betty's eyes.

"I was so scared. I don't know how much more I can take."

Red came over and put his arms around his mother.

"Maybe it's time for you to come visit me in Ireland until this is all sorted out."

She dabbed her eyes with a tissue from her pocket.

"I can't abandon my home."

"No, of course not," he assured her. "I'm thinking maybe…" He looked at Liam. "…six weeks?"

"There are no guarantees," Liam said darkly.

Wilma carried the pizza to the table.

"Anyone hungry?"

She instructed them to use the paper plates stacked on the table then carry them out to the patio.

⊷——⊶

"That was really good pizza," Permelia said. "Where did you get it?"

"It's a place called Pizzeria Otto's. It's a ways from here, but fortunately, you can get almost anything delivered in this town."

Ben got up and went to sit beside Liam.

"What's on your mind, buddy?" the detective asked him.

Ben's bottom lip quivered as he tried to speak.

"What's going to happen to those men that tied up Permelia and Red's mom?"

"Right now, they're in jail. They'll be charged with assault and maybe kidnapping, breaking and entering. But I have to be honest, they'll probably be given bail."

"Do you think they'll try to come here?"

Wilma laughed.

"Honey, stick with me. No one is getting in here unless I want them to."

"What about Red's mom?" Ben asked.

Permelia set her iced tea down.

"I'm pretty sure that man Mark really is looking for his book. He has no reason to look for it at my house."

"What's this journal ledger he's looking for?" Red wondered.

"As I told Permelia," Wilma said, "I've been digging around on the internet and, keeping in mind there's no guarantee the figures I'm finding are correct, the group of franchise businesses this guy owns seem to be consistently underperforming compared to other similar businesses in the area. One explanation is that he's been cooking the books. This ledger he's looking for could be the key."

Liam pulled a small notebook from his shirt pocket and jotted something down.

"I'll speak to our white-collar crime people and see if they can check it out."

Harold wiped his hands on his napkin and crumpled it up, tossing it on his plate.

"If that's true, and Edward was the accountant, maybe he was on to the scam and was going to turn them in. That would give Mark a motive to kill him. But why Sylvia?"

Permelia stacked her empty plate on Harold's and gestured for Liam and Red to hand theirs over.

"Maybe Edward told Sylvia what he'd discovered. But then Mark would have to know that he had."

"Dad never talked about his work, except to say he was going to be gone," Ben said. He hung his head. "I don't think Mom was interested in what anyone else did."

Red put his arm around Ben's shoulders and gave him a hug.

Liam stood up.

"Hopefully, we'll learn the answer to that mystery as we talk more to Edward's boss and his associate. And speaking about that, I'd better get back to the station and see what's going on."

He shook hands with Harold and Red and ruffled Ben's hair.

"Ladies," he said and gave them a mock salute. Fenton swiped at his ankle from under the table.

"Excuse me," he said, "I didn't mean to forget you." He reached down and scratched the cat's ears. He straightened up. "I'll be in touch."

⊷──⊶

"Would anyone like some Italian ice?" Wilma asked. Permelia and Betty had cleaned the pizza plates up, and they had all settled around the kitchen table.

"Sure," Ben said. "It'll cleanse our palates."

"Where did you learn that?" Red said with a chuckle.

"Sitting around the hotel room watching cooking shows while my mom was out with her new boyfriend."

Wilma set cartons of lemon, raspberry, and mango ice on the table beside a stack of small glass bowls and then served the flavor combinations each person requested. Red sat back in his chair. He took a spoonful of raspberry ice then used his empty spoon as a pointer.

"You know, Dad's been sending a lot of stuff to me in Ireland."

Betty looked surprised.

"He has? What kind of stuff?"

177

"I don't really know. Some of the boxes look like bankers file boxes. And just after the first of each month a smaller box comes. That one is heavy for its size. I was wondering if the book that Mark guy is so desperate to find is in one of the boxes in Ireland."

Betty frowned.

"What did your father tell you to do with these boxes?"

"He asked me to stack them in the spare bedroom."

"Did you open them?" Permelia asked.

"No, they were my dad's."

Wilma put the cartons of ice back in the freezer and sat down with her own dish.

"Given the current circumstances, do you think you could get someone to open the boxes and look?"

Red took another bite and thought for a minute.

"I could call my cousin Declan."

"Do it," Betty said.

Red pulled out his phone.

"It's a little early there, so I'll send him a text and ask him to call me when he wakes up."

"You tell me as soon as you hear from him," Betty ordered.

"Yes, ma'am,"

+←——←+

Harold insisted on walking Permelia and Betty to her door.

"Are you sure you ladies are okay after what happened today? I mean, I could sleep on your couch, if it would make you feel safer."

Permelia smiled.

"That's really sweet, and today *was* upsetting, but the bad guys are in custody, at least for now, so...." She stopped talking as she noticed the broken glass that covered her step.

"Where did that come from?" Betty gasped.

Harold looked up at the stairwell window ten feet above the door.

"Looks like someone chucked a rock through the window up there."

Permelia shook her head.

"My day is complete."

She slipped her key into the lock and opened the door. A rock wrapped in paper lay at the base of the stairs. She picked it up and unwrapped the paper.

leaVe

it read in the familiar letters cut and pasted from a magazine. She handed the note to Harold.

"My day is complete," she said again.

◆━━◆

Permelia filled her teakettle with water.

"You two go sit in the living room, and I'll bring the tea in when it's ready."

"My offer still stands," Harold said when she joined them a few minutes later.

"I appreciate your offer, I really do, but I'm sure this is not related to what happened today. I've been getting these notes ever since I moved here. I really think it's a prank."

Harold sipped his tea.

"I hope you're right."

Chapter 41

Permelia and Betty sat on the deck the next morning watching the city wake up while they sipped their tea. Betty held her cup with both hands and blew across the surface to cool its contents.

"It's so peaceful up here, watching everything come to life."

"It is." Permelia spread strawberry cream cheese on her bagel. "Too bad we can't stay up here all day."

"I've been thinking. Do you think Mark Murphy killed Eideard?"

"I don't know. In my mind, killers are crazy and out of control, but that's not based on anything real. I suppose someone might appear completely normal right up until they kill. Mr. Murphy was really upset about his book. Maybe it's worth killing for."

"What if they never figure out who killed him?"

"Let's not go there."

They sipped their tea in silence. Finally, Permelia stood up.

"I'm going inside to get my knitting. Want me to get yours?"

Betty did, and Permelia returned with her socks and Betty's scarf.

"I read somewhere that knitting is the only thing that puts your brain into theta waves. And the only other activity that does that is when highly trained monks meditate."

Betty laughed.

"And these theta waves? They're supposed to be a good thing?"

Permelia started knitting.

"That was the implication. I'm about to find out."

<hr/>

Betty held her scarf up for Permelia to inspect.

"This looks great," Permelia said. "Your cables are very uniform."

"I don't know about that, but my thetas have been waving. I haven't thought about anything but my stitches for the last hour."

Permelia's cell phone rang as she was about to start her next row.

"Yes, hi, Eddie. Ben is staying with my neighbor, but he's anxious to see you." She paused and listened. "Eleven o'clock will be fine." She pressed the end button. "Eddie is finally back and got our messages. He's coming over at eleven."

"Ben will be happy to see his brother."

"I'd better call Wilma and let them know,"

<hr>

Harold was on Permelia's porch peering up at the broken window when she opened the door to let Ben in.

"Is Eddie here?" he asked.

"Not yet, honey, but Fenton's upstairs."

He grinned and ran up. Permelia continued down.

"Harold, you didn't need to come over here on a Sunday just to clean this up."

He stopped working and leaned on the broom he'd brought in case any glass had fallen outward.

"I know I didn't, but I wanted to make sure things were okay over here."

She smiled and put her hands on the broom.

"I'm fine, if that's what you're asking."

His cheeks flushed.

"If you must know, I feel a certain amount of responsibility for putting you in harm's way. If you'd never moved here, you'd never have met Betty, which led to your assault and kidnapping."

"That's ridiculous. I could have rented an apartment elsewhere and met Betty at the supermarket or coffee shop or anywhere. None of this is your fault."

"Still, I'll understand if you want to move somewhere safer."

"Please, don't you start, too. It's hard enough convincing my eldest daughter that I'm not disabled just because I'm past sixty-five years old."

He smiled.

"I definitely don't want to be in the same category as your daughter."

"I raised eight children on a wheat ranch in the middle of nowhere. I don't scare easy. Now, I'd better get upstairs and see what mischief Ben and the cat are getting up to."

<hr>

Ben and Fenton were on the living room floor playing with a stray piece of yarn.

"Is Eddie here yet?" Ben asked again as he jumped up.

"Not yet, honey. It's still a few minutes until eleven."

At fifteen minutes after eleven, Eddie still hadn't arrived. Finally, the doorbell rang. Ben ran downstairs and opened the door, but it wasn't Eddie. Henri stood on the doorstep.

"Can you come hang out?"

Permelia, who had followed him, suggested, "I could call you when Eddie gets here. Will you be staying at your house?" she asked Henri.

"I was going to show Ben my new game."

Permelia looked to Ben.

"What do you think?"

He thought for a moment. "Okay, but call me as soon as he gets here."

The two kids turned and trotted across the parking lot.

Thirty minutes later, Permelia stood in her living room. Betty had gone across the street to talk to Red; and she'd done the breakfast dishes, cleaned Fenton's cat box, and run the vacuum over the rugs while her guest was gone. Eddie still hadn't arrived.

The downstairs door opened, and moments later Betty came in.

"How's Red doing?" Permelia asked her.

Betty crossed the room and plopped down on the sofa.

"He's convinced I should pull up stakes and go back to Ireland with him."

"Weren't you planning on moving there when your husband retired?"

"I was, and I'd still like to go, but not like this. It doesn't feel right to let these people chase me out of town. I'd always be looking over my shoulder. If I can go to Ireland, so can Mark Murphy or his minions. I need to see this through."

"Red's worried about your safety. And I'm not sure his idea is a bad one. You could always come back for Mark's trial."

"I told Red I'd think about it. Any word from Eddie?"

"Nothing. He said he'd be here by eleven, but now it's...what?" She looked at her watch. "Almost twelve, and not a word. Ben went down the street to hang out with a girl he knows from music school."

"Poor kid. Eddie is all he has left. He hasn't said anything about either of his sisters that I've heard."

"Me, either. I wish Eddie was a little more interested in him. Then again, maybe I'm selling him short. He just lost his parents, too."

"I suppose. And if I'm being honest, I'm probably more than a little judgmental, given our rather unique circumstances. Eddie can't be more than two or three years older than Red."

"Would you like to go for a walk? I'm tired of being held hostage by Eddie, and I think Fenton will benefit from some exercise. I'll leave a note on the door."

"That sounds good. Let me go put on my tennis shoes."

Permelia wrote her note and put the harness on Fenton. She figured they could walk by Henri's treehouse and see how Ben was doing on their way.

"I've never seen a cat walk on a leash," Betty commented as they went down the stairs and into the parking lot.

"His breed is very active, and if you don't keep them exercised, they get into mischief—something he does on a regular basis even *with* walks. Still, I think it helps."

Ben and Henri dropped from the big oak tree as Permelia and Betty passed by.

"Can we come with you?" Ben asked.

"Yes, but Henri needs to check and make sure it's okay with her mom."

Henri ran to the house and disappeared inside, returning moments later.

"She says it's okay." Her braids bounced on her back as she skipped alongside Permelia. "Can I hold his leash?"

"After we cross the street," Permelia answered. "And be careful, hold it tight."

Henri and Ben walked with the cat in front of Permelia and Betty, chatting about Fenton and the possibility that he really was a wild cat.

"When do we lose that ability?" Betty asked.

"You mean that one where they can have their world falling in on them one minute and be skipping down the sidewalk the next?"

Betty smiled.

"Yeah, that one."

"After watching my group grow up, I'd have to say it's an inborn resilience that some kids have, and others don't. Some do acquire resilience as they experience life, but others are just more able to cope with life's rough patches. I think Ben is one of the resilient ones."

Betty sighed.

"Poor kid is going to have to be."

"Can we go to the park?" Ben asked.

"Not today, sweetie. There are too many dogs in the park on weekends. Let's go the opposite way up ahead and see what we find."

They walked two more blocks and turned around to come home. Fenton was still pouncing on bugs, but his pace had slowed.

"I'm going to go see if my brother's here yet," Ben told Henri when they got to her house. "Can we play your new game again tomorrow?"

"Sure," she said and raced up to her front porch. "See you tomorrow," she yelled before heading inside.

Permelia's note was still in place when they returned to the morgue. Ben threw his hands in the air then dropped them dramatically to his sides.

"Eddie's still not here?"

He crumpled to his knees and hugged Fenton, rubbing his face in the cat's fur.

"Let's go get something cool to drink, and you can call him," Permelia suggested.

Chapter 42

Ben called Eddie and came back into the kitchen where Permelia was peeling potatoes and cutting them into quarters before dropping them into a bowl of ice water.

His shoulders drooped.

"Eddie got tied up with something, so he can't come right now. He said he'd call later when he's free."

Permelia wiped her hands on her apron and pulled the boy into a hug.

"I'm sorry, sweetie. I know you miss your brother, but he's having trouble dealing with your parents' deaths, too. He might need to lean on a friend more his age right now. Does he have a girlfriend, maybe?"

Ben had started to cry and swiped at his eyes, nodding.

"I have an idea. Let me finish peeling these potatoes, and we'll go across to Wilma's and see if she can help us with something. Why don't you go wash your face with a cold cloth in the bathroom? Open the linen closet, and there's a stack of facecloths on the middle shelf."

She knew she was taking a bit of a gamble, assuming Wilma wanted to help and then would be able to do what she wanted. She had said she was better than average with computers, so just maybe she could help Ben out.

* * *

Wilma ushered them into her kitchen, where she'd set out glasses and a pitcher of iced tea.

"Help yourself and then tell me what you need."

Permelia filled glasses for herself and Ben.

"You said you were pretty good with computers," she started.

"I am," Wilma agreed.

"Could you find Ben's sister and rig up a face-to-face call?"

"That shouldn't be too hard. Ben, you know where she's working, right?"

"She's in Africa," he answered.

Wilma and Permelia smiled.

"Honey, do you know which country?" Permelia asked him.

"I'm pretty sure it's Uganda. She's with the Peace Corps, I think."

"That helps," Wilma said. "Give me a few minutes. Let me see what I can find."

She left the kitchen, going through the parlor and farther into the large house. She returned fifteen minutes later; and Permelia was all but certain she hadn't searched on her computer to find the info but instead had called one of her mysterious contacts.

"Got it," she said. "We can call her this evening."

Ben's lower lip started to quiver. Wilma reached out and patted his hand.

"It's after midnight there. Your sister might not appreciate it if we wake her up. We'll call her at nine p.m., how about that?"

"Okay, I guess," he said.

Permelia thought for a moment.

"What about your other sister? Are you allowed to visit her?"

"Yeah, I think the place she stays likes that, but my mom didn't want her to be a bad influence, so she never took me."

Wilma smiled.

"As it happens, Ben and I looked up the place she stays last night. He wanted to see what it was like. I can get the number, if you want." She got up and went back to her office again. Returning in a few minutes, she handed him a piece of paper and pointed him to her telephone.

"You'll probably have to talk to a receptionist first. Tell her who you want to talk to."

He looked skeptical.

"Go ahead," Permelia urged him.

He had made the connection, had a brief conversation, and hung up. His cheeks were pink.

"They let me talk to her. She has to ask her floor supervisor if she can have visitors today, and she'll call back. She says she thinks it'll be okay, though."

Ben paced while Wilma and Permelia chatted. Wilma watched him cross the room.

"Was that the good doctor I saw hanging around your door this morning?"

Permelia sighed.

"Someone threw a rock with a note wrapped around it through the stairwell window. Harold is worried all the nonsense is too much for me to handle."

Wilma grinned.

"That's very sweet. And having someone after you *is* a little worrisome."

"I know I should be worried, but it just has the earmarks of a juvenile prank. In fact, there's something familiar about it I can't put my finger on."

Wilma shook her head.

"If you say so. You could put a camera on that doorstep. Maybe one of those doorbell cameras."

"If I can't figure it out, I will," she promised. "Now, how's your knitting coming along?"

Wilma brought her scarf out, and Permelia examined it. Wilma had dropped a stitch two rows down, and Permelia again showed her how to correct it.

"Keep going," she said, "You're making good progress. Now, I'm making a big batch of potato salad, and I was thinking I could bake a pan of chicken to feed everyone, if that's okay."

"That sounds perfect," Wilma agreed. "I can pick some greens and tomatoes and cucumbers from my garden and make a big salad to go with."

The phone rang. Wilma answered, and held it out to Ben. He listened then covered the receiver with his hand.

"Can we go visit around four?"

Permelia glanced at her watch.

"Perfect," she said, and he finished his call. "Come on, Ben, we have some shopping and cooking to do."

<hr />

They had to hustle, but Permelia got the chicken bought and baked, the potatoes boiled, along with a few eggs, for the potato salad. She would assemble it after the potatoes had a chance to cool.

"Do you think she'll like the flowers I bought her?" Ben asked when they were in the car and headed for Silver's residential treatment facility.

"You said she likes flowers, and you picked a pretty bouquet. She should love it."

Silver was waiting in the lobby area when they arrived; she ran up and hugged Ben as soon as he came through the door. She grinned at him.

"You remembered." She looked at Permelia. "I love flowers."

They stood there looking at each other, smiling, as if none of them knew what to do next. A tall, slender woman in jeans and a white long-sleeved shirt joined them.

"Silver, why don't you and your brother go to the kitchen and ask the cook for a vase for your flowers?"

Ben followed his sister down a hall and disappeared. The woman turned to Permelia.

"My name is Janet Brown. Could I talk to you for a minute?"

"You can, but I have to tell you, I'm not related to Ben in any way. I'm merely a friend."

"I have to make a very difficult decision regarding Silver, given that both of her parents have passed away. I'm just looking for any information that might help."

"I've only known Ben for a few weeks; I don't know Silver at all."

"I hope I can trust you to be discrete. I could lose my job for even talking about this."

"Maybe you shouldn't, then," Permelia cautioned her.

"Look, Sylvia and I were both in Kappa Kappa Gamma at university; otherwise, Silver would have been removed a year or more ago."

"Why is that?" Permelia prompted.

"First and foremost, Silver doesn't need to be here. Sylvia reported a lot of behavioral problems that frankly, we've never observed. She doesn't need to be in residential treatment. But more important, Silver's account is seriously in arrears. I hate that money has to enter the equation, but Silver doesn't qualify for a scholarship because her need for services is minimal to nonexistent."

"What happens to her in a case like this?"

"We contacted the family lawyer, but the parents didn't specify what should happen to any minor children in the event both parents died. We contacted Sylvia's parents, but as Silver is adopted from a foreign country, they aren't interested in taking guardianship. Ed's mother lives in Ireland, so that isn't an option.

"Our next step is to contact the older siblings to see if they can provide a home for her. We've been unable to reach the sister in Africa and are waiting for a response to our message to the brother."

"I can see why you're feeling pressured."

"I've talked the board into letting her stay until the end of the month as a bereavement gesture, but then, if we can't locate a relative, she becomes a ward of the state."

"Foster care?" Permelia asked.

"Foster care," Janet said grimly. She sighed. "Can I get you a bottle of water?"

"I think I need one."

Janet led her into an alcove off the main lobby that was furnished with chairs and a small refrigerator. She retrieved two bottles of water from the fridge and handed one to Permelia.

"What's going to happen to Silver's younger brother?" she asked and sat down.

Permelia sat down opposite her.

"I don't really know. We've managed to reach his brother Eddie with not much success, and we're going to call Tiffany in Uganda tonight."

"Could you ask them to call me regarding Silver?"

"I can do that."

They sat in silence for a few minutes, then Janet stood.

"I'd better check on the kids."

"I'll join you, if that's okay. I need to see how Ben's doing."

"No problem, the kitchen is down the hall."

Chapter 43

arold's car was still in the parking lot when Ben and Permelia returned. She gave Ben the keys.

"Will you go up and check on Fenton? I'm going to see if Dr. Grace wants to come to dinner."

She walked around to the front entrance and, finding it locked, rang the buzzer. Harold smiled when he opened the door.

"Is everything okay?" he asked.

Permelia felt a long-forgotten sensation in her stomach. Could that be butterflies? It had been so long since she'd felt anything like it. Had Michael ever looked at her like that? She wasn't sure.

Their relationship had been about working together to make a success of their farm, and to provide children. If romance had been a little lacking, she'd always thought her babies made up for it. They loved her unconditionally—at least until they grew up.

She wondered if Michael looked at the young nubile Heather like this man was looking at her.

Harold reached out and touched her arm.

"Are you okay," he asked, his concern evident.

"I'm sorry, I'm a little distracted today," Her cheeks felt hot. "Things are fine enough. I noticed your car when Ben and I came in. We're going over to Wilma's to eat and wondered if you want to join us. I baked chicken and made potato salad, and Wilma's making a salad with vegetables from her garden."

"Can I bring something? I just restocked our freezer with Tillamook ice cream and before you ask, it's a different freezer. On difficult days, we find ice cream helps."

"I think that would be very welcome."

"What time is dinner?"

"I'm not sure when we'll eat, but I'm going to go over to Wilma's in about an hour. Would that work?"

"That sounds great. I'll see you in an hour."

As she walked around to her door, she made a mental note to be a little more guarded with her thoughts when she was around the good doctor. She'd just gotten out of a bad relationship, and she had no business thinking the thoughts she'd had on the porch about a man she'd only just met.

⊬⊱⊰⊹

Betty had left a note on the kitchen table saying she and Red were going to go do some shopping and would meet them at Wilma's. Permelia told Ben she was going to put her feet up and rest a little bit, and he asked if he could do the same on the sofa with Fenton. It wasn't quite the quiet time she'd envisioned, but when she looked at his sweet face, and thought about all he'd been through, she couldn't say no.

She sat on her bed, her feet propped on a pillow, and leafed through the latest copy of *Interweave Knits* magazine. She listened for sounds from the living room; and when all was quiet, she slipped out of her room and tiptoed through the kitchen to peek around the wall.

Ben and Fenton were curled around each other, sound asleep. She tiptoed back to her room, set an alarm on her phone, and was asleep before her head hit her pillow.

⊬⊱⊰⊹

"Can I leave a note on the door for Eddie?" Ben asked her when nap time was over.

Permelia handed him a notepad and pencil. He wrote a simple message and took the masking tape she gave him.

Dr. Grace was waiting in the parking lot, an insulated bag over one arm.

"Can I help carry something?"

Permelia was carrying the chicken in a covered baking dish with the potato salad balanced on top.

"Can you take the bowl?"

He did, and they waited while Ben taped his note on the door.

Wilma was waiting at the big oak doorway when they crossed the street.

"Come on in, the gang's all here." She stepped aside and waved them in.

Ben went up to his room, and Betty watched until he was out of earshot. She turned to Permelia.

"Did you learn anything from Ben's sister?"

191

Permelia slid the chicken into the oven and set it on warm.

"We didn't learn much from Silver, but the social worker gave me an earful."

Wilma stopped what she was doing and came over.

"What did she say?"

"I tried to get her to save her story for a more appropriate person, but she insisted on talking to me," Permelia said.

"But what did she say?" Wilma pressed.

"First, she said Silver didn't really need to be there. Sylvia described behavior problems that the clinic didn't observe. The social worker let her stay as a favor to her sorority sister, Sylvia. Second, she said Silver's account was seriously in arrears. She managed to get the board to approve a few more weeks due to bereavement, but then Silver has to leave; and so far, they can't find anyone who wants her."

Betty put a hand over her mouth.

"That's terrible."

"Maybe the sister we're calling tonight will have some idea," Wilma said.

Permelia turned back to her potato salad and started taking the top off the large bowl.

"Let's hope so."

Harold cleared his throat.

"Where would you like the ice cream?"

Wilma took the bag from him. "Here, I'll put it in the freezer, and thanks for bringing it."

⊷――――⊶

Dinner had just started when the gate buzzer sounded. Wilma got up and went into the kitchen to look at the security screen.

"It's Eddie," she called and went out the back door to let him in.

Ben jumped up and ran to his brother as soon as he appeared in the dining room door.

"Eddie, you came." He turned to Permelia. "Can he have dinner with us?"

Permelia smiled.

"Of course."

Wilma retreated to the kitchen, returning a moment later with a plate and silverware. She set it at the table next to Ben's place. Eddie smiled gratefully and sat down.

"Sorry I'm late, little man. I had to meet the insurance adjusters at our house."

"It's okay," Ben said, "We went and saw Silver."

Eddie closed his eyes, finally opening them as he blew out a breath.

"I haven't even thought about Silver. How is she handling everything?" Ben's face became serious.

"She's scared. She doesn't know what will happen to her."

Eddie was silent.

"What *is* going to happen to Silver?" Ben asked in a tiny voice.

"I don't know. I need to talk to Tiffany so we can figure it out."

Ben brightened.

"We're going to do a computer call tonight at nine."

"Sweet," Eddie said. "We should probably eat this great-looking food now. We can talk more about the future after dinner."

Permelia was relieved. She wanted a chance to talk to Eddie without Ben to find out what the possibilities actually were. Eddie was young himself, and she wasn't sure he would present whatever the answer was in a way that wouldn't traumatize Ben. She also wasn't quite sure Eddie was going to be able to take two adolescent siblings home to his studio apartment.

"This chicken is wonderful," Eddie told her when he'd sampled a bite.

"Thank you," she said and attended to finishing her meal.

⊷───⊷

Red and Eddie got up after dinner and cleared the dishes from the table.

"What sort of work do you do?" Red asked as they worked.

Eddie gave him a long look before answering.

"I'm in real estate. I've got my license and was learning the business from my mother."

"I'm sorry," Red said.

"Ben said you're still in school." It was a statement, not a question.

"I'm in graduate school in Ireland."

"You'll be returning soon?"

"Unfortunately, yes. Classes start again in a couple of weeks. I'm trying to talk my mother into going to Ireland with me."

"I wish I had another country to escape to," Eddie said, quietly enough that Ben couldn't hear him. He didn't need to worry. Ben was occupied grilling Harold about dead bodies.

"It's such a nice evening," Wilma said. "Why don't we go outside while we wait for call time. I've got coffee or tea or lemonade."

They all made their choices and retreated outside.

⊷───⊷

Permelia stood in the doorway of Wilma's computer room once Ben and Eddie were settled in front of the monitor. The rest of the group moved into the parlor.

"Tiffany," Ben shouted as soon as her image appeared.

"How are you doing, Bennie-boy?"

Ben's eyes filled with tears.

"I need you to come home."

"Me, too," Eddie chimed in. "I need help with all this stuff."

Tiffany smiled at her brothers.

"It's so good to see your faces. I'm working on getting home. I'm the lead engineer on a project that's bringing water to a whole village. They need clean water to be able to fight the Ebola outbreak. The Peace Corps is getting a replacement engineer as fast as they can, but the project is at a critical point, and I can't leave until he gets here. It should only be a couple more days. Then it'll take me a day or two to get back."

"Grandmother doesn't want Silver to come stay with them. Any ideas?"

"I've been thinking about that. I'll email Mom's attorney and see what we have to do to get custody of the kids."

Ben visibly relaxed.

"You'll stay home when you get here?"

She smiled.

"I won't lie. I was hoping to finish this water project, but yes, I'll come home and do whatever it takes to get custody of you kids. Eddie," she asked. "Do you know anything about Mom's and Dad's estate?"

"Not really."

"Okay, I'll figure it out when I get home. Hey, Mom told me we have a new half-brother. Have you met him?"

"He's here," Ben said. "And he's really cool. He's Irish. I'll go get him."

He jumped up and went to the parlor, grabbing Red by the hand and leading him to the computer room.

"Meet our sister Tiffany," he said.

Tiffany smiled.

"You definitely look like an Anderson," she said.

"And you a FitzAndreu," Red answered, his Irish lilt apparent.

"Touché," she said, still smiling. "I look forward to meeting you in person." She looked to her left, off-screen. "I have to go."

"Bye," Ben said.

"Let us know when you've made your arrangements." Eddie added.

The screen went blank.

Chapter 44

E ddie didn't sit down when they returned from the computer.
"Thanks again for dinner. I spent all day at my parent's house, and I've still got hours of work tonight, setting up a couple of new listings I got and transferring my mother's clients over." He patted Ben on the back. "Be good. And let me know if you talk to Tiff or Silver again."

Ben followed him into the kitchen where Wilma unlocked the door.

"Bye, Eddie," he said.

Eddie raised his hand in a wave without turning around.

Red stood up when Ben came back in.

"Let's get you upstairs and into the shower. You can read a while, but you need to get in bed."

"Can I have ice cream first?"

"Sure," Red said and went to the refrigerator to get the ice cream.

•◄───►•

"Okay, you need to brush your teeth and hit the hay," Red said when Ben was finished.

"Will you come with me?" Ben asked him.

Red took Ben's bowl and put it in the sink."

"I'll help you get started."

Permelia watched them leave the room.

"He's really good with kids."

Betty beamed.

"He's an Eagle Scout, and he did a project working with underprivileged kids. He'll make a good father someday."

Harold sipped his lemonade.

"You must be very proud."

"It's too bad Eid couldn't be here to see him finish college, marry, and raise a family." A tear slipped down her cheek, and Wilma silently handed her a tissue.

"It's interesting how differently Eid's child turned out—from what we've seen, anyway," Wilma said.

"I think it's a testament to the different mothering they got," Permelia said. "Betty has done a fine job with Red, and Sylvia..." She trailed off as Red came back into the room.

Red looked at the ceiling, as if he could see through the floor to where they heard the faint sound of the shower running.

"I've got to get back upstairs to tuck him in, but while he's in the shower, I wanted to tell you what he just said when we were gathering his jammies."

"Don't keep us in suspense," Betty urged him.

"He asked me how insurance worked." He stopped and listened to make sure water was still running. "I asked him why he was asking, and he said he was confused about Eddie being at their house with the insurance adjuster. He said he overheard his mother and Eddie fighting after the house burned because his mom said she'd let the house insurance lapse a few months ago."

"That *is* interesting," Permelia said.

They heard the pipes creak as Ben shut the water off.

"I better go."

Harold looked at Permelia.

"What do you think Eddie was really doing at the uninsured family home all day?"

Permelia set her empty glass down.

"Assuming he *was* at the family home, my guess would be he's selling everything that isn't nailed down."

"He's a realtor," Wilma said. "Maybe he's getting it ready to show. In that location, they'll still get a good price, even as-is."

"If it isn't mortgaged to the hilt," Harold added.

"On that happy thought," Wilma said with a grin. "Anyone ready for ice cream?"

⊷──⊶

Permelia and Harold scooped ice cream into bowls and carried them to the kitchen table. Wilma warmed a jar of chocolate sauce in the microwave and set it beside a spray can of whipped cream in the center of the table.

Red returned to the kitchen as they brought the last bowl to the table. He nodded as Harold handed it to him. His mother slid the chocolate to him.

"How do you think the boy is doing?" she asked. "Has he said anything you can share?"

Red spooned chocolate sauce on his ice cream.

"He just went on about how happy he was to see his sisters today, other than that bit about the insurance."

"Children that age can be pretty resilient..." Permelia's cell phone rang before she could finish. She glanced at the screen. "Excuse me, I need to take this. It's my daughter." She got up and went into the kitchen. "Jennifer, what's up?"

"I thought I'd check in on you, now that you've been at that horrible apartment for two weeks, to see if you've come to your senses yet."

"My apartment is not horrible, and for your information, I'm settling in quite nicely. I actually just finished dinner at a neighbor's house."

"Katy told me you've been having trouble. And I'm not talking about the woman whose husband was murdered. I don't know why you insist on befriending a person like that."

"Honey, it's not her fault her husband was killed."

"Anyway, Katy said someone has been harassing you—spraying graffiti on your door and breaking a window. It would be so much safer for you to live in a group setting."

"I don't want to argue with you, Jen, but I'm not moving. I'm perfectly safe in my apartment. And Fenton loves it."

Permelia could envision her daughter rolling her eyes.

"Don't even get me started on that creature you insist on living with."

"Listen, honey, I need to get back to my dinner. Did you have anything else to tell me?"

"Yes, I was calling to see if you wanted to come over for Bea's birthday a week from Wednesday."

"I'd love to. Let me know if I can bring anything."

"If it isn't too much, Bea was hoping you could make that lemon blueberry cake she loves so much."

"I would be happy to make her a cake."

"I'll send a car for you."

"Thanks, but I'll drive myself. Bye, Jen, love you." She hung up before her daughter could say anything else.

Harold looked up when she returned to the kitchen.

"Is everything okay?"

She smiled. "As okay as it ever is with my eldest."

Betty cleared her throat loudly, and everyone else stopped talking.

"You all have been so wonderful with your hospitality and all your support, but I think it's time for Red and I to move back to our house."

Harold set his spoon down in his bowl.

"What do the police think about that?"

"They're okay with it. Mark Murphy admitted he was responsible for the break-in, although he claims he didn't do it personally. He swears he was just looking for his book, and had nothing to do with Eid's murder. He makes the good point that he'd never kill Eid as long as he didn't know where his book was."

"Makes you wonder what's in that book," Wilma commented.

Red looked away from the table, his eyes cast downward.

"What is it, son?" Betty asked.

"I'm pretty sure *I* have the book," he said.

"What?" Permelia and Betty said at the same time."

"When I first got home, I found this leather-bound book wrapped in the old pajama pants I left in my bedroom dresser. I couldn't make heads or tails of it. It was a bunch of numbers in some sort of code. One of my schoolmates in Ireland is really good with codes, so I sent it to him to see if he could figure out what it meant.

"Since Dad really liked baseball and played fantasy sports, I thought it was probably statistics about that, and he'd put it in code so his buddies wouldn't know what he was up to if they were watching games together.

"By the time the break-in happened, and we learned about the book Dad's boss was looking for, it was already in the mail."

Wilma leaned forward. "Have you heard anything?"

He shook his head. "Since I thought we were dealing with fantasy baseball, I told him there was no rush."

"Could you check with him, and maybe get him to prioritize the project?" Permelia suggested.

"Of course," Red said. "I'll email him now." He pulled his phone from his pocket and started tapping.

Harold pulled out his phone as well.

"I think I'll send Liam a message. He'll want to know the book's been found. Depending on what those numbers actually are, they could provide Mark Murphy with a motive to commit murder."

"Back to my original statement," Betty said. "While we've very much appreciated the hospitality of Permelia and Wilma, I think it's time to return to our own home."

"What about Ben?" Red asked immediately.

"That's a good question," Permelia said. "We don't really know who has custody of him. Eddie could make a claim, I suppose, but he doesn't seem very interested."

"What about the sister?" Harold asked her.

Permelia twirled her spoon in her fingers.

"Tiffany said she would do everything she could to get custody of Ben and Silver, but she won't be home for a week, probably."

Wilma pressed her lips together.

"What if Ben and Red stay put until she arrives? And if Permelia and Betty don't mind, Betty should stay close by, too."

"Fine with me," Permelia said. "And if you wanted, Betty, you could go to your house during the day to work on whatever projects you've got going."

Harold put his phone back in his pocket.

"I agree it's a good idea for everyone to stay put. I think the boy needs the stability, at this point. And we don't want to be in a position where we have to ask who has custody."

"I guess if Permelia doesn't mind I could stay put for another few days," Betty said, "but I'm going home tonight to do laundry, collect the mail and water my plants. With Mark Murphy in jail, I'll be perfectly safe, and I'll come back in the morning before Ben even knows I've been gone."

Permelia stood up and started collecting ice cream dishes.

"Now that's settled, I'd better go see what Fenton's been up to in my absence."

Chapter 45

Permelia and Harold had just reached the morgue parking lot when his phone rang. He answered it, spoke briefly, and with a sigh slid it back in his pocket.

"No rest for the weary. A couple of bodies have been found across town, and they suspect murder."

"Shall I make you a thermos of coffee for the road?"

He smiled at her.

"That would be nice. I fear it's going to be a long night."

"Can I do anything else?"

"I appreciate it, but no. I'll stay on the scene and then accompany the bodies back here. Coffee will be enough."

He followed her to the apartment and up the stairs. They could hear Fenton yowling before Permelia got the door open.

"I know you're feeling neglected," she said as she brushed past him and filled the water kettle. Harold picked him up and scratched his ears while Permelia ground coffee beans, set up her large pour-over cone with a filter, and balanced it on her stainless-steel coffee thermos.

"Do you always grind your own coffee?" Harold asked her.

"I do now. On the ranch we always had an industrial pot brewing with whatever was on sale in the three-pound cans at the grocery store. When I started the fiber co-op, I decided we needed an upgrade. It was our little secret—the men never came into our building. I ordered beans online along with some really nice teas."

The kettle whistled, and Permelia poured the water, watching as it slowly trickled into the thermos, adding more water as it went.

"Do you want sugar or cream?"

"I think I better go with black for this trip."

She removed the filter cone, wiped the sides of the thermos, and screwed first the cap and then the cup that covered it.

"Here you go. Can I send anything else? Cookies? Scones?"

"Maybe just a few of your chocolate chip cookies."

She loaded a bag and sent him on his way. She watched out the kitchen window until she saw the medical examiner's van pull out of the lot and into the dark night.

Permelia woke when she heard the van return and the unloading bay doors open. Dawn was just starting to light the eastern sky. She used the bathroom and went back to bed, but sleep evaded her, aided by Fenton. He sat on the pillow next to hers and poked his paw in her ear. She pushed him away, so he moved to the end of the bed and started pouncing on her feet. She tried calling him to her and petting him in the hope he'd fall asleep, but he wasn't having it. She wasted thirty minutes, by which time sunlight was filtering through her window.

"Okay, you win," she said in disgust, but then she couldn't help but smile as he grabbed her left slipper and ran across the room before she could stop him. She pulled on her bathrobe and brushed her teeth and found her slipper sitting on Fenton's dish when she reached the kitchen.

She laughed.

"Message received. You're ready for your breakfast."

While he ate, she mixed up a batch of cream scones and put them in the oven. Fenton was still batting pieces of dry food around the kitchen floor when her scones came out to cool. She never understood why some mornings he was able to eat his food like a normal cat while other times an extended battle with each kibble was required.

She noticed several police cars in the parking lot along with Harold's car. Whatever had happened would likely be on the morning news.

She fixed a cup of tea and took it with a warm scone out to her deck. She didn't mind having Betty stay with her, but was enjoying having the place to herself.

She sipped her tea and watched as a man came out of the house next to Henri's, dressed in business wear, and walked to the corner bus stop. A young man with four dogs on leashes walked up the block—clearly the neighborhood dog walker. A woman dressed in maroon nurse's scrubs joined the man at the bus stop. In spite of Jennifer's misgivings, she was pretty sure she was going to like her new neighborhood.

She finished eating her scone and heard Fenton batting at the door. He would be happy when Robert finished the catio but for now, he was going to insist on going for a walk.

"Allright," she told him as she came back inside. "Let me get dressed, and we'll go out."

Henri was in her treehouse when Permelia and Fenton walked by.

"Can I come walk with you?" she asked.

"Ask your mother, and if she says it's okay, you can join us."

"She won't care," Henri assured her.

"Humor me and ask anyway."

Henri hopped out of the tree and skipped to the front door.

"Mom," she hollered through the screen door.

Her mother answered, and Henri went inside. Permelia guessed Eleanor had instructed her daughter about the need to make requests without shouting and face-to-face.

Henri returned a moment later.

"She says I can come as long as I'm not making a pest of myself."

Permelia smiled.

"You're not being a pest. I think Fenton enjoys your company."

"Can I hold his leash?"

"Sure," Permelia said and handed it over.

They strolled down the block, stopping every few steps to wait for Fenton to poke at a stick or a leaf, or pounce on an imaginary foe.

Henri studied the cat intently.

"You know how you told me I shouldn't spy on people from my treehouse?"

Permelia looked at her.

"Yes, I do." She waited for Henri to elaborate and was beginning to think she wasn't going to, when Henri looked up at her.

"What if I *accidentally* saw something?"

"I guess that would depend on how accidental it was and what, exactly, you saw."

Henri thought for a moment.

"You know the other day when someone threw a rock through the window over your stairs?"

"I do. Go on. Did you see who threw the rock?"

"I didn't mean to."

Permelia stopped and turned to look at her fully.

"Henri, this is an exception. If you know who broke my window, tell me. Right now."

"It was Beatrice's mom."

"My daughter, Jennifer? Are you sure?" Permelia's voice rose and she could feel the blood rushing to her face.

Henri's eyes got round, and her face paled. Permelia put a hand on her arm.

"Honey, I'm sorry I shouted. Thank you for telling me. This is a case where it was good to tell someone what you saw. Now, you're sure it was Jennifer?"

Permelia knew it was the truth before Henri nodded. She realized what had been nagging at her memory since the first note—that she'd seen a note made from cut-out magazine words before. When Jennifer was in the fifth grade, she'd sent similar notes to a boy she had a crush on. It had been easy for him to figure out who the sender was, since she'd taken a piece of paper from the recycle bin to paste her note on, and hadn't realized the back side of the paper had the ranch address on it.

"I'm sorry I told you," Henri said. "Now you're upset. I didn't mean to upset you. I just thought you'd want to know."

"Henri, you did the right thing. Yes, I'm upset, but not at you. I'm unhappy that my daughter resorted to such childish pranks to try to scare me into moving into the senior living home she picked out for me."

"You're not old enough to live in one of those places," Henri said. "My mom's grandma lives in one, but she's ninety. And it smells funny there. Plus, they wouldn't let you have Fenton there."

"Don't worry. Fenton and I are quite happy right where we are. I am going to have a talk with Jennifer, though, and don't worry—I won't tell her how I know it's been her."

Fenton meowed at the sound of his name.

"Okay. I'll deal with that when I get home. We can enjoy our walk first."

Henri smiled and skipped a few steps, Fenton trotting along beside her.

Permelia silently chided herself for not realizing it was Jennifer sooner. She was the only one who was disturbed by her mom living over the morgue. No one else cared. She sighed. It was not going to be a fun conversation.

Henri giggled, breaking into Permelia's musing. Fenton had climbed into a small tree and was batting at a leaf. He could be a real clown when he wanted to, and Permelia was pretty sure he had sensed Henri's distress and was trying to cheer her up.

"Come on," she told him. "We need to get on with our exercise."

"Can we take him to the park?" Henri asked.

"Sure, it should be quiet this early on a Monday morning." She lifted him out of the tree, and they headed to the park.

Chapter 46

Permelia poured Fenton a fresh bowl of water and tossed a few treats on the kitchen floor. She wouldn't make him bat his treat ball around since he'd had a longer-than-usual walk. When he was settled in the living room chair, she pulled her phone from her pocket and dialed Jennifer's number. It went to the message machine.

"Jennifer, I expect to see you at my apartment as soon as you get this message. Don't try to tell me you've got appointments all day. Cancel. And bring your checkbook."

She ended the call and settled down at her spinning wheel in the living room. Her doorbell rang an hour later, and she went downstairs, ready to give her daughter a piece of her mind.

"Je—" She stopped when she realized it was Red standing on her porch, not her eldest daughter.

"Is this a bad time?" he asked.

"No, I'm expecting my daughter sometime today, but I'm not sure when. Come on in. I baked cream scones this morning. Can I tempt you?"

"Indeed, you can. There's nothing better than a fresh-baked scone."

"Eaten with tea or coffee?"

"Tea, please."

"Go on into the living room, and I'll bring it in when it's ready."

Red was sitting on the sofa, Fenton curled on his lap, when she carried in a tray laden with a pot of tea, cups, sugar and cream, napkins, and a plate with three scones on it.

"This looks fantastic." He poured his tea, stirred in a spoonful of sugar, and picked up a scone with a napkin. Permelia poured her own tea and waited for Red to settle in and tell her why he was here.

"You're probably wondering why I'm here," he started. "I found something out, and I want an impartial opinion before I tell my mother or anyone else."

"Are you sure I'm the right person to be hearing whatever it is?"

"Positive. I haven't known you long, but with all that's been going on, you haven't resorted to hysterics, tears, or anything else."

"Go on, then." Permelia sipped her tea to prepare for whatever he was about to reveal.

"The book," he said. "The one Mark Murphy was looking for. The one I sent to Ireland to have my friend look at. My friend just answered the email I sent last night." He hesitated.

"Don't leave me in suspense," Permelia urged.

Red looked down at the floor.

"If my friend is right, having two families wasn't my father's only secret. My friend says he's pretty sure the company my father worked for was cheating on their taxes. They were underreporting their income. They paid taxes on only a fraction of the revenue from all their businesses. My dad had to keep two sets of books—one that reflected what they were willing to pay taxes on and his book that kept track of their actual income."

"He was cooking the books?"

Red nodded.

"That isn't the worst of it. It looks like Dad was the only one who really knew how much money the corporation was making. That being the case, he was apparently skimming money from the untaxed funds."

"I guess that explains how he afforded two families. He must have been pulling down a pretty good salary, being the top financial guy at the corporation," Permelia said, more to herself than to Red. "And according to my daughter, Sylvia was one of the top realtors in the city. Why would he need to resort to stealing?"

Red took a bite of scone and followed it with a sip of tea.

"Maybe it wasn't about the money. If Mark Murphy forced him into cooking the books, maybe he skimmed the money as payback."

"I wonder if that's why he was killed. We've been assuming Mark Murphy wouldn't kill him without first getting the book, but with your dad dead, there's no one to report the tax evasion. And if the book is missing and heavily coded, maybe he decided to take his chances that no one would find it or be able to interpret it if they did."

"What I don't understand is where the money went. The amount he was skimming was potentially substantial. Mom certainly didn't benefit. If Sylvia was so broke she stopped paying the insurance on her house, it doesn't sound like she was benefiting, either."

Permelia set her cup down on the coffee table.

"Sylvia's money woes mean she was spending more than she had, but that could still be a substantial amount. She might have been supporting her boyfriend. He certainly wasted no time in joining her at the hotel, at least according to Ben."

"I suppose if Dad was doing it just to spite Mark, he could have donated the money to a worthy cause."

Permelia smiled.

"I guess anything's possible."

She poured more tea into their cups, and they sipped in silence for a few minutes. Red picked up another scone.

"The real reason I came to you with all this is I need advice about what, if anything, to tell my mother."

Permelia let out a breath.

"That's a tough one. Ordinarily, I'd say honesty is the best policy, but I'm not sure what would be gained telling her, now that your dad is dead. Especially since you don't know where the skimmed money is, if there is any skimmed money. And that's a big if."

Red ran his hands through his hair.

"I wish my dad were here. He always knew what to do."

Permelia chose to not say anything to that, but she couldn't help thinking that Red's father was the reason for the problem in the first place. He clearly had been a very complicated man.

"If you want my advice, I'd hold off saying anything about the book or the possible money to anyone. If your friend's analysis is proved to be true, you'll have plenty of time to tell your mother then, if you think she needs to know. I do suggest you consider giving the book to the police."

"I'll have to think about that. If I leave the book in Ireland, no one need ever know what my dad was involved in."

"If you leave it there, Mark Murphy might never be held to account for his crimes."

"They have him on breaking-and-entering and for attacking you and my mom, and for burning Ben's house. That should be enough to put him away for a while."

Permelia gave him a long look.

"I know your parents raised you right. I'm sure you'll do the right thing. Now, would you like another scone?"

Red blushed.

"I suppose one more wouldn't hurt."

Permelia smiled and returned to the kitchen to refill the plate.

⊢──⊣

Red stood and picked up his plate and cup, carrying them to the kitchen.

"I told Ben I'd take him shopping. He hasn't been able to get anything from his parent's house since the fire. We're also going to go visit his dog at the boarding kennel. I'm a little worried that no one is paying the fee, so Mom and I decided we would. We don't want to risk anything happening to that little dog. Ben can't take one more loss."

"That's very kind of you."

"It's the least we can do. And he is family."

Permelia patted his arm.

"You are a good boy. Ben is lucky to have you as a brother."

Red blushed.

"I'd better get going."

Chapter 47

Permelia watched Red walk back to Wilma's and waited until she saw him and Ben drive away. She called Wilma to make sure it was okay to come for a visit.

"It's such a nice day, shall we sit outside?" Wilma said as she let Permelia in through the big oak door.

Permelia smiled.

"That sounds great."

"You can get seated, and I'll bring the tea out. I started the water as soon as I hung up."

Wilma returned with a tray with two steaming mugs, sugar, and a plate of oatmeal raisin cookies and set it on the table.

"What's on your mind?"

"I'm sure you noticed that Red came to visit me before he took Ben shopping. He was seeking advice, and I gave it to him, but I'm not sure I'm right, so I wanted to see what you think."

Wilma sipped her tea while she listened to Permelia relate what Red had told her. She set her cup down when Permelia finished.

"That *is* a tough call."

Permelia swallowed a bite of cookie.

"Part of me thinks Betty needs to know the cold, hard truth and deal with it, but the other part thinks she's had so much to deal with that one more thing might drive her around the bend."

"The money is a whole other problem," Wilma said. "If Mr. Murphy has been cheating the government out of tax money, someone needs to be held accountable. And they should be paid back."

"I'm not sure how you determine how much might be owed. All Red has is a coded book, and we don't know how accurate that is."

"The government will send auditors, but if the records have been falsified from the get-go, it could be hard to establish what the actual income of the businesses is," Wilma said.

Permelia sipped her tea and thought. Finally, she set her cup back on the table.

"What are you thinking?" Wilma asked her.

"I keep wondering about the stack of empty boxes Betty and I saw in Eid's garage. The one where he kept whichever car he wasn't driving, depending on which persona he was being."

"What about them?"

"Red mentioned that they looked like the boxes his dad sent to him in Ireland. Eid asked him to save them for him. For when he and Betty moved there. I can't help but wonder if those boxes were used to ship money he'd been skimming overseas. Not as cash, I'm guessing. Red did say the boxes were heavy for their size; I'm thinking they contained gold or silver or some other valuable but difficult-to-trace form of currency."

"Huh…I wonder if Sylvia's money problems were due to Eid cooking the family's books."

Permelia sat back in her chair.

"If he was channeling money from the Anderson accounts to Betty's, and Sylvia found out, that would give her motive to kill him."

Wilma took a bite of cookie and chewed it thoughtfully.

"True," she said finally. "But if she killed Eid, who killed her?"

"Well, that would be the question, wouldn't it?"

Permelia tipped her cup up but found it empty.

"I can heat more water," Wilma offered.

"That's okay. I need to get back home. I'm expecting my eldest daughter. With Henri's help, we've solved the mystery of who has been harassing me."

"Uh-oh. I'm guessing she wasn't going to give up on moving you to a senior residence."

Permelia shook her head.

"She always has been a strong-willed one. Now, back to my original question. What, if anything, do we tell Betty?"

"I'm not sure you have enough information to tell Betty anything. Think about it. Red found a book and sent it to a friend for interpretation. He made some assumptions when he sent it, but he has no proof the book belonged to his dad. Maybe Eid took the book from his boss and hid it in his home.

"And, for all we know, the gold, or whatever is in the boxes, was, in fact, money he took from his first family to fund his life in Ireland with his second family. Technically, transferring money from family one to family two isn't a crime—it's all his money."

Permelia stood up.

"You're right. We have been assuming the book was Eid's. Maybe it's not. In any case, I think the police need to end up with that book."

Wilma picked up their teacups and started for the kitchen.

"That we agree on."

Permelia picked up the empty cookie plate and followed her.

+-----+

"Jennifer," Permelia said.

"Mother," her daughter replied. "What's so important I had to cancel my afternoon appointment?"

"Let's sit down.

"I'll stand. I'm not going to be here that long."

"Sit. Down."

"Okay, already," Jennifer said, sounding more like her teen-aged self than the mother of two teen-aged children.

They both sat down in the living room, Permelia in her customary chair and Jennifer on the sofa. Permelia looked at her hands and took a deep calming breath.

"Jennifer, I know you've been worried about my choice of places to live." Jennifer started to speak, but Permelia held up a hand to silence her. "You've stated your objections, and I heard them, and then I made the choice to stay here. It is *my* choice, not yours. Now, as you know very well, I've been tormented since I've been here by a series of threatening notes and vandalism, including a broken window.

"This morning I found out from a twelve-year-old girl that my own daughter has been the one breaking my windows and painting threats on my door. I am going to have to tell my landlord that a grown woman is responsible for the damage and offer to pay for the repairs. After that, I may well have to go looking for another situation. And read my lips—I am not moving into a senior residence. I am so ashamed of you. Your father and I raised you better than that."

Jennifer hung her head.

"I'm sorry, Mother. I just felt very strongly that you'd be safer in a se-cure facility."

Permelia threw up her hands.

"Listen to you. I'm neither a child nor a criminal. I do not need to be in a 'secure facility'. There may come a time when I am unable to take care of myself, and at that point, I will go willingly to some sort of assisted-living facility. But I'm nowhere near that time.

"And for your information, both your father and I have paid into long-term care insurance for years. When the time to make that decision comes,

I've documented with our lawyer that your sister Lizzy, being a nurse, will make the decision with your brother Michael if your father or I are unable to make it. Your father may change that now, but that's his business."

Jennifer sank back into the sofa.

"You put Lizzy in charge?" she whispered.

"She is in charge of our medical power of attorney. She's a nurse. She's in a better position to evaluate medical conditions than you are. And clearly, my decision was the correct one, given your behavior."

Jennifer's eyes filled with tears.

"I'll pay for the damage."

"Good. I was hoping you would take responsibility for your behavior."

"I'm sorry, Mother. I just worry about you."

"I accept your apology, but I will expect better behavior from you in the future. Now, would you like a scone while you're here?"

Her daughter smiled.

"I'd love a scone."

Chapter 48

Permelia cleaned up the dishes from Jen's visit and paced around the apartment, too unsettled to sit and spin. Finally, she returned to the kitchen and looked out at the parking lot. The police cars were gone, save for Liam's unmarked car. Harold's car was in its usual spot. She thought about waiting until Liam left, but finally put half a dozen scones on a plate, covered it with plastic wrap and headed downstairs.

"Is Dr. Grace busy?" she asked the receptionist. "If he is, I can just leave these," she said, holding up the plate.

"You can go on back—he's in the break room with Detective James having coffee right now." The young woman smiled. "Those look good."

"Do you have a napkin?" Permelia asked and pulled up the edge of the plastic wrap. She slid a scone out and put it on the tissue the girl held up.

"Thanks, I'm Ella," the girl said and smiled again. "I think we're all going to like having you upstairs."

At least someone's glad I'm here, Permelia thought.

"Knock, knock," she said when she reached the open breakroom door. Harold stood up.

"Come on in. Can I fix you a cup of tea, or coffee?"

"Tea would be nice." She set the plate of scones on the table. "I brought you these." She removed the plastic wrap and slid the plate toward Detective James. "I thought you guys might need a little pick-me-up after being here most of the night."

Liam took a scone from the plate and took a bite. He closed his eyes briefly, savoring the flavor. Permelia smiled. Her scones tended to have that effect on people.

Harold set a teacup on the table while the water was boiling.

"This is very thoughtful, but I can't help thinking you've got something on your mind. If you wind that plastic wrap any tighter around your finger, I might have to surgically remove it."

Permelia dropped the rope of plastic wrap.

"I think I need some tea before I tell you."

Liam laughed. "That sounds ominous."

"It's more embarrassing than ominous," she said with a rueful smile.

Harold brought the kettle to the table, topped off Permelia's cup and held it up in front of Liam, silently asking if he wanted a refill, too. Liam shook his head, and Harold returned the kettle to the stove.

"Now, what's going on?"

Permelia cleared her throat.

"As I said, this is very embarrassing. I've discovered who has been vandalizing the property here and sending me threatening notes."

"Go on," Harold encouraged.

Permelia took a deep breath. "It turns out it's my daughter, Jennifer," she said in a rush.

Liam chuckled and stood up.

"I think you two can figure out a suitable restitution without my help." He picked up another scone and left.

"I am so sorry for my daughter's behavior," Permelia told Harold. "Of course, she will reimburse you for the cost of the repairs."

He reached across the table and took her hand.

"It's not your fault. And her heart was in the right place, however misguided her actions. She cares for you and is worried for your wellbeing."

"She has a funny way of showing it. I gave her a talking-to and told her she needed to not only repay the cost of repairs but also needed to come apologize in person."

"You're a tough one."

"With as many children as I had, I needed to be. I still can't believe Jennifer resorted to such childish behavior."

He squeezed her hand. "At least it's one less thing to worry about. "Any new developments with your house guest and her family?"

Permelia finished her tea and debated what, if anything, she should say.

"You don't have to tell me if it puts you in an awkward position."

She pressed her lips together. "It's just that it's not my story to tell."

"I understand. But just know that if you ever need to talk, I'm a good listener. And if you do tell me anything, I will keep it between us."

"I appreciate that, and I may take you up on it. For now, would you be willing to come with me to Sylvia and Ed's house?"

"What are you looking for there?"

"I'm curious. Red and Betty have been shopping for Ben, since he doesn't seem to have salvaged anything from the fire. That leaves me wondering if Ben is taking advantage of Red and Betty, or if someone told him his belongings were burned up."

Harold took their cups to the small sink and rinsed them, setting them on the drying mat.

"Who would have told him his stuff was gone?" he asked when he'd finished cleaning up.

"His mother or his brother, I suppose."

"I can't imagine his clothes and books would be worth selling, if that's what you're thinking."

"I'm thinking he's a child of privilege who probably had all the latest electronics—computers, tablets, music devices, and video games."

"I suppose. Or maybe something's going on at the house no one wanted him to see."

"That's what I was wondering. I know it's none of my business, but I'm curious."

Harold took his car keys from his pocket and jingled them. "One way to find out."

Permelia picked up the empty scone plate. "Let me get my purse."

⊷⊷

"Do you think the Anderson children—or at least the boys—could have conspired to kill their parents in order to inherit the estate or the insurance money?" Permelia wondered aloud as they drove out of the parking lot. "Assuming Ed and Sylvia had life insurance, that is."

Harold glanced at her then back at the road.

"Are you serious?"

"Only a little. I'd like to reassure myself that Ben is not scamming the FitzAndreus'—which I don't really believe he is—but I'd also like to see what Eddie's been up to at the house."

"No matter what we find, it won't tell us anything unless we know what's in the will. It's quite possible the house and its contents were left to him, in which case he has the right to do whatever he wishes. Even if it was left to all the children, with the older girl out of the country, Eddie would be the logical one to dispose of the contents and sell the house."

"Are you telling me it's none of my business?"

Harold smiled.

"I would never do that. I just don't want you to get your hopes up. No matter what we find, it may not tell us anything."

Permelia smiled to herself. She liked the way he said *us*.

The gates to the Anderson property were open, and a hand-lettered sign reading ESTATE SALE hung at an angle on the right-side gate panel. Harold pulled his car to the curb across the street and turned off the engine.

"Be honest," Permelia said, resting her hand on his arm. "am I sticking my nose in where it doesn't belong?"

He took a deep breath and was silent for a moment. "I'm trying to think of the best way to say this."

"Spit it out. If I shouldn't be here, let's go home."

"Hear me out. From the police point of view, you should let them do their job. You're in a unique position here, though.

"You have people staying with you and with Wilma who are in the middle of two murders. They may be innocent victims who deserve your help, or they may be part of a murder conspiracy involving some or all of them, in which case you could be in jeopardy. Given that, I think you are justified in attempting to find out what's going on. As long as you're careful and don't risk your own safety."

"The estate sale sign does make it seem like they're inviting the public in."

Harold pocketed his keys.

"Let's go look. I'm curious to see who's running things."

Permelia looped her purse over her arm and got out.

The door of the garage where the firemen had rescued Ben's dog was open, and a table with a cash register sat in the opening. The space behind it was empty.

"Hello?" she called out. No one answered. They went to the front door and knocked, but again, no response.

"Let's go around the back. I got Ben out through the French doors onto the patio. You can see the kitchen and hallway and into the living room."

They followed the path around the house to the patio. The large hole Permelia had made with the garden gnome still gaped open.

"I'm surprised no one has boarded over that hole," Harold commented.

"From what Ben's said, Sylvia was distracted by her boyfriend, and Eddie doesn't strike me as the home-repair type." She reached through the hole and unlatched the door, sliding it open and stepping in.

"They've definitely sold stuff," she said. "There was an expensive-looking espresso machine on the counter over there."

She gestured at an empty stretch of tile counter. There was another empty space where the Sub-Zero refrigerator/freezer unit had been.

Harold crossed the kitchen and went into the formal living room. Two paintings and a small tribal rug were all that was left in that space. He looked back at Permelia, who was opening cabinets.

"I'm guessing the living room had furniture in it when you were here?"

Permelia joined him and looked around the mostly empty room.

"The house was fully furnished with top-of-the-line furniture, rugs, and statuary in every space. The firemen put the fire out so quickly, I'm sure the furniture wasn't damaged."

"Someone has held a fire sale, it would seem."

Permelia peeked into the office. It was as charred and soggy as one would expect.

"Let's go upstairs and see if we can figure out which room was Ben's," she suggested.

They climbed the central staircase and turned to the right, opening doors and looking in. The first few rooms looked like guest rooms; they had beds and nightstands and little else. At the end of the hall they found a room that had to be Ben's. Posters of football teams and their schedules, local high school teams as well as the state's public universities, adorned the walls. A lacrosse stick stood in a corner.

Permelia stroked her finger across the surface of the desk.

"The desk looks like it used to hold a computer, judging by the pattern in the dust."

Harold opened the closet door. A jumble of clothes lay on the floor, but no electronics of any sort were in evidence.

"Looks like anything of value was taken downstairs and sold."

Permelia shook her head.

"No wonder no one wants Ben to come near this place. As long as he doesn't see it, they can keep telling him his stuff all burned up."

Ben's room had his own bathroom, and Permelia went in to rummage in the cabinets. She only found the usual items you'd expect—Band-Aids, antibiotic cream, skin cleanser.

She came back into the bedroom.

"I hadn't thought about this before, but according to Ben, Sylvia was seeing her boyfriend before his dad died. If she was supporting him, he'd have a motive to come get anything of value he could cart away."

Harold leafed through a stack of video game magazines on the nightstand.

"On the other hand, maybe she wasn't delivering enough, and he decided to cut his losses and move on."

"I wonder if the police even know who the boyfriend is."

"I can ask Liam when I see him. Of course, he can't really do anything about our speculations."

"Let's go down to the garage and see if there's anything telling in or around the cash register."

The cash register was locked. They'd just concluded there was nothing more to be learned when a stout blonde hurried toward them from the street.

"Can I help you? The sale is pretty much over—just a few clothes and things left."

"No," Permelia told her. "We saw the estate sale and wondered what was going to become of the house."

"I'm sure I don't know. They just hired me to sell the small goods. I can tell you, though, most people who have an estate sale are doing it because they want to move on. Family who are taking over a house usually keep a lot of the stuff. And if they have a sale, they do it themselves."

Harold put his hand in the small of Permelia's back and pressed gently, guiding her toward the car.

"I think we're coming away with more questions than answers," he said as he opened her car door.

"I got the answer I was looking for. Ben is not trying to scam Betty and Red out of expensive electronics. He really doesn't have anything left."

"That's something, I suppose."

Chapter 49

Permelia left Dr. Grace in the parking lot with a promise to call him if anything else developed. Her cell phone chimed as she reached the top of her stairs. It was a text from Betty. She'd made Red's favorite homemade mac and cheese as well as a fruit salad and was bringing it to Wilma's for dinner and could she come by at five-thirty. Permelia clicked her phone off and opened her door.

Fenton meowed loudly.

"I know, you've been home alone for hours, but don't forget, you had a nice long outing this morning." He wove between her legs as she made her way to the kitchen.

She refreshed Fenton's water bowl and poured herself a glass of water, carrying it into the living room. Fenton ran in and jumped onto the arm of her favorite chair, waiting for her to sit down before climbing into her lap. She stroked his head absently.

"What do you think, cat? Why are they in such a hurry to sell off the estate and presumably sell the family home? Are they all broke? Is that why the parents were killed? Do the kids all inherit life insurance or something?" She stroked his head as she spoke aloud, organizing her thoughts.

"And what's going to happen to poor little Ben? Do you think his sister will take custody? And what about those boxes Eid was sending to Red in Ireland? Is that what set this whole thing in motion? Did Eid send money from his first family to the point that he was bankrupting them?

"And Fenton, the biggest question of all, why would a man have two families in the first place? I get that he could have been pressured by his father to marry Sylvia and produce an heir to clear a gambling debt, but why not just divorce her once the deed was done?"

Fenton raised up and rubbed his mouth against the side of her hand.

"I agree, that whole forced-marriage business sounds a little fishy, and we will probably never know what the truth is. I just hope for the sake of Betty and the kids that Liam can figure out who killed Eid.

Permelia stroked Fenton's head, and he settled in and started purring.

+——+

The last thing Permelia remembered was Fenton purring. The next thing she knew an hour had passed, and she was sitting with her feet on the ottoman and her head against the back of her chair, her mouth open, catching flies. She looked around the room to be sure no one had caught her in such a state, but of course, no one was there.

"Let's get your dinner, shall we?" she asked the cat. He ran into the kitchen and stood by his bowl.

Betty arrived as Permelia was putting Fenton's wet food back in the refrigerator.

"Oh, good, you're still here. I was afraid you'd already be at Wilma's. I left dinner in the car and need a little help carrying it over."

"Give me a minute to freshen up, and I'll be right there."

Red and Ben drove in as Betty was pulling dinner from the back seat of her car.

"Perfect timing," she called out to Red. "Would you two boys please carry our dinner over to Wilma's?"

Red grinned. "Are you sure you can trust me not to run off with all that mac and cheese?"

Betty looked up at her son with the first real smile Permelia had seen on her face.

"Try it, and I'll box your ears."

Ben had a shopping bag looped over his arm and tried to pick up the big bowl of fruit salad without setting it down.

"Here, let me carry that," Permelia offered and took the bag without waiting for an answer.

"Wilma gave me her old iPad," Ben said as he bounced along beside her. "She dropped it and broke the corner. She has insurance, but she needed to bring it in to the store to get the replacement. She ordered a new one instead, and let me and Red take the old one to the store. And guess what?"

"It suddenly started working?" Permelia guessed.

Ben laughed.

"No, silly, they took the old one and gave me a brand-new one."

"That's pretty amazing, and very generous of Wilma. Be sure and thank her. More than once," Permelia advised him.

"This has been the best day ever. I got a new iPad; we spent an hour with Puppy, and Eddie said he could come to dinner tonight."

"Yes, he asked me first," Betty said before she could ask.

Wilma was waiting at the gate and ushered them in, taking the bowl of fruit from Ben as he went by.

"That was a very generous act, giving Ben that iPad."

"It was the least I could do. He's been through a lot. And I needed to get a new model in any case."

Ben and Red went into the dining room to set the table, and Betty joined them to supervise. Wilma slid the mac-and-cheese pan into the oven and turned it on to warm.

"I meant to tell you earlier—the police figured out who threw the Molotov cocktail into my courtyard. Apparently, someone put my address on an online treasure-hunting website claiming there's gold buried under my patio. Some kids were trying to get in. They tried to come over the wall the other night and tripped the silent alarm. The security company caught them and called the police."

"Another mystery solved then."

Permelia watched Wilma as she pulled glasses from the cupboard and set them on the table. She didn't make eye contact, and Permelia was pretty sure that was because she was trying to sell a false story. It was possible that kids threw the Molotov cocktail, but somehow, it didn't ring true. How would that result in them finding buried treasure?

And then there were the shadowy figures who had come and gone silently, erasing all evidence of the event.

Whatever was going on, Permelia was pretty sure Wilma wasn't your average agoraphobic being pestered by youthful treasure hunters. When all was said and done, it wasn't any of her business, and if there came a time when Wilma wanted to explain what was going on, she'd be all ears. Until then, she'd keep her own council.

Permelia carried the glasses to the table; Wilma followed with two pitchers—ice water and iced tea.

"Anyone know when we can expect Eddie?" Wilma asked.

"He said he'd be here by six o'clock," Ben said.

Wilma looked at Permelia, then Betty. Permelia knew they were all thinking the same thing—they hoped Eddie wasn't going to disappoint Ben again. They didn't need to worry. The gate chimed ten minutes later, and Eddie joined them.

Red rubbed his hands together.

"Does this mean we can eat now?"

Betty patted him on the back.

"Yes, it does. Everyone can sit down, and I'll go get the food."

Red leaned back in his chair and patted his belly

"Mom, you've outdone yourself. That was fantastic."

"Yes," Eddie chimed in. "This was great."

Betty's cheeks pinked.

"Well, thank you. It's nothing special, but Red has always liked it."

"We never got to have mac and cheese at home," Ben said. "My mother always had us on some weird diet."

Eddie smiled ruefully.

"By that, he means we ate a lot of kale and chia seeds."

Wilma set her fork down.

"How did it taste?" she asked.

"Some of it was good. We had a food delivery service, so all you had to do was assemble the ingredients as the recipe card instructed."

Ben twisted his napkin in his fingers, looking down at his hands as he did.

"Why can't I go get my books and stuff from our house?" he asked Eddie.

"The house isn't safe. And besides, our stuff that wasn't burned outright was smoke-damaged beyond use."

"But couldn't we put my books outside until the smell goes away? I was re-reading my Harry Potter books, and I was only halfway through."

"When the house sells, I'll buy you new books."

Ben started to protest, but Eddie gave him a look, and he sighed and said nothing more.

Wilma got up and started clearing dishes away. Permelia joined her.

"Anyone up for a game of dominoes?" Red asked.

"I'm in," Eddie said and stood up.

"Let's go to the parlor," Red said, leading the way.

Permelia scraped and rinsed the dishes while Wilma put them in the dishwasher.

"Correct me if I'm wrong," Wilma said, "But didn't you say the fire at Ben's house was mainly in the office?"

Permelia lowered her voice to a whisper.

"Harold and I drove over to the house, just out of curiosity. There was an estate sale going on. Almost everything was gone—kitchen appliances, furniture, all the electronics."

"Were Ben's books gone?" Wilma said in an equally quiet tone.

"There were books in his room. No computers or gaming systems or anything electronic. I suspect Eddie doesn't want Ben to see that he's sold everything."

"It'd be nice to know if Eddie's the executor. If he is, he's got the right to liquidate the assets. The question is whether he's supposed to share the proceeds with the other kids or not."

Permelia dried her hands on a dishtowel when the washer was full.

"I feel sorry for Eddie. Having both parents die and leave behind two minor children for him to deal with is rough. And I know Eid had no way of knowing he and Sylvia were going to die, but it does appear he was planning to leave the first family without much when he moved to Ireland."

"Even with the fire, Eddie should be able to get a good price for the family home. In that neighborhood, the property alone is worth a mint."

Permelia hung the dishtowel on the oven handle.

"At least that's something, I guess."

Chapter 50

P ermelia and Wilma joined Betty and the boys in the parlor. The group was gathered around a dark cherry game table that sat in the corner of the room.

Eddie looked up as they came in.

"Oh, good, we need reinforcements. Red's mom is cleaning up."

Betty smiled.

"It's luck of the draw. I've had very good tiles."

Red chuckled.

"That's what they all say."

Wilma sat down on the sofa.

"Has anyone heard from Tiffany?"

"She texted me," Eddie said. "She says she thinks she'll be able to get a flight out at the end of the week. And she'll video chat with us one more time to see where everyone's at before she leaves."

"That must be a relief. You'll have some help dealing with all this," Permelia said.

"I suppose. Tiffany and I don't see eye-to-eye on most things, so it may make things more difficult."

Permelia glanced at Ben, who was watching his brother closely. He looked like he was about to protest but thought better of it.

"Hey, does anyone want to play cards? Gin rummy? Canasta?" Red asked, distracting Ben.

Wilma pointed to a drawer in the table in front of Ben.

"Open that drawer, and you'll find several decks of cards as well as several sets of dice."

"Cool," Ben said and pulled a double deck of cards out and put them on the table.

"Would you ladies like to join me on the patio for some after-dinner tea?" she asked Permelia and Betty.

"Sounds good to me."

"Me, too," Betty agreed.

+——+

The sound of laughter floated on the breeze from the open parlor window. Permelia smiled.

"They sound like they're having a good time."

Betty studied her hands as she twirled her wedding ring around her finger.

"What's wrong?" Permelia asked her.

"I feel so guilty. I don't know for sure, but I'm pretty sure Eid left all his life insurance to Red and I. And he was well-protected. So far, it looks like we're going to get it all. Eddie doesn't seem to have any money. How will he take care of the younger kids with no money?"

Wilma picked up her iced tea and took a sip.

"They aren't exactly destitute. As I was saying earlier, that house will net a good profit, even with the fire."

Permelia slid her chair closer to the table and set her glass down.

"Hopefully, they didn't have a lot of debt."

"Eid didn't believe in carrying debt, other than the mortgage." Betty said and then chuckled darkly. "I wonder if Ed had the same philosophy."

"I think the issue will be what Sylvia believed. I can imagine her spending more than she earned," Permelia commented. "My daughter said she was a successful Realtor, so it's surprising she was so poor she didn't have insurance on the house."

"Who knows, maybe Sylvia was going to run off with the boyfriend, torching the house as she went and leaving it uninsured so Ed would lose out," Permelia suggested.

Wilma laughed. "You should consider a career in fiction writing."

"After what I've been through, I can imagine anything being possible."

"I hear you," Betty said.

"What's so funny?" Eddie asked from the kitchen door. The three women laughed louder.

"You had to be here," Permelia finally choked out.

"Did you need something?" Wilma asked.

"I was just checking to see if it was okay for me to make a cup of coffee."

Wilma stood up.

"Come on, I'll make it for you."

Permelia waited until they were both in the kitchen before speaking. "I wonder how long he was standing there listening to us?"

"Hopefully, not too long," Betty said, worried.

The party broke up after Eddie had his coffee. Ben and Red stayed with Wilma, and Betty followed Permelia back to the apartment.

"I didn't want to say anything while we were at Wilma's," Betty began when they reached the kitchen. "Red told me he found the book Mark Murphy was looking for and mailed it to his friend in Ireland. He said it was a bunch of numbers—a code, he thought."

"Did he know what it meant?" Permelia hoped her face didn't reveal that this wasn't news to her.

"He said his friend was working on breaking the code."

"Are you going to tell the police?"

"I think we have to. Whatever was in that book was important enough to Mr. Murphy for him to break into two houses and to threaten you and me. I want to make sure he gets jail time for scaring us like that."

"I think that's a wise decision. The police probably have contacts in Ireland that will allow them to take possession from Red's friend."

Permelia wondered silently if there was any way the police could use the information in the book without Betty discovering her husband's possible role in criminal activities. It was unlikely, she surmised. She and Wilma would have to support Betty as best they could when and if that happened.

"A penny for your thoughts?" Betty said.

"Oh, I was thinking about what a mess this all has been, and how hard it's been for you and your son, and Ben as well." And it was all true, just not what she'd been pondering.

Fenton jumped off his living room climbing post and thundered into the kitchen, meowing loudly.

Permelia picked him up and laughed.

"Did you think Betty was offering a penny for *your* thoughts?" she asked as she scratched his ears.

Betty reached over and rubbed his head.

"You probably have all the answers, don't you? If only you could talk."

He meowed agreement.

Permelia put her nightgown on and got ready for bed, but her mind was too busy for her to fall asleep. Fenton wove through her ankles.

"What do you think, cat? Shall we knit for a little while?"

He headed for her favorite chair and climbed onto the ottoman.

"I'll take that as a yes."

She pulled a fluffy mohair, wool, and silk-blend yarn from her bag and cast on the stitches for a simple shawl. She knitted for almost an hour, relaxing more with each stitch. She was thinking about going to bed when Fenton jumped up and ran to the kitchen, jumping onto the counter. She followed him and saw Harold getting out of his car in the parking lot. The phone hadn't rung, so someone must have called him directly. That probably meant the police wanted to see the body and hear Dr. Grace's observations right away.

Liam's unmarked car pulled in and parked beside Harold's. The two men stood together talking—waiting for the ambulance, she supposed.

Without thinking, she started making a pot of coffee. She warmed her air pot with hot water and filled it with coffee.

"You wait here," she told Fenton and pulled on her robe before carrying the pot and two mugs down to the parking lot.

"You're a saint," Liam said.

"Did we wake you?" Harold asked her as she handed him a mug of coffee and then pumped one out for Liam.

"No, I couldn't fall asleep, so cat and I were knitting in the living room. He's the one who heard you."

"Has anything happened across the street?" Harold asked.

"Betty will be contacting Liam tomorrow with an interesting development, and that's all I can say."

Liam shook his head.

"You're lucky I've got my hands full with this..." He gestured toward the morgue. "...or I would be demanding you tell me what you know."

Permelia backed up.

"I'd better get up to bed," she said before he could change his mind. "Good night, Harold, Liam." She nodded to both and walked back to her porch.

"Come on, cat. Time for bed." She turned off the lights and got in bed, but sleep still did not come quickly.

Chapter 51

Permelia was up early after her restless night. There was no sign of movement from Betty's room, so she crept around the kitchen making a cup of tea and then retreated to the living room. She'd brought the current novel she was reading with her and read in the morning light coming through the front window. She'd just reached the point where it was revealed that the innocent missing woman had a wild side no one knew about when her downstairs doorbell buzzed.

She wrapped her robe more tightly and retied the sash as she descended the stairs.

"Harold," she said when she opened the door. "Is everything allright?"

He blew out a breath.

"Everything's fine. It's just been a long night." He held up her empty air pot. "I saw you sitting in the window and thought I'd return this."

"I'm glad you came by. After tossing and turning all night, I've decided I need to tell you what Betty knows. I hope I can trust you with the information."

He scraped his toe in the debris at the bottom of her stairs.

"If it's something that will impact Liam's investigation, I'll have to tell him."

"I understand. That's what I was wrestling with. In the end, I decided I trust your judgment."

"Thank you for that."

Permelia looked back at her stairway.

"I'd invite you up, but Betty's still sleeping, and I hesitate to disturb her."

"We can go to my office."

She looked down at her tattered robe.

"No one will be in the office for at least an hour."

She shook her head but followed him around the building to the front door.

"Tea?" he asked. "If you don't mind, I think we'll be more comfortable in the break room."

He led the way, and while she sat down, he busied himself filling the kettle and setting out mugs and teabags. She waited, gathering her thoughts while he made their drinks. Black for him, one sugar for her.

"Now, what is it Betty knows?"

Permelia blew on her tea then set it down without drinking any.

"It's Red who knows something. And Betty only thinks she knows everything. Red talked to me first. He says he found a journal wrapped in his pajamas in the bottom drawer of his dresser when he came home. He said it was filled with strings of numbers. He couldn't make any sense of it, so he sent it to a friend of his in Ireland who is skilled in coding and ciphers."

"And?" he prompted.

"And the friend contacted Red yesterday. He can't be sure, of course, but he thinks Eid's boss was under-reporting the income from his businesses in order to avoid paying full taxes. He thinks what's in the book is the real information, plus he suspects Eid may have been skimming a percentage of the unreported income for himself. It's all speculation on his part, but he thinks that's what makes sense."

"Wow. That certainly gives Mark Murphy a motive to kill Eid."

"But not Sylvia," Permelia pointed out.

"Not Sylvia."

"Betty told me last night she's going to tell Liam about the book."

Harold was silent for a moment.

"Liam does need to know about the book, but I think we need to give Betty time to do the right thing. I'm willing to wait a day or so to see what she does."

Permelia sipped her tea.

"That's fair."

Harold reached across the break room table and took her hand.

"I'll bet you'll be glad when this is all behind us."

She smiled.

"When I was preparing to move, I used to try to imagine what living in the city would be like. I saw myself visiting yarn stores and struggling to figure out a wool-dying setup. I imagined walking in the park. Not once did I imagine myself in the middle of a murder investigation."

"I deal with murder victims all the time, but apart from the initial identification, I don't ever see the effects on the victim's families. I feel so sorry for poor Ben."

"I feel sorry for Betty and Red, but I'm with you—Ben's whole support system has been kicked out from under him."

Permelia pulled her hand back and picked up her teacup, sipping slowly.

"I'd better get back upstairs. I haven't fed Fenton yet."

Harold ran his hand through his hair.

"I'm going to go home and try to grab a few hours' sleep. We were at it all night last night. Criminals are learning a lot from watching all the forensic shows on television. When I first started, we never saw victims with their fingerprints removed and their faces destroyed. And last night's victims seem to have been bathed in bleach as well. And in court, juries are now reluctant to convict without DNA or fingerprints. They call it the 'CSI effect'."

"I guess I never thought about the bad guys sitting around and watching TV."

"They do," he said. "But don't listen to me. I get frustrated sometimes."

"It's understandable, given the state of the world these days."

Permelia stood and picked up the air pot.

"I better get upstairs. I'll see you later, I guess."

"I'll check in with you when I come back. We need to see where we are with Betty and the book. Oh, and thanks again for the coffee. It was a real lifesaver."

"You're very welcome," Permelia said, smiling to herself as she walked away.

※—————※

Betty was awake when Permelia arrived back upstairs.

"I'm sorry, did I disturb you? Harold brought the air pot back, and then we went to the morgue break room to have tea in the hope we wouldn't wake you."

Betty shuffled around the kitchen in her fuzzy slippers, making toast and coffee.

"I didn't hear a thing. I just woke up a minute ago. Surprisingly, I slept pretty well last night."

"That's good. Maybe you can start to establish a new normal, whatever that's going to look like."

"It certainly felt a little more normal to be at my own home again yesterday. I started sorting through Eid's things and boxing stuff up for donation and setting things aside for Red, and even a few things for Ben. It's sad. I've had to stop and cry a few times, but at the same time, it feels final, somehow, to be moving his things out. I know he's only been dead a few weeks, but I'm starting to realize it may be a long time if ever before we find out who killed him. I can't stop, stuck, while I wait for answers. I'm facing the fact that I may have to live with never knowing. I think I'm ready to start my new life, whatever it's going to be."

Permelia set the air pot on the counter and unscrewed the pump parts, rinsing them in the sink.

"I can't imagine the pain you're going through, losing your husband the way you did. And even though my ex-husband is a louse, I can't imagine him dying suddenly. I can relate to starting life over without the husband you thought you'd grow old with, though."

Betty sat down with her breakfast.

"I thought I'd go back to the house and continue my clean-up. In a way, I have Mark Murphy to thank for moving the process along. I know we did the basic cleanup, but it inspired me to reorganize everything and make the place mine, if you know what I mean."

"I do understand. After everything that's happened, you deserve a fresh start. You and Red. Have you decided about going to Ireland?"

"I'm still thinking about it. In the end, I think it's the right thing to do, but I need to live in my own house for just a little while before I go. It may sound silly, but I need to leave on my own terms, not because circumstances are pushing me out. I'm not sure how long it'll take for it to feel right—weeks, months? No more than a year."

"Well, you do what you need to do. There's no rush."

"Red is anxious for me to get there, but he'll be okay."

"I'm going to spend the day spinning—I've been neglecting my work these last few weeks. I need to make some samples and then start visiting the local yarn stores."

"That sounds fun. When you get to the store visits, I'd be happy to go along. If that won't interfere with your work, that is."

Permelia smiled.

"Not at all, and it would be nice to have company."

"It's a date. Now, I better go get cleaned up and on to my housework."

"See you at dinner?"

"Sure."

Chapter 52

Permelia came into the kitchen thirty minutes later. Betty was gone, and Fenton pounced on her foot, chewing on her shoelace and flopping on the floor in front of her.

"Okay. Just a short walk." She got his leash and harness and strapped him in.

The day was sunny, but the morning was cool. Henri had on a bright-red sweatshirt when she jumped out of her tree.

Permelia and Fenton stopped.

"What are you doing up so early?"

Henri bent down and stroked the cat's head.

"My dad has to go to work early, and he's been working late, so I decided to get up and have breakfast with him."

"That's sweet of you."

"I think he likes it. He doesn't get to read his newspaper, but he says he can read it on the bus on his way into town."

"I'm sure he'd rather eat with you than read his paper."

Henri stood up.

"Is Ben still staying across the street? Without spying on the courtyard, I can't tell if he's still there."

"He's still there."

"How long does he get to live there?"

"I'm not sure. It's a temporary arrangement until his family can sort things out."

"I know it will be better for him to live in a real house with his family, but I'm going to miss having him so close. There aren't any other kids my age on this block."

"Will you be home today?"

Henri sighed.

"Yes, my mom's working on her project, so we can't do anything until she finishes."

"Let me finish walking Fenton, and then I'll stop by Wilma's and see what they have going on."

"Thanks. I'll be in my treehouse if you need to find me."

Permelia smiled and wished she had a treehouse to retreat to.

"I'll let you know."

<hr />

True to her word, Permelia stopped at Wilma's gate and pressed the buzzer when she'd finished walking the cat.

"I'll be right there," Wilma called through the speaker, and moments later the gate opened.

"Do you have time for tea or coffee?"

"No, not this morning. I need to get some work done. I saw Henri when Fenton and I were walking, and she asked me if Ben was still in residence and if he is, could they play."

"Hasn't she seen him through her binoculars? She usually watches my courtyard like a hawk."

Permelia smiled.

"I told her she had to stop doing that, although right after that she told me she'd seen my daughter vandalizing my entrance."

Wilma laughed.

"I don't have a problem with her spying. I make sure nothing happens in the little slice she can see. Not that anything interesting ever happens over here."

Permelia was pretty sure that wasn't true but kept that thought to herself.

"Fenton," Ben yelled as he thundered downstairs and into the kitchen. He dropped to his knees, and Fenton pushed him into a sitting position and climbed into his lap.

"Do you have any plans today?" Permelia asked him.

Ben looked to Wilma. "Do I have plans?"

Wilma smiled at him.

"I don't know, have you and Red planned anything?"

"We haven't," Red said as he joined the group in the kitchen. "I have some ideas, though."

"I just talked to Henri, and she wanted to know if she and Ben can play. Her mom is working at home, so she's stuck there."

Red rubbed his chin with his hand as if stroking a goatee.

"If Henri's mom is agreeable, I was thinking of taking this one…" He gestured at Ben. "…to the Museum of Science and Industry. They've always got good interactive displays."

"That sounds like fun," Permelia said. "What do you think, Ben?"

"It sounds great. Can I call Henri and see if she can come?"

Permelia looked at Wilma, who gave a slight nod.

"Go ahead."

"If she can, tell her we'll be ready to go in thirty minutes," Red told him.

Permelia picked Fenton up.

"My work here is done," she said with a smile. "I will see you all later."

⊷──⊶

Permelia had just filled her second bobbin and was stretching her back when her phone rang. The readout said *Betty Fitzandreu*.

"Hello, Betty. What's up?"

A series of rustling sounds came over the speaker before a faint voice said, "I'm in trouble," before the call was abruptly cut off.

"That was weird," she said to Fenton, who lifted his head briefly before going back to sleep. "I wonder if it was a pocket dial." She hit the top number on the recent calls list and listened while Betty's phone rang and then went to voicemail. She left a brief call-back message and hung up.

She stared out the window, reviewing the call in her mind. It really had sounded like a pocket call, but still…she was sure she'd heard the word *trouble*.

Taking her phone from her pocket again, she dialed Wilma. She described the call.

"You could ask the police to do a welfare check on her," Wilma suggested.

"That seems a little excessive. Still, given everything that's happened, maybe I'll just drive over and confirm it was a pocket dial. She's not answering her phone, and I won't be able to concentrate on my work until I know she's okay."

"Are you sure you should go alone?"

"If I see anything suspicious when I drive over there, I'll call in the cavalry before I go inside."

"Let me know what you find. And if I don't hear from you in thirty minutes, I'm calling the police."

"Will do," Permelia said and rang off.

⊷──⊶

The drive to Betty's seemed to take hours. More than once, Permelia thought about turning around and going back home. She pulled over halfway there and rang Betty again with the same result as before.

233

She turned onto Betty's street, and it looked much like it had the last time she'd been there. A yard crew mowed and edged the lawn two houses before Betty's, and across the street a woman sat on a quilt with a baby and a scattering of toys. Betty's car was parked in the driveway.

Permelia parked beside Betty's car and got out. She paused and looked around, but nothing seemed out of order.

Well, so far so good, she thought and went up to the front door and rang the bell. She waited, but no one answered. She tried knocking, first a normal tap then pounding with her fist.

"Open up, Betty, I know you're in there."

She heard shuffling from the other side of the door and then nothing. She pounded on the door again, and finally it flew violently open and she was yanked inside.

"Eddie, what are you doing?"

"Why didn't you just go away when no one answered the door?"

He motioned her into the kitchen with the gun that was clutched in his right hand. Betty was sitting at the table, a laptop computer open in front of her. Permelia immediately noticed zipties holding Betty's legs to the chair's.

"Sit down," Eddie commanded.

"What's going on?" Permelia asked.

"Betty here has decided that my father made a mistake leaving all his insurance to her. You heard her. She said so. I heard her tell you. She hasn't admitted it yet, but he cleaned out our bank accounts and put the money in hers. She's going to give that to me, too.

"I know Father didn't mean to leave Tiff and I and Ben with nothing." He paced the kitchen, running his free hand through his hair, then returned to stand behind Betty, face glowering.

"Eddie, what are you thinking? Betty isn't going to hand over her money."

He glared at her.

"That's where you're wrong. Given the choice of parting with her money or parting with her life, I think she'll do the right thing."

Betty cleared her throat.

"You can have all the money I've got, but it's really not that much. I received a ten-thousand-dollar death benefit when Eid passed."

"Don't call him that," Eddie interrupted. "His name is Ed. Say it—Ed."

"Okay, when *Ed* died, I received ten thousand dollars, and I spent some of it on his memorial service. But nothing else, if there is anything else, has come to me."

"Don't lie to me. A bunch of money is missing from our family accounts, and you have it. Transfer it to your checking account, and then you can write me a check."

"I don't know what money you're talking about," Betty said with a sob. Eddie hit her in the head with the barrel of the gun.

"Stop saying that," He screamed at her.

"Wait," Permelia said as he started to hit Betty again. "That isn't going to help anything. I cleaned Ei—Ed's office and found some files. Maybe the financial information is in there."

He looked at Betty and then at her.

"You..." He pointed at her with the ugly gun. "Go find the files in the office. And you..." He shoved Betty. "Open your bank account on the computer." He watched as Permelia stood up and headed for Eid's office. "Don't try anything funny. Oh, and hand over your cell phone."

She'd touched the screen in her pocket as she'd started to walk away. It opened to her phone app and she brushed her thumb over Wilma's number as she handed the phone over. He tossed it onto the table, his attention on Betty. She could only hope he didn't notice the screen light up when Wilma answered.

"I moved some of the files that were in the top drawer to the closet," Betty said softly.

Permelia went into the office and sat down at Eid's desk, scanning the room, looking for something—anything to help get her and Betty out of this situation.

Chapter 53

She slid the top desk drawer open. It still held the same pencils, paper clips, rubber bands, and scattered business cards as it had the first time. Why would Betty call her attention to the desk drawer? She pushed it shut and opened the other drawers, one at a time. Nothing useful presented itself. The stapler was too small to throw at Eddie's head. There was Scotch Tape but not duct tape.

There hadn't been files in the top drawer when she looked the first time. Why would Betty have put files in the thin drawer only to move them to the closet?

She stood up. Maybe Betty wanted her to look in the closet for some reason. When she'd opened it before it had been lined with shelves containing sheaves of printer paper in various weights, spare printer cartridges, and other general office supplies. She crossed the room and opened the door.

Everything was as it had been with one exception—Betty's sewing basket sat on the floor. This was the message. She quickly rifled through the contents, tossing aside the tape measure, pin cushion, needle case, small hoop with an embroidery project barely started—and at the bottom found a pair of wicked-looking dressmaking shears.

Permelia crossed back to the desk and credenza, pulling open drawers until she found a likely looking file. She picked up two more file folders and slipped the scissors between the second and third one. She tried to think through the most vulnerable points on the body, but she couldn't be sure what position she'd be in or he'd be in, and she didn't want to seriously hurt him, just disarm him until they could call for help.

"What's taking so long?" Eddie called. "Get out here now, or I start hurting Betty."

Permelia brought the files to the table where Betty was sitting, giving her a slight nod as she handed her the first file.

"Okay, here's the bank account number. I don't know his password," Betty said.

Eddie pressed the gun into the back of her neck. She grabbed it with her hand.

"I can figure it out. He always used variations of Red's name and birthday. I can't do anything with that thing jammed in my neck. Now back up, and I'll see what I can do."

Surprisingly, he took a step backward.

Permelia took a deep breath. It was now or never. Eddie was focused on the computer screen as Betty typed various combinations into the window.

She slid the scissors from between the files, and in one smooth move reared her arm back and stabbed the scissors down into Eddie's back beside his arm socket. He screamed and dropped the gun, spinning toward Permelia, who danced back out of his way. Blood was spurting from his shoulder.

Betty tipped in her chair, landing on her side with a thud. She quickly started scooting in the direction the gun had gone, extending her right arm and dragging the chair along with her. Eddie glanced at her, and Permelia took the opportunity to grab the ceramic cookie jar from Betty's kitchen peninsula and, using both hands, smash it into his head. He fell to the floor as Betty made it to the gun, grabbing it and clutching it to her chest.

"Is he out?" she asked, her voice raspy from her fall.

"He is. Here, let me cut your legs free." She picked up the shears from the floor where they'd fallen. They were slick with blood. She cut the zip ties from Betty's legs.

"Do you have anything we can tie him up with?" Permelia asked.

Betty stood up.

"I've got some kitchen twine in the utility drawer; let me get it."

They had just trussed him up like the turkey the twine was intended for when there was a knock at the door. Permelia looked at Betty.

"Stay here and watch him while I see who it is."

She looked through the peephole in the door and then immediately swung the door open.

"We're here to do a wellness check on Mrs. Betty Fitzandreu," said a uniformed police officer. "Are you Mrs. Fitzandreu?"

"No, but thank heaven you're here. Betty is in the kitchen along with the man who tried to kill us both."

She led the way to where Eddie was starting to return to consciousness. The policeman twirled a dial on the radio attached to his shoulder.

"I need an ambulance and backup at..." He recited Betty's address and described the situation.

"Did Wilma call you, Officer...?" Permelia asked when he was through reporting.

"It's Officer Kelly, and I don't know who Wilma is, but we were sent by our sergeant. We're going to need you and Ms. Fitzandreu to come to the station with us and make a statement."

"Can I call my son?" Betty asked.

"Sure," Kelly said. "And we'll have the paramedics look at that bruise on your arm, too. Did the guy on the floor do that to you?"

Betty shook her head.

"I must have bruised it when I tipped the chair I was tied to over. I was trying to get to the gun after Permelia stabbed Eddie with the scissors."

"These two crazy women attacked me," Eddie shouted. "I was only trying to help them fix their computer."

"Save it," Officer Kelly said.

Any further conversation was interrupted by the arrival of the paramedics.

⊷──⊶

Permelia sat down at the table. All of a sudden, she wasn't feeling so well.. One of the paramedics was working on Eddie, but Officer Kelly glanced at her then touched the one who wasn't on the arm, nodding toward her.

"Put your head between your knees," the man said as he closed the distance between them. "Take a deep breath. You're feeling the aftereffects of an adrenaline rush. Kelly, can you get her a glass of water, please?"

Officer Kelly did as asked and brought it over.

"Here, take a few sips of this," he told her.

The paramedic rubbed her back then set about measuring her blood pressure and taking her pulse.

"I'm Brian, your friendly local paramedic. Are you feeling a little better? We can take you to the hospital to do a more thorough checkup, but I think you've just had a bit of a shock."

Permelia sat up straighter.

"That won't be necessary, Brian. I just felt faint there for a moment, but I'm feeling better. She looked around. "How's Betty?"

Betty was in the living room, where additional police had gathered. She was sitting on the sofa beside a female officer, her head between her knees.

"Can I go talk to her? It might help."

"Stand up slowly." Brian advised, and then held her arm while she walked to the living room to sit beside Betty and pat her hand.

"Are you okay?"

Betty raised her head slowly.

"Did we really catch him?" she said in a whisper.

Permelia smiled.

"We did. And you were brilliant. That was quick thinking, letting me know where the scissors were."

"I'd have never been brave enough to stab him."

"I wasn't going to let him shoot you. It was the only thing I could do. And I am sorry about your cookie jar."

Betty started laughing.

"You saved me from certain death, and you're worried about the cookie jar?"

"It looked like it came from Ireland."

"It did, but little good it would have done me if I was dead." She stopped laughing and took a deep breath. "He really did almost kill me, didn't he?"

Permelia patted her hand again.

"Try not to think about that part of it. We prevailed, that's what matters."

They sat in silence as Eddie was wheeled out of the house and into the waiting ambulance.

Permelia stood up and returned to the dining room.

"Officer Kelly, can we go home before we come make our statements?" She explained that Betty was staying at her house because of the previous break in and the aftermath of the murders. "Everyone's going to wonder what's going on."

"You can call them, but I'm afraid we need to go get those statements done."

"Can we get our purses?"

"For now, we need you to leave them here. This is a crime scene. Don't worry, our people will be here for hours, and your purses will be safe."

They followed him out to his car and got in the back seat.

"I've always wondered what it was like to ride in the back of a patrol car," Permelia whispered to Betty.

"Me, too."

"Now, ladies, when you're finally finished, where is home?"

"The morgue," they both said with a laugh.

Chapter 54

It was dark when Detective James pulled into the morgue parking lot with Permelia and Betty in his back seat.

"I know you two are probably beat, but there's a group of people waiting to see you over at Wilma's."

Permelia rubbed her face with both hands.

"I wonder if anyone's told poor Ben. He's had so much to deal with, and he's done so well. This may break him."

Betty sighed.

"Kids are resilient, or so they say."

The gate in Wilma's wall opened as soon as Permelia was out of the car.

"Come on over here, you both must be starving." Wilma called to them.

Permelia led the way across the street and into the courtyard. Harold stepped out from behind Wilma.

"Are you okay? It must have been horrible for you."

Permelia was suddenly unable to find words.

"I'm sorry, what am I thinking?" Harold said. "Come in and sit down. I hope you don't mind, Liam called me while you were at the station giving your statement. He didn't tell me much other than that you and Betty were okay."

Wilma stepped between them, an arm on each of their shoulders.

"Harold, let the woman come in. I'm sure she'll tell you everything once she's had something to eat and drink and maybe just a few minutes to process what she's been through."

"Oh, of course, I didn't mean to—"

"Harold," Permelia interrupted, putting a hand on his arm. "It's okay. You were worried. Why don't you find me a glass of water or iced tea or something while I find somewhere to sit and put my feet up?"

Red brushed past her to get to Betty.

"Mom!" he shouted and grabbed her in a bear hug, lifting her off her feet in the process.

"Pwwt. Meh...." Betty mumbled.

"Oh, sorry." Red set her down, loosening his grip in the process.

"Whew," Betty said. "You just about hugged the life out of me. Now, before we tell you what happened, can you point me to a bathroom so I can freshen up a little?"

"How about we eat dinner, and then Permelia and Betty can tell their story." Wilma suggested. "And Liam, I've already set a place for you, so don't argue."

The way she said it, Permelia guessed Wilma and the detective had more than a passing acquaintance. She'd have to ask her about it, but not tonight.

<hr>

Wilma had prepared angel hair pasta with fresh garden vegetables, feta cheese, and avocado tossed with olive oil and Parmesan cheese. It was served with crusty bread and dishes of herbed olive oil to dip it in. Their dinner was finished with a light custard topped with fresh raspberries.

The group at the dinner table kept the conversation light, Harold and Liam regaling them with tales of bungling burglars and ridiculous robbers.

"Ben, why don't you go take your shower while we adults talk," Red suggested.

Ben looked like he was going to argue but thought better of it. He got up and slowly went out of the dining room.

"I'll go first," Liam said when they heard a door close upstairs. "Eddie Anderson was arrested this afternoon for killing his parents and attacking Betty and Permelia and holding them against their will."

"Eddie killed Eid," Betty said with a gasp.

Permelia sipped from her after-dinner cup of tea.

"I think it's safe to assume Eddie found out about his dad's second family. And if I'm right, Eid was transferring all his and possibly Sylvia's money to his accounts under his Fitzandreu identity. I think Eddie figured out his father was taking the money and moving with his second family to Ireland, leaving him and his mother and siblings with little or nothing."

"You're right on the money," Liam said. "Once Eddie started talking, we could hardly get him to shut up."

Red leaned back in his chair, his brow furrowing.

"Why would my father do that?"

Permelia reached over and patted his hand.

"We may never know what motivated him. I can only guess."

"That's more than we have now," Red said. "Let's hear it."

"Your father was forced into a loveless marriage to settle his father's gambling debts. Once he produced the required heirs, he probably started planning his escape. Now, this next part is pure speculation, but it wouldn't surprise me if Sylvia's father is the one who set your father up with Mark Murphy. Your father must have felt trapped. His only relief was the life he created with your mother.

"I think he'd been skimming money from Mark Murphy for a number of years. I also think *Sylvia* may have been the one draining the Anderson accounts, to pay for her boy toy. Eid must have decided that Red's graduation was the perfect time to go back to Ireland and forget Sylvia."

Betty wiped her mouth on her napkin.

"How could he leave his children behind?"

Wilma put her coffee cup down on the table.

"You don't know he was going to leave his other children behind. Obviously, Tiffany and Eddie were already out on their own, but with Sylvia cheating on him, and her clearly not interested in Silver anymore, maybe he was planning on taking the younger kids with him. That could be why he was consolidating his resources. And with Red having a year to go in graduate school, Eid probably figured he had a year to execute his plan."

"Good point," Permelia said.

"I can't really say anything," Liam said. "But Eddie's ranting at the station makes me think you may not be far off the mark."

Harold sipped his coffee.

"I'd like to know how these two lovely ladies escaped Eddie and then subdued him until the police arrived."

Permelia and Betty laughed and then told them the story.

<hr />

"I'm glad you two escaped without injury." Harold said.

Red stood up.

"Wilma, could I use the computer in your office to contact Tiffany. I texted her earlier, and we agreed to talk when I knew what had happened."

"Sure, I'll set it up for you," Wilma said and followed him out of the room. She returned and sat in her favorite chair in the parlor. Permelia was looking at Wilma's knitting when Red returned briefly, signaling to Betty to join him in the office.

"What do you think that's about?" Harold asked.

Permelia sipped her tea.

"I imagine they are up there deciding the fate of the two youngsters. Red seems like a responsible young man, and he's become pretty attached to Ben in the time he's been here."

Harold looked into his coffee cup and found it to be empty. He stood up.

"That sister in Africa seemed like she was willing to help the kids. Anyone else want coffee or tea?"

Liam raised his cup.

"Coffee, please. The sister may want to take care of the kids, but I happen to know that she's not making any money to speak of working for the Peace Corps. If her dad drained the family coffers, she may not have anything to support them with."

"I know Red's only been staying here for a little over a week," Wilma said, "but we've talked a fair bit, and I think he will want to do the right thing."

It was another thirty minutes before Red and Betty came downstairs.

"Ben's upstairs playing on his iPad." Red said as he passed through the parlor and on to the kitchen. "I'll be right back."

Betty sat on the sofa next to Permelia.

"I think everything is going to work out fine for the kids," she said then took the glass of iced tea her son handed her, looking up at him with a smile.

He set his glass down on a side table and ran his hand through his hair before sitting down.

"I know you're all anxious to hear what all we discussed, so I'll try to relate it in a way that makes sense.

"First, Tiffany is willing to do whatever it takes to protect Silver and Ben. Second, it turns out Dad set her up with a savings fund as soon as she turned twenty-one. He told her he would deposit funds into it each year, as long as she didn't tell her mom or Eddie. He told her that Eddie had a gambling problem and spent every cent he could get his hands on, and he was through bailing him out.

"He told her Sylvia also spent everything she made and more on her boyfriends, partying, and everything else. He put money in college funds for Ben and Silver that could only be used for education.

"As most of you know, Mom and I were beneficiaries of Dad's life insurance, and he had a lot. So, I'm saying, we all have enough funds to take care of the kids.

"Next, we talked about our ability to care for Ben and Silver. We know we need to talk to lawyers and stuff, but with Mom's approval..." He smiled at Betty, and her cheeks turned pink. "With her approval, Tiffany will come home and get a job and then take Silver to live with her. She's pretty sure the rehab where Silver is staying will keep her for a few more weeks while Tiff gets set up, especially if they're paid.

"Lastly, Mom has agreed we can take Ben. She'll do the heavy work until I finish my last year of graduate school. We will all go to Ireland, at least for a while. I think it would do Ben some good to get away from all the awful stuff his family has done. Once things are settled, he and Mom can return to the states if they want, or maybe they'll fall in love with Ireland as I have."

Liam stood up.

"I'd better get going. If I can do anything in the way of putting in a good word with Children's Services or anything like that, let me know. I doubt you'll have any trouble, though. Good homes for children are hard to find, and you *are* family."

Harold and Permelia both stood as well.

"It's been a long and eventful day, so I think I'll toddle off, too," she said.

"I'll walk you across," Harold said—a statement not a request.

"Thank you once again, Wilma," Permelia added. "The food was delicious."

Liam and Harold said their thanks, and they all left Betty and Red to refine their plans under Wilma's watchful eye.

Epilogue

A month passed, and things remained quiet in Permelia's new neighborhood. She'd observed Wilma leave her compound for a late-night run a few weeks after Betty, Red, and Ben had left for Ireland. She decided it wasn't her place to ask Wilma what she was doing and figured her friend would tell her if she saw fit.

As Liam had predicted, there were no problems with Red and Betty gaining temporary custody of Ben, with permanent custody to follow after a time period.

She was boiling water for a nice pot of tea one morning when Harold knocked on her door.

"This letter was delivered with the morgue mail yesterday afternoon. I found it on my desk this morning. Judging by the stamp, it's from your friends in Ireland."

"I was just making some tea and am going out to the patio to drink it while Fenton enjoys time in the catio. Would you care to join me?"

"That sounds great. Shall I take his nibs out while you finish the tea?"

"He'd like that."

She poured the water into a pot she'd pre-warmed. She'd made shortbread the evening before, and put several pieces on a plate before loading everything on a tray and joining Harold and Fenton outside.

"I can't wait until we've finished our tea to read this," she said and picked up the envelope. She opened it and pulled out a card with a hand-drawn picture of a farmhouse with a stone fence surrounding it and a great leafy tree in the garden.

"'Dear Permelia,'" she read. "'Ireland is great! Red is in school and busy a lot, but I have Irish cousins. Please hug Fenton for me. Bye, Ben.'"

Below Ben's message was a note from Betty.

> I just wanted to let you know that we've arrived and are settling in. I was already acquainted with Eid's mother and sisters, which helps a lot. Ben loves having cousins his age, and seems to be doing okay in school so far, although he still struggles with the accents a bit. I can't thank you and Wilma enough. Have a cup of tea and think of us.
>
> Warm regards, Betty

"There's a PS," she said and continued reading. "'The boxes were filled with gold coins. A nest egg. I haven't decided what to do about them.'"

Harold poured a cup of tea and handed it to her.

"You must miss your friend."

"I do, but things are better for her over there."

"I talked to Liam when he was here yesterday. I asked him how the case was going against Mark Murphy, and he said the white-collar group got a lot of good information from that book Eid left his son. What they didn't find was any indication that Eid had been skimming money."

"But Red's friend said he had been."

"The information was heavily coded, so maybe the friend was mistaken. Or, it might be that Eid was skimming before he recorded any income."

"I suppose there's always the possibility Red's friend carefully removed a critical page or two."

"Hmm," Harold said, "I hadn't thought of that, but that's the more likely explanation. Whatever the case, you might want to let Betty know that, without any record of the funds, there is no way of knowing what part of the gold is from the Anderson family and what, if any, is from embezzling from his crooked employer. Liam says he's not a lawyer, but as far as he's concerned, the money belonged to Eid and now to Betty."

"She'll be relieved to hear that. And I'm glad she's taking care of Ben and hopefully can find, if not happiness, then peace."

She gazed over the edge of her deck to the trees beyond, picturing Betty in her new garden. With that in mind, she picked up her cup and sipped.

END

Acknowledgments

I'd like to thank everyone who supported my idea of writing a second series while keeping the first one going. Thanks also go to my family and friends who have their lives disrupted by my writing and promoting schedules. Special thanks to Deon Stonehouse of Sunriver Books and Music for her enthusiastic support of this new book. And last but not least, thanks to Liz and Zumaya Publishing for everything they do.